EXECUTED IN PARADISE

PARADISE SERIES

BOOK 9

DEBORAH BROWN

This book is a work of fiction. Names, characters, places and incidents are either the product of the author's imagination or used fictitiously. Any resemblance to actual persons, living or dead, or to actual events or locales is entirely coincidental.

Cover: Natasha Brown

ISBN-13: 978-0-9903166-9-5

ISBN-10: 0-9903166-9-6

PARADISE BOOKS
PRINTED IN THE UNITED STATES OF AMERICA

PARADISE SERIES NOVELS

Crazy in Paradise
Deception in Paradise
Trouble in Paradise
Murder in Paradise
Greed in Paradise
Revenge in Paradise
Kidnapped in Paradise
Swindled in Paradise
Executed in Paradise

Starfish Island – A standalone romance

EXECUTED IN PARADISE

Chapter 1

"What the hell?" I screeched, loud enough to be heard on the next block. I held down my skirt with one hand as another blast of wind came in from across the Gulf, blowing sand in its wake, and tried to toss it up and give the neighborhood a peep show of me in skimpy underwear.

Fab covered her ears. "Language, Madison Westin," she said and shook her finger at me. "What would your mother say?" She tugged on one of my red curls.

"Why is there a dead body in the trash?" I glared at my best friend, struggling not to hyperventilate.

Damn her. That Fab could look so hot first thing in the morning was annoying. She wore skin-tight blue jeans and knee-high black boots, a white dress shirt covering her handgun. The Sig Sauer P229 was a new purchase, since both our guns had been booked as evidence by the Miami Police Department during our last case and had yet to be returned.

I didn't bother to look down at my own outfit, which I was forced to pair with a jacket due to a nip in the air. Cold weather should be illegal in Florida, with a mandate of no days below seventy degrees. I had lived here long enough that my blood had thinned to water, and any temperature below that left me grumbling, "It's freezing."

Ignoring Fab, I stomped around in a circle, almost running into my property manager, Mac. "Why, why, why?" I bent over slightly to calm my nerves. *No other property in the neighborhood boasted the occasional dead body.*

The ten-unit beachfront property I'd inherited from my Aunt Elizabeth scored high in curb appeal. The individual cottages, painted in bright, art deco colors, were wrapped around a circular driveway, each with a flowerbed that ran along the front and sides. Those beds got regularly trampled by tenants and their friends squeezing out the bathroom windows to escape law enforcement; a few had even been successful, for a short time anyway. The property boasted beach access and a swimming pool with a tiki bar. It was a classic example of looks being deceiving; from the street, you wouldn't suspect all the neurotic people that occupied the units in the past, present, and probably future.

"If it makes you feel any better, it doesn't appear that he was killed on the property." Mac peered into the bin, studying the corpse dispassionately, then turned her attention to the ground in front of it. "No blood trail. I'll have to explain to our crime scene cleaner dude that the reason we didn't call him was because there was no mess. Don't want him thinking we took our business elsewhere."

Nothing fazed my property manager, Mac Lane. All I could say was thank goodness I'd had the sense to hire her on the spot. The big, bosomy brunette had changed her look today, trading in her usual ankle-length skirt for an orange, knee-length full skirt, with what looked suspiciously like an aquamarine tutu underneath, and camo high-top tennis shoes. She hadn't given up her overly small shirts; this one was a bright yellow, and in addition to letting everyone know that "I ate the worm," it wrestled her assets together and held them in place with no room to move.

"Yeah," I drawled, "wouldn't want to offend that creep-nut."

Fab whipped out her phone and snapped photos of the deceased in all his middle-aged glory. She must have quite an impressive array of crime scene photos hidden away on a thumb drive somewhere. No one would ever suspect the hot French woman of a little ghoulishness.

"Fabiana Merceau," I hissed. "Respect for the dead."

"It's not like he's going to know." Fab pulled an elastic band from her pocket and pulled her long brown hair into a ponytail before taking one last look. "I don't think he's been dead long; rigor hasn't set in and his skin hasn't turned some unsightly color yet."

Too late to stick my fingers in my ears.

"Seen him around anywhere?" Fab asked Mac.

"Don't recognize him." Mac shook her head. "I forwarded his pic to Shirl. She showed it around and no hits."

Shirl, our resident RN, would help anyone, anytime, and always with a friendly smile. She worked at Tarpon Cove Hospital and had been best friends with Mac since grade school. She became a tenant after a messy break-up with her boyfriend, and soon after she arrived, I forbid her to ever move. Now she was the resident nurse, her reassuring bedside manner making tenants and guests love her.

Fab rushed to the curb, waving away the approaching trash truck. The driver never braked as he drove on past. She turned around and closed the space between us to stand by my side. "I assumed we weren't going to look the other way and let Mr. Doe go to the dump."

I banged my head against her shoulder and pointed to Mac. "You call."

* * *

Sirens could be heard from a block over as they came screaming up Gulf Boulevard. One cruiser turned the corner and rocketed into the small parking lot, coming to a halt beside the dumpster, a second close behind it.

Deputy Kevin Cory jumped out of his police car, having snagged the only available parking space for himself, and the other car parked half on the grass behind him.

I ground my teeth at the tire marks that now marred the green lawn, but held my temper and chose instead to glare at the deputy, who ignored me. I didn't budge an inch, not wanting to be any closer to the dumpster.

Kevin squeezed in at around six feet, filling out his uniform in a way that wasn't hard to notice; women always gave him a second look. Instead of his usual uptight, slicked-back do, the wind had whipped his hair into an unruly mess. Kevin was a by-the-rules guy who relaxed his standards when it came to his preference for strippers. He was someone that I would never have rented to, but my brother, Brad, had snuck him in, arguing that, since Brad was hot for Kevin's sister, the deputy was almost family.

Kevin and I managed to maintain a chilly relationship despite the fact that he thought I was guilty of multiple felonies and belonged in jail. The problem with his theory was that I didn't have a record and any charges against me in the past had always been dropped.

"You murder this one?" Kevin peered at me over his shoulder, half-amused by his own attempt at humor. He held his flashlight steady as he checked out the inside of the trash bin.

"First of all, I've never murdered anyone." Shot a few people, true, but decided that now wasn't the time to point out that I didn't make it a practice to shoot to kill.

Fab grabbed the back of my jacket, holding me in place. "Florida has the death penalty," she whispered.

"Second." I held up my fingers, changing my mind at the last second and holding up two instead of just the middle one. "You can move. Your stay here was supposed to be temporary, and it's over."

"Evict me," he said stonily.

"No eviction necessary. I can get rid of you without stepping one foot inside a courtroom." If only I could hire some thug for relocation services, but good sense said my only recourse was to let my brother handle it.

"Are you threatening a deputy?"

Before I could respond, *Just pointing out a fact,* Mac stepped between us. "Behave, you two. I found the body earlier when I came out with the office trash." She pointed to a knotted white plastic bag lying off to one side. "I didn't think it was appropriate to dump it on top of him, all things considered." She waved her hand, cutting Kevin off. "And no, I've never seen him before." She wisely kept it to herself that she had disseminated his picture to her phone list; most of her female friends were frequent drinkers at Custer's and knew all the locals.

Custer's, a popular rat-hole bar across from the beach, attracted mostly lowlifes and tourists who wanted their picture taken in front of the "D" rating sign from the Health Department, which was proudly displayed on the door, with another one above the bar where the cat slept. The feline was popular and had his own set of groupies, who showed up just to see him. Due to the low cleanliness standards of the bar's namesake owner, the liquor license had been revoked, and now they were only allowed to serve screw-cap wine and beer, though some said the revocation had more to do with local contractors salivating to get their hands on the valuable property.

I gave Fab the friend-to-friend meaningful stare that hopefully she correctly translated as, "Let's get the hell out of here." Unfortunately, before I could take a second step, Kevin yelled, "Don't go anywhere."

Fab linked her arm in mine. "We'll be out by the pool," she yelled back and snapped her fingers at Mac, motioning for her to follow.

Mac bounced over and held out her arm. "We could pretend this is the yellow brick road and skip over to the pool," she suggested.

Fab gave her a confused look and ignored her. I bit back a laugh, wondering if the convent school graduate had ever watched the Wizard of Oz. Mac had to know by now that Fab didn't do touchy-feely unless it was me or Mother, and that was only after we'd adopted her into the family and passed our trial period. Now she held the title of honorary sister/daughter. For his part, my brother found her amusing, but only when we weren't getting into trouble.

Due to the numerous pool keys that had gone "missing" over the years, I'd changed the lock and had a security pad installed. Since then, the incidents of drunken locals passing out by the pool had stopped. Mac had obviously made the enclosed area the first stop of her day today, as it was free of towels and the chaise lounges and chairs were not strewn around or floating in the water. Even the tiki bar had been cleaned.

The three of us kicked off our shoes, Fab rolled up her jeans, and we plopped down on the concrete at the shallow end of the pool, sticking our feet in the water. The only thing missing was the margaritas, but I reminded myself it was still morning.

I broke the silence. "Dead body is better than murder, don't you think?"

Chapter 2

"Hello, ladies." Professor Crum rode up on his newest acquisition, a pink Barbie two-wheeler, his thin, well-over-six-foot frame hunched over the handlebars. "The police are here. You need a place to hide, my door is always open." He cackled.

"You steal that off some little girl?" Fab asked.

"He's a regular dumpster diver." Mac looked impressed with his current find.

His rubber boot thrust the kickstand into place. Standing ramrod stiff, shirtless and smoothing down a skirt that barely covered his backside, he looked down his nose and said, "I don't steal. And I am tired of having to remind you of that."

The professor was another gift from my brother, having been snuck in when one of Brad's real estate deals required his eviction from his previous residence. No one ever believed that he had taught engineering at a private highbrow college in California. And yet, I'd verified the employment, and the woman on the phone had been effusive in her praise of

Crum.

"Know the dead guy, by any chance?" I asked.

"You know I don't have any friends except you three." He gave us a toothy grin. He used his code to get in the gate, shoved a recliner into place with his foot, and straddled the seat.

"Why don't you go find out what's going on with the investigation?" Fab suggested.

Crum shook his head. "I gotta stay away from that weasel-sucking turd. Kev says he's going to arrest me for being cross-eyed. Which I'm not. Not my fault he has a single-digit IQ."

"Pointing out that Kevin's dumber than a rock isn't conducive to good neighbor relations. If you want to be helpful, find an affordable place for him to live and give him the address. If you want to stay on my good side, keep my name out of it," I said.

"I'll get on that." He stretched out, craning his neck to the sun.

Thankfully, the man crossed his legs. He was under a new dress code–no more strutting around in his form-fitting underwear and ugly shoes; he had to cover up. I'd hoped for shorts or pants, but no. He'd hustled up a couple of what appeared to be used bath towels and pinned them around his middle. When I suggested more tasteful attire, he'd gone on a rant about chafing, and I'd walked away, wondering if the pharmacist sold ear bleach.

The gate opened and two couples, guests from England, strolled in. They waved to Mac and dragged chairs over to the back corner, which afforded a sliver-view of the dumpster.

Crum stood. "Excuse me, ladies." He swept a low bow. "Just remember: mi casa, your hideout, anytime." He dragged a chair over to the foursome and plopped down. They greeted him like an old friend.

"You'd think he'd be bad for business." Fab stared at the group in disbelief.

"Oh, hell no." Mac laughed. "Crum knows everybody, and whether they like him or not, they all speak to him."

I caught movement from the corner of my eye and turned to check out the cottage that backed up to the pool. "Joseph just flipped up the blinds; is he okay?"

Joseph, a war veteran, was one of two original tenants I'd inherited from my Aunt Elizabeth. According to his doctors, he was supposed to have died long ago from his myriad health issues. He never listened to anyone, so it made sense that he ignored them too.

Mac craned her head back against her chaise, rocking it around to try to get a glimpse of his back window. She waved. "He's happier since Svetlana came into his life. Ever since a couple of jerk-offs tried to kidnap her, he's stopped dragging her around by the arm everywhere he goes. Now he stays close to home, and he hasn't been arrested in a long time."

I shook my head, thankful I'd finally called a halt to picking up Joseph from jail in the middle of the night; the end of the free rides had also helped to deter his wandering. "Who knew a rubber doll would keep him out of trouble."

Svet was a favorite among the guests; they liked to think of reasons to stop by and leer at the anatomically correct buxom blond. Joseph had inherited her—along with her impressive wardrobe, shoes, and several wigs—from Twizzle after he'd gone on to find out what his final reward was. I hoped, if Twizzle had found out that cigarettes and liquor weren't served in the afterlife, that he wasn't disappointed.

"Why do we have to sit here when we haven't done anything?" Fab stood, kicked water on Mac, and hopped out of the pool.

I splashed a handful of water at her back, but she scooted out of range and threw herself into a chair. "Go ask Kevin if we can be excused," I suggested. "Don't pull your gun; you know it irritates him that we have concealed carry permits."

Fab held out her hands. "Toss me your phone; I'll ring him up."

"If it breaks, you're buying me a new one." I steadied my breath and sent it airborne in a crappy underhand pitch, whooshing out a breath when Fab easily caught it.

We both carried handguns. I never left the house without mine anymore, having found out the hard way that it paid to be prepared. My favorite gun, my Glock, had recently been confiscated, along with Fab's. But my boyfriend, Creole, had surprised me with a beautifully wrapped square box containing a Five-SeveN, a semi-automatic handgun originally restricted to law enforcement and military. Creole and I had sat cross-legged on the bed as I displayed it in my palm, liking that it was lightweight and had a large magazine capacity. In short, it was badass, and I loved it.

Fab, frustrated by several attempts to get Kevin to answer the phone, sent a text.

Mac held up her phone. "Text from Shirl. Her sheriff's department sources say this is the third middle-aged man to be dumped in the Keys in the last year."

Fab and I exchanged looks of surprise, both wondering "what the heck..." and why hadn't we heard about the dead bodies before.

"Are they linked?" I asked.

We waited in silence for Mac's phone to ping again with the answer. It didn't take long.

"Law enforcement is tight-lipped on their working theory. As of now, the men aren't linked, the crime scenes differ, and they're looking hard at one man's business associates," Mac read.

Fab held up my phone. "We're free to

go." She got up and pulled me to my feet.

"I want tacos," I said and looped my arm in Fab's.

"I want a martini, two olives," Fab said.

We waved to Mac.

Chapter 3

Fab whizzed around the corner in my black Hummer. "You have a house full," she said, maneuvering the SUV into the driveway next to her latest ride, a black Porsche 911. Her previous car, a Mercedes, had been returned under the agreement she had with her client, Brick Famosa, who owned a luxury car lot. They had a secret deal that included fancy sports cars. Not wanting to be indebted to Brick in any way, I'd pressed for a good deal on my SUV instead.

"Neanderthal is here." Fab smirked and tossed a glance at the oversized pickup truck parked at the curb, her boyfriend's gleaming Mercedes behind it.

"Your calling my boyfriend names is old already. Stop it." I climbed out, slammed the door, and stomped to the front door of the house that I'd also inherited from my Aunt Elizabeth. The Key West-style two-story white house sat on a street off the main highway in Tarpon Cove, the first town at the top of the Keys off the Overseas highway.

I held the door open for Fab, tossed my bag on the bench in the entry, and sent my flip-flops in a skid across the floor. The living room was unoccupied, but the French doors to the patio stood open.

I started towards the stairs to my bedroom. "I'm not going out there. I need a nap."

Fab jerked me off the bottom step by my shirt. "What's the worst that can happen?"

"They're going to ask what we've been doing." I rubbed my temples. "I forgot to call, and I know you didn't because you never do. I can't bear a lecture right now about how we broke yet another promise to call when things go awry."

Fab pulled me by my arm. "We'll lie."

"That's a great idea." My words dripped with sarcasm.

Fab propelled me out the door. "We're home," she announced, dropping my arm and running towards her supermodel boyfriend, Didier—just the one name.

He stood in time to catch her as she propelled herself into his arms. They looked like a Hollywood "it" couple. He was over six feet of sexiness; she fit perfectly in the crook of his arm. They were both blue-eyed, her brown hair long and hanging almost to her waist, his black hair a rumpled mess.

When I inherited the house, I turned the backyard into an outdoor entertaining space with a small kitchen area, an oblong table with seating for twelve, and comfortable cushioned furniture that overlooked the pool.

"What have you two been up to?" Creole held out his arms. Luc Baptiste, AKA Creole, was an undercover detective with Miami's finest. He used the name "Creole" when dealing with the criminal element of society, and there were only a handful of people who knew it wasn't his real name.

Both men were in running shorts and sand-covered shoes; they'd been for one of their infamously long runs on the beach.

I wrapped my arms around his bare torso and looked up. "Breakfast, shopping, three pairs of shoes." A deep chuckle rumbled through his chest, and he planted a soft kiss on the side of my head. I snuggled deeper into his embrace; his lips looked firm but so kissable.

Creole pushed me back, his cobalt blue eyes tinged with amusement. His bold gaze moved down my body and back to my face again. Little sparks danced like flashes of light across his eyes. "That isn't the truth."

"I know, but it sounds really good. It's the way I *wish* the day had gone." I pressed closer, and his arms tightened.

"What do you have to say for yourself, young lady?" Didier asked Fab in his stern voice.

Fab beamed up at him, running her finger across his chest. "You need a shower." She entwined her fingers with his and headed toward the house. They quietly made their getaway.

"What time are we having dinner?" Mother called. She was standing in the patio doors, looking perfectly put together in black knee-length shorts and a black silk button-down shirt. Now that she had a younger boyfriend, her perfectly coiffed blond hairstyle was gone, replaced by a sexier windblown look.

I groaned and whispered, "Did I forget again?"

Creole laughed in my ear. "She called, irate that she couldn't get ahold of you, and then announced that she'd invited the usuals for dinner. The upside: news of the dead guy has swept through your family, so no need to repeat the shopping story."

"We can use the shower excuse too." I ran my eyes over him from head to toe, a hopeful look on my face.

Creole stared in amusement. "As long as you promise that you won't attempt to sneak out the door with me."

"You okay?" Mother came up behind us, putting her arms around me.

"Not a scratch." I kissed her cheek. "If your morbid curiosity gets the better of you, Fab has pictures. Creole smells bad," I added, as he leaned over and kissed Mother's cheek. "I'm going to make sure he gets clean." I winked.

"Hurry back and set the table. That way,

you won't look at it and sigh, making me feel bad that I don't have your attention to detail."

I loved setting the table. I collected odds and ends of dishes, as many seashell ones as I could find, from flea markets and second-hand stores. I used to enjoy candles until my cat swiped his tail through the flame. I'd had visions of the house catching fire and now used battery-operated light strings.

"That's nonsense. You're the detailed one, and I get it from you. Look at you; you always look amazing." I pointed to the black-and-tan leather slides that graced her feet. "My shoes look good on you."

Mother made a noise that sounded like a snort she'd tried to recapture. "They're mine," she said. "You borrowed and didn't return them, so I *borrowed* them back."

The clouds had lightened to a light grey but were still ominous. "We may have to eat inside. It's been threatening rain all day."

"Nonsense, that storm is ripping its way up the middle of the Gulf, and we're getting treated to the outer edges." Mother licked her finger, holding it out as if to predict the weather that way.

The three of us moved into the living room, a large open space that encompassed the kitchen and a large island that easily sat six, a couple more if we angled the stools just right. I'd eliminated the dining room since we mostly ate outside on the patio.

"What's for dessert?" I asked.

"Your brother is bringing it." Mother went into the kitchen and started unpacking the shopping bags that sat on the counter.

I gave Creole a quick shove. "Hurry, before she brings up babies."

"I heard that," Mother yelled after us.

* * *

When Creole and I came downstairs hand in hand, the room was filled with family. I waved to my brother, Brad, and at that moment, the doorbell rang.

Brad opened the door and shot me a "behave" look as Kevin crossed the threshold, a stupid smile on his face. He'd changed into his surfer attire: wrinkled shorts and a tropical shirt.

I leaned into Creole and said tightly, "What's he doing here? Pitch his ass to the curb."

"Your mother invited him." Creole's lips crinkled up, but he knew better than to laugh.

"Fine," I seethed. Kevin had a lot of nerve, showing up for a free meal after I asked him to move out. "Hey, Kevin," I called, "long time no see. Where's your stripper girlfriend?"

Kevin glared at me.

"I knew she was a stripper," Liam said, stepping around the corner from the kitchen and clapping. "Besides having giant—" He held his hands out like platters. "—her name is Boots."

"Liam," Julie hissed.

Julie was Kevin's sister and my brother's girlfriend. Standing alongside Kevin and Liam, her teenaged son, you could pick them out of a lineup as related; tanned, with sun-bleached hair, the three of them looked like they'd just strolled in off the beach.

"Margarita anyone?" Fab headed my way with one in her hand, handed me the salt-rimmed glass, and mouthed, "Try to be nice."

"Don't go anywhere." I pulled on her hand. "I'll be needing a refill." I turned to Kevin. "Dead guy have a name?"

"Where?" Julie jumped, looking around.

"Denton Newlin. Now that you've got a name, does that jog your memory; you remember him now?" Kevin turned to his sister. "How many times have I told you to move out of that hellhole she calls The Cottages? You never listen, no matter how many felonies get committed there. "

Spoon spoke up. "I knew Denton, or about him anyway. Fisherman. Lived down in Marathon. Kept to himself."

Mother smiled at her boyfriend, Jimmy Spoon, looping her arm through his. She'd hardly dated after our father died when we were pre-teenagers. But now there was Spoon, who made her laugh and kept a smile on her face. I'd liked him right off; it had taken Brad a little longer and was still a work in progress. He'd never envisioned his mother hooking up with a reformed badass.

Kevin switched his attention to Spoon. "Know of anyone who would want to put six bullets in his back?"

"What a waste of ammo. Or a piss-poor shot." I sucked down the last drop of my drink.

Liam laughed.

Mother clucked in a disapproving tone, wiggling her nose; her way of letting a person know to check their language.

"Is Dead Dude connected to the other dead ones?" I held my empty glass out to Fab.

"One drink is enough for you today," Creole growled in my ear. "Kevin is family, even if he's an ass at times—you need to learn to tolerate him. If you don't behave, I'll toss you over my shoulder like a sack of potatoes and haul your sexy behind out of here."

"You promise?" I gave him a hopeful look.

Having heard none of our whispered byplay, Kevin said evenly, "Details on open cases are 'need to know,' and you're not on that list."

I wiped away a non-existent tear.

"Bet you-" Fab stood, and Didier hauled her back down by his side. "-we'll know more than you do by tomorrow."

Mother jumped up. "Dinner's ready. Grab a plate off the island, help yourself, and take a seat outside."

Mother and I were both excellent cooks, and we'd both stopped cooking when we moved to South Florida. Mother favored takeout, which suited this group just fine.

Fab and I exchanged raised eyebrows. She held up her phone, motioning with her head.

I stood and bent down, cupping Creole's chin. "Would a food fight get me hauled out of here?" I brushed his lips with a kiss.

He frowned and shook his finger at me.

"You like the idea just as much as I do." I winked and followed Fab to a private corner on the opposite side of the pool.

No eavesdropping possible at this location, as anyone trying would be seen as they approached. Before I could question her about who'd called, however, Creole and Didier joined us.

"Listening in isn't beneath us," Creole said. "This way, we don't have to fight over which of us is the last to know." He knuckle-bumped Didier.

To my surprise, Fab's phone rang just then; unless she was psychic, which I doubted, she must have called someone and asked them to call back. So it hadn't just been a ruse to keep me from telling Kevin off.

Fab answered and hit the speaker button.

"Hey boss, I've got a pen," Phil said.

Philippa Grey, aka Phil, was a third-year

law student who bartended at Jake's, the bar I owned on the main strip. She also sold hard-to-procure information to a select clientele and had proven herself to be reliable.

Fab was a licensed private investigator. I was officially her unofficial backup, having not worked enough hours to get a license of my own. I also excelled at planning all the details that Fab found pesky.

"Before we get started," I said, "you're on speakerphone - Creole and Didier are here." When Phil didn't object, I told her about this morning's find. "Denton… something."

"Newlin," Fab and Creole said simultaneously.

"Got a tidbit from Mac," I added. "There've been several unsolved murders recently—all men; no women, as far as I know. This isn't a rush. I just want to lord it over Kevin that we know more than him."

Phil laughed. "Kevin's a lot of fun when he hangs up the uniform. The other night, he orchestrated a sing-along to whatever popped up on the jukebox."

Why couldn't I get along with him? "We just rub together in an infected, uncomfortable way. I'll make more of an effort after he moves out of The Cottages and I don't have to see him. Except when he gets invited to family gatherings."

Chapter 4

I stood at the kitchen sink, the morning sun shining in the garden window, watering and shifting plants around. Part of my attention was on surveilling the driveway; I didn't expect to find anything out of the ordinary, but it paid to check once in a while.

Jazz meowed, brushing his furry tail along my lower legs as he twined himself between my feet. I scooped up the long-haired black cat, cooing, "Hungry, old man?" I reached into the refrigerator and grabbed a can of tuna, having switched from the deli meats Auntie Fab spoiled him with. Tuna seemed to agree with his twenty-year-old system.

The front door opened and Mother came in. "Ready to go? We'll miss out on the good stuff."

"Who the hell gets up this early to root through junk?" Fab asked in a surly tone, coming into the kitchen from the patio.

Liam, who was right behind Fab, laughed. He'd stayed the night so Brad and Julie could sneak off for some alone time, not wanting the savvy teenager to realize they were having sex.

It made me laugh that everyone in the family was engaged in hiding the fact that they had a sex life.

I tugged on the end of Fab's hair. "Good thing you get to stay home with Liam. Make damn sure you don't shoot anyone."

Liam folded his arms across his chest. "I'm going. I've been wanting to go to the flea market."

"We don't have your mom's permission." I hugged him, pointing at a bakery box on the counter. I felt guilty offering only a muffin to a growing teen. "It's a big step that you got to stay here; I'm certain she'd object to a road trip. She thinks we're unsuitable role models—flying bullets and all."

"Nonsense." Mother finished off her latte and threw the paper container, missing the trash. Liam retrieved it for her with a wink. "We're all going. I'm the mother here; I'll tell you what to do and you'll do it, got it?" She looked at each of us.

I needed a real coffee; my mix wasn't strong enough for this morning. *We better hit the drive-through.*

"As for you—" Mother fixed Fab in her sights. "—get in the car; we need you to drive and haggle. It doesn't embarrass you to squeeze the last dime out of those vendors."

Fab liked to whine and complain, but one

thing she wouldn't stand for was being left behind. Especially since Didier had left earlier for an appointment in Miami. Another giveaway that she wasn't planning on sitting at home by herself was that she was dressed in black skinny jeans. Plus, I'd seen her drop her purse on the couch.

"We'll take my SUV—more room," I said as we headed across the driveway.

Fab squealed out of the driveway, and her lips curled up in satisfaction when Mother smacked her in the back of the head. "Slow down or I'll drive."

After a detour through our favorite drive-thru coffee place, Fab sped up the Overseas Highway out of the Keys, making a sharp turn onto the turnpike that would take us to one of the largest flea markets in Miami.

My phone rang, which I ignored. Then it rang again. Sighing, I fished it out of the bottom of my bag, and of course, it stopped ringing. I didn't have to wait long for it to ring again. My brother's face smiled back at me. I thought briefly about sending it to voicemail, but instead handed it over the seat to Mother. "Here, it's for you."

She said she'd take the heat; time for her to step up.

"Hi," Mother said way too cheerfully, hitting the speaker button.

Fab and I had trained her well—there

wasn't anyone in the family who didn't like to listen in on phone calls.

"Where's Liam?" Brad asked in exasperation.

"Right here," Liam answered.

"Where are you? How soon before you get back?"

Mother frowned at me, shaking her finger, for forcing her to deal with Brad and Julie. "We're almost at the flea market and will be back this afternoon."

Brad covered the phone, relaying the information; he kept rubbing his hand across the mouthpiece, creating static and making it hard to eavesdrop.

Mother cut in before he could say anything. "You don't have a problem with my spending the day with Liam, do you?" she asked, a tinge of hurt in her voice.

Score one for Mother. Go on the offensive.

"No, no, it's fine," Brad said, clearly lying. "Text me, and we'll pick him up at Madison's later. In the future, let me know ahead of time so we don't worry."

Mother ended the call on a phony cheerful note and handed me the phone. "Okay everyone, we're on our best behavior so we don't get our Liam privileges suspended."

"Thanks." Liam leaned sideways and kissed her cheek.

Fab careened into the parking lot, sliding

into the line to pay behind about twenty-five other cars. There was lots of good parking left; only the hardcore showed up this early.

"Fab's the go to girl. If we get separated and you need her services, text. She knows better than to dawdle. Right?" I smirked at her in the rearview mirror.

* * *

I wanted to gloat that our adventure had gone off flawlessly. But today wouldn't be the day. Double damn. I knew it wouldn't count in our favor that we had nothing to do with Miami PD showing up. Thankfully, no one got shot.

Fab had just wound up her negotiations on an old leather doctor's bag, a birthday gift that Mother wanted for her friend Jean. Once Mother determined that it was similar to one in Jean's collection, she ordered Fab like a drill sergeant to get it for her at the lowest possible price and not allow anyone to slip in and overbid. Fab scrutinized the piece and pointed out that it was locked and didn't have a key. She assured Mother that it wasn't a big deal; she could pick it without any damage and get a new key made.

Fab barked at the vendor, "Any idea what's in here? It must weigh fifty pounds."

The vendor waffled around and spit out, "Books."

I refrained from calling him a bald-faced liar. He didn't have a clue what the contents were and didn't care. Without lock-picking skills, he would destroy the lock getting it open, and then he wouldn't be able to sell the bag to anyone.

Mother was pleased at the negotiated price and cash exchanged hands. The four us were headed down the aisle when the police arrived en masse. Dressed in jeans and identifying t-shirts, with Glocks holstered at their sides, they scattered in different directions.

As soon as they passed, Fab cocked her head and motioned for us to follow as she cut down a different aisle. At the end, we slipped through a space between the tarps and hustled across the broken concrete to the parking lot. The police who'd passed us must have been the backup crew because the cops were already herding a line of people in our direction—mostly men, a few women, all in zip cuffs—heading toward the police bus that had just pulled in and parked next to a row of unmarked sedans. Business came to a standstill, shoppers and vendors alike stopping to gawk. There were a few others who, like us, had bypassed the excitement and were hustling to their cars, and some swarmed for the exits already.

Liam took out his phone to snap pictures.

Fab waved us around the drama; she too had her phone in hand.

"I don't think so." I jerked on Liam's arm. "If your mom sees pics, she'll think we were ringside for the trouble. Besides, Fab is the picture taker." I pointed to where she was doing just that.

Liam shook his head. "Mom caught me looking at the close ups of the dead guy in the trash. She thought Fab left her phone on the counter in the kitchen and told me never to touch her phone again. She doesn't know that Fab said I could look at her phone anytime, but if I got caught, I wasn't to rat her out. Pretty much decided I don't want to end my life in a dumpster."

"That's a good goal." I smiled at him.

I used the key fob on the back of the SUV, clicking it open. Liam threw the doctor's bag in the back. It was then I noticed that Fab had disappeared.

"Get in the car," I told Mother and Liam. "We'll wait for Fab behind tinted windows." She was in a big hurry to hustle us out of the tents and now she disappears. "Wonder why she took off?" I knew her well enough to answer my own question; she wouldn't leave without knowing why the police had been called out.

Finally Fab came out through the entrance and ran back to the SUV. "The cops are conducting a crackdown on counterfeit designer goods," Fab announced, out of breath, as she slid into the driver seat. "They hauled the vendors off to jail and are confiscating their merchandise."

"Fab, did you get pics?" I winked at Liam.

I got a snort in response that I translated as a yes.

Mother had hopped in the front seat and hung her legs out the door while we waited for Fab; now she shaded her eyes with her hand, surveying the parking lot. "The front entrance has got a backup of cars trying to get out on the busy boulevard, which doesn't have a signal. There are two exits at the back with no wait; if we hurry, we can get out before other cars start to converge on them."

"Get in the car, young lady," I said to Mother, sliding in next to Liam. "I'm not going to ask how you know these things."

Once Fab maneuvered out of the lot, Liam cleared his throat and said, "I see no reason to mention that we had a close-up view of a police sting. If we don't say anything and Brad or Mom hears about it, they'll think we left before the arrests went down."

No one said a word. We all liked the idea, but if we were found out, we'd be sent to major time-out.

"Mother, call Brad and find out if we need to bring dinner. Or are they fetching the kid and running out?" I made a face at Liam and he laughed. "So, what did everyone get? I got a clamshell purse. Dickered the price down from twenty to ten. My mentor would be proud." I pulled gently on a strand of Fab's long hair.

"I got a couple of DVD's. One is a movie that just came out." Liam shot his fist in the air. "But I was long gone before the police showed up. You know, just in case."

"Brad's barbequing," Mother announced, ending the call.

"Do we need dessert?" The whole Westin family was dessert-obsessed. If left to decide, my brother wouldn't buy any, but if it was sitting on the counter, he never said no. "I wanted another one of those strawberry shortcakes on a stick this morning, but they were gone. Even the bakery box had been tossed."

They were half-dollar size shortcakes with bright-red ripe strawberries and whipped cream tucked inside. Not standing on ceremony, I always ate mine off the skewer, licking the confection off my lips so as not to waste a bit of it.

"Didier's on his way home," Fab announced.

Mother grabbed her phone out of her hand. "No talking, texting, or anything while driving—ever!"

"Encourage her to get an earpiece. I did, but she ignored me." In Fab's defense, she never texted while driving; I read incoming messages to her.

"Hang on, everyone." Fab waved her arm. "We're going to break the record getting home."

"Yeah!" Liam stuck out his knuckles for a fist bump and I reciprocated.

Before closing my eyes and leaning my head back, I saw Mother poke Fab's arm and point at the dashboard, so I knew we would stick close to the speed limit.

Chapter 5

"I made you coffee," I said, hearing Creole's footsteps behind me. I had my feet propped up on one of his double chaise lounges as I soaked up the view of the Gulf from his patio.

I hadn't bothered with party manners the night before, when the whole family showed up for the second night in a row. I packed a picnic basket with two plates piled high with food and wrapped for transportation, stuffed in Creole's favorite beer and a flavored water for me, yelled, "Good-bye," and flew out of the house before anyone could stop and question me. A sweet tooth to satisfy, I'd stopped at The Bakery Cafe on my way to Creole's house.

Creole had returned after I'd gone to sleep. Now he shuffled slowly through the door and sat down next to me, coffee in hand. "Sorry I wasn't any fun last night."

"You feeling better?" I put my palm on his forehead. "No fever. Go back to bed, and I'll be your private nurse." I playfully smacked his ribs.

He hunched over with a low, groaning

growl.

I jumped to my feet, trying not to yell and barely succeeding. "What the hell is the matter with you?"

"Too loud," he whined. "It hurts my head."

"Baloney on your head hurting. What's wrong with your ribs?"

"You need to improve your bedside manner."

His labored breathing shot my anxiety level through the roof. "Take off your shirt," I said softly.

"Don't flip out. It's only some bruised ribs." He unbuttoned the single button on his shirt.

My knees went weak. I covered my mouth, taking in the bruising on his entire right side. "Is the other guy dead?"

He took so long to answer, I wanted to smack his head but didn't, knowing that would hurt too.

"Stakeout last night—I wasn't paying attention and took a fall over a fence," he said.

"You'd be so mad if I lied to your face like you just did to me. But then, maybe it doesn't count when it comes from you. You need to get tips on selling a lie from Mother. She can recognize one before you get the whole BS story out." I flounced inside.

My tote still sat on the floor where I'd left

it. I shoved my hand to the bottom and fished out my phone. Scrolling through the numbers, I found the one I wanted, pressed the call button, and went back to the patio, the phone ringing.

"Who are you calling?" Creole demanded. "Hang up." He tried to take the phone from me, but the sudden movement left him hissing and leaning back against the chaise.

"Is now a good time?" I asked when my call was picked up.

"Shoot." Shirl laughed.

"How do I figure out if ribs are just bruised and not broken? If the former, what's the treatment?" I ignored the dirty look Creole flashed me. He closed his eyes, but I knew he was hanging on every word.

"I can come to your house, check you out myself," Shirl offered.

"It's not me."

Creole's eyes snapped open, and he glared at me.

"Aww..." She paused and told me to lightly run my hands over Creole's ribcage. The area around a cracked or bruised rib might feel swollen, but she said I shouldn't notice any huge protrusions or dents.

I put her on speakerphone so Creole could hear. "Are you going to do it or do you want me to?" I asked him.

"Already did," he said gruffly. "They're bruised. I've had broken ones and know the difference." He ran his hand gingerly over the affected area.

"Ice, aspirin, and rest," Shirl advised. "And do not wrap his chest with a bandage or anything like that. Keep him off his feet for the rest of the week." She giggled. "I remember how attentive you were the time he was in the hospital."

"Madison's bossy," Creole complained.

"I'm sorry I was such a nuisance, but at least I'm not as bad as Mother." I sighed. "I felt like I held my breath the entire time until he regained consciousness."

"You weren't so bad. Now your mother..." Shirl laughed. "Call me if you have any questions, no matter what time it is. I'm like a cat and can go right back to sleep. One more thing: no jungle sex." She laughed again and hung up.

"You in pain?" I asked.

He brushed off my outstretched hand. "Kind of," he mumbled. "I want someone nicer."

"Piffle!" I ignored his raised eyebrows. "Me is what you get. And you're going to rest, like Shirl said, or I'll take advantage of your weakened state and cuff you to the bed. I know you have a pair here and where you keep them." I disappeared inside without waiting for a response. Not happy that his beautiful bathroom held only the basics, I'd remedied that by filling the vanity with sweet-smelling soaps, lotions, and bath gels to make bubbles in the clawfoot tub, which had an amazing view from the picture window. I'd also stocked the necessities, which was a good thing or there would have been no aspirin for his banging head.

I heard him groaning as I crossed the threshold back out to the patio. "Here." I thrust a bottle of water at him along with the painkillers. "You don't have any ice. Anything you want from the store?"

He unscrewed the top and sniffed the inside.

"You and Fab need to stop that sniffing nonsense," I grouched. "The damn bottle was sealed."

"I just need a nap, and I'll be fine."

It took two adjustments to lower the back of the chaise into a position where he was comfortable. "Listen up, grumpy, you better be on your best behavior while I'm gone, and that means rest. Don't think you'll pull one over on me; I'm Madeline Westin's daughter, and I'll know."

"I'm not six." He hissed when his crossed arms put pressure on his chest.

I leaned in and brushed my lips across his. "If I didn't love you, I'd tell your whiney-ass self to call me when you were feeling better. Here's your phone." I took it out of my pocket and laid it on the table.

"Bring me tacos," he yelled after me.

* * *

When I walked in the door, I found him on the couch, one leg slung over the back, the television on and the sound muted. I made a face when I realized that, despite trying to be quiet, I'd woken him up.

On my way back, I'd called Jake's for a takeout order and had them put together a plate of all Creole's favorite foods. Before I could hand it to him, both of our phones rang, so I left the food on a table next to the couch where he could reach it. I walked out on the deck and dropped into a chair to give us both privacy.

"I can hear you breathing," Fab said

She never appreciated my juvenile antics. "This better be good."

"Brick wants us in his office tomorrow morning."

"Why can't he send job details in an email?" I cut off her response. "I can't—Creole's hurt, and I'm not going anywhere."

"Hangnail?" She laughed.

I hung up on her.

My phone rang again, and once again, I answered without saying anything.

"Sorry. I'll stop with the jokes."

"Have you thought about how our foursome would work if I were to trade him in for another model? He and Didier are best friends. I guess I need to remind you that Creole tolerates you and has never once suggested that you move out," I said with an edge.

She dropped her teasing tone and said, "Bring him here, and we'll have your mother look after him."

"You know Mother will drive him crazy with her hands-on nursing approach. Besides, his moving around is not a good idea." I gave her a quick rundown.

"He's not half-dead," Fab said in exasperation. "It's only a couple of hours."

"I'll get back to you."

"I've got a meeting in the morning," Creole informed me as I crossed the threshold.

"Fine," I said in annoyance. "Me too. But the difference is: I can walk to the bathroom without shuffling and stopping to catch my breath."

Men!

"You can drive that ridiculously big pickup truck of yours in pain?" I yelled from the kitchen. I grabbed my plate and slid onto a stool, fishing my phone out of my pocket. "Turns out my calendar is empty," I said when Fab answered.

"Be here early. I'm buying the lattes, and I'll throw in one of those iced scones you love."

"Two scones and you're on." I grinned at the phone.

"Heck, I'd buy a dozen to get you back here and to the meeting on time." She made a kissy noise and hung up.

I only made it halfway through my dinner before I had to stop because I had an upset stomach. It wouldn't go to waste; I was a big fan of leftovers. Creole had gone silent, so instead of going back outside with a book, which would have been my first choice, I settled in a chair across from him. We stared at each other like we were on an awkward first date. Finally, I decided on a Westin family trick in an uncomfortable situation and changed the subject. "Anything good on television?"

Chapter 6

Fab and I rounded the corner from different directions. I braked so that she could pull into the driveway ahead of me, then rolled up behind her Porsche. Instead of getting out and going around, I slid over into the passenger seat. I gave her a thumbs up through the windshield when I saw the lattes resting on top of the pink bakery box that meant more than two scones. I restrained myself from licking my lips.

Fab opened the driver's door and handed me the drink tray, and I transferred the cups into the console. "Am I the best friend or what?" She smirked.

"Even without coffee." I lifted the lid and licked whipped cream off the top.

Fab hopped into the driver's seat and took a swig of her dark brew before pulling out; most people said double espressos put hair on their chest - luckily, Fab had escaped that side effect.

"How's the BF?" Fab asked, making a complete stop at the sign. Everyone in the neighborhood now knew we were right around the corner from one of the sheriff's speed traps, since Fab had passed the word around.

"He's a stubborn old mule. I wanted to shout, 'I told you so,' when he could barely get out of bed this morning. I ignored his groaning, gave him a crappy kiss, and banged the door behind me."

Fab shrugged. "Hmm… I don't know what to say."

"Try something sensitive."

"Um… can I get a hint?" Noticing the foul look I directed at her, she said, "He's not going to die." She patted my shoulder.

"That's the best you can do? If I said that about Didier, you'd shoot me."

"Listen up. In this duo—"she pointed to herself then me. "—I'm not the nice one; that's your job. And a crappy, thankless one it is."

I chuckled. "What would I do without you and these sensitive tidbits you feel compelled to share?"

"Grab the sissy bar," she said and jammed on the gas. "You know Brick hates it when we're late."

* * *

Hitting the signals just right - all green, well mostly, but none were red - we blew into Famosa Motors in record time. The high-end luxury car lot situated on some pricey real estate in a highly sought-after commercial area also did a brisk rental car business. Fab made a grand entrance, skidding up in front of the rolled-up doors where new cars were on display. It was too early for car buyers, and the renters, I suspected, showed up in the dead of night with freshly printed bags of hundreds.

"I love how you always get us the best parking spot." I slid my feet into my red flip-flops; the straps lined in petite conch shells, they matched my sleeveless top. My work attire rarely deviated from skirt and top, only changing to crop sweats and tennis shoes for those jobs where I might need to run to avoid getting arrested, or taking a bullet, or some other unfortunate surprise.

Fab hated my choice of shoes but had stopped reminding me that I had no sense of shoe fashion. I laughed to myself, thinking that if I glued four-inch heels to the bottoms, she'd still hate them.

"Let's not dawdle," I said. "We've got better stuff to do. Brick doesn't need to know that we don't know exactly what that is at the moment."

The glass door was unlocked, but I pushed the annoying night bell anyway. I looked up at the second-floor domain of the boss himself; he stood at his office window, from there, he had a view of the entire property and busy boulevard.

"Good morning, Bits-ee," I said and slowed in front of the receptionist's desk. "You weren't here the last time we came in. We've missed you." I puckered my lips, a look of fake concern on my face.

"I heard you had to leave town," Fab said. "You screwed someone who didn't care that you had Brick's protection. Sucks for you when he decides to stop straightening out your life." Fab stared her down.

The heavily made-up blonde sat up straight in her chair, pushing out her double D's. "You change your attitude, or I'll tell Brick it's you two or me."

Fab laughed.

I flashed her a phony smile, knowing that when I overdid the expression, it turned into a lopsided sneer. "I wish you would. Just a word of warning: There are more big-chested pole twirlers where he found you."

Bitsy had been promoted from her job at Brick's strip club for her obvious assets; she was here to swing her charms, to provide a distraction for male buyers.

Fab tugged on my arm, and we went up the stairs to the inner sanctum.

Brick's muscled bulk was stuffed into a chair behind his desk, his feet on top, a cigar between his lips. He waved his arm toward the oversized leather chairs in front of his desk. "Why don't the two of you sit down at the same time for once, instead of one of you lurking around the office?"

Fab ignored him and took up her post at

the window. I sat down and perused the walls to see if Brick had added another Cuban businessman plaque to his growing collection. He'd been awarded a few for his philanthropy, but not anything to do with his businesses, which ran to the seedy. He'd gotten his start with a local bail bonds office and soon after had opened locations up and down the state, then parlayed those into a string of pawn shops and his crown jewel, the strip joint in Alligator Alley that he'd named The Gentleman's Club.

Fab pushed away from the ledge, opened the refrigerator, and handed me a water. She took one for herself, then sat in the chair next to me.

"What's the job? We've got two other client appointments today." I maintained eye contact, the first rule in selling a lie.

"Car retrieval—Lamborghini. During the day, it's parked at a deserted warehouse surrounded by barbed wire with Rottweilers on duty. At night, I never have an exact address. She's constantly on the move; she did stop for two hours last night, but neither of you would answer the phone."

"She?" Fab arched her brow.

"And here I thought you were sexist and only rented your lux cars to male criminals," I said.

Brick took a deep breath and appeared to be counting, resting his head on the back of his chair. "Go get the Lambo. I've got an app that can be installed on your phones so you can tail her; at some point, she's got to stop for gas." He handed me a folder that had been sitting in front of him.

"Nice ride." I admired the two-hundred-thousand-dollar red sports car in the photo. "Any info you can give us on this Tracy Corn? Such as—is she crazy? Dangerous?"

Instead of shouting his usual insistence that this was a case of search and find, Brick hesitated.

Fab noticed and jumped to her feet. "If you don't fess up and we get ambushed, we'll never work for you again. And I will sneak up on your ass some night and shoot you."

He shot to his feet. "How dare you fucking threaten me!"

"Sit down," I yelled, "both of you." I stepped in front of Fab and turned to Brick. "I promise you she won't kill you—my boyfriend will. Now let's play nice."

"I had every intention of telling you." Brick settled back down in his chair. "I… uh… oh hell, she's Briscoe's girlfriend, and he wants her back unharmed. He has a soft spot for the thieving witch."

Another man who didn't need a last name. Unless it was "Scary Drug Dealer."

"Thieving?" I stared him down. "The Lamborghini? Or something much worse, like from Briscoe himself?"

Brick opened his desk drawer, uncapped an aspirin bottle, and threw two in his mouth. "Tracy embezzled funds from Briscoe's business. He's willing to overlook her indiscretion. You know—a man in love."

"Love." I rolled my eyes, mentally making a retching noise.

Fab kicked the side of his desk so hard the bottled water he'd failed to screw the cap back on tipped over, the water running out and puddling on his paperwork.

I enjoyed the look of irritation that settled on his face. "You act like he's a respectable businessman. News flash—he's not."

"How does some chick just walk in and rent one of your cars?" Fab asked, grabbing the file off the desk and flipping through the notes.

I looked at Fab, rubbing my fingers together. "Cash!"

"Anything we should know about her?" Fab asked. "Nutjob? Felon?" She slammed the file back on the desk.

"Considering Ms. Corn's boyfriend—a drug addict?" I asked.

"I'm not hiring *you*." Brick glowered at me. "The quality of her work has suffered since she hooked up with you." He thrust his finger in Fab's direction. "She used to be much more focused. Never made these petty demands; just went and got the job done. What is it that you contribute anyway?"

That caught me off guard - reduced to a sidekick or worse. I'd put myself on the line for his stupid jobs more than once. I restrained myself from saying anything, not wanting to unleash an F-word tirade. I stood to storm out, but Fab grabbed my arm, propelling me back into the chair in an ungraceful sprawl.

Fab leaned across the desk. "Back when I started working for you, I embraced danger and made many foolish decisions. At the time, I had nothing to lose. That has changed. You're lucky we—" she gestured between the two of us, "—take your jobs. Hire someone else. I'm not going anywhere without backup and the only backup I'll accept is Madison. Good luck getting anyone to work for you when word gets around that your jobs stink."

Brick growled out a sigh, running his hand through his jet-black hair.

"We're a team, and if you don't like that—oh well. One more thing, if you ever again insinuate that Madison is a useless part of the team, our relationship, business and otherwise, is over."

Brick smiled conciliatorily and handed her a sticky note. "This guy will put the new app you need on your phones." He held up his hand. "Before you go..." He reached into the credenza and pulled out a trash bag, then stuck his hand into the cabinet, withdrew the candy bowl, and upended it in the bag, which he handed to me.

I smiled down at the bag, wanting to pet it like a beloved animal. This was way better than an apology.

"Thanks for the sugar. I'll call when we're ready to go." Fab tugged on my arm as we walked downstairs. "Peanut butter cookies in there?" She pointed to the bag.

Once we got outside, I flicked through the bag. "Thanks for sticking up for me. Means more than the Oreos I spotted in here."

"What I said is true. Not leaving home without my gun or you." Fab patted my head.

I laughed and brushed her hand away. "I'm going to remind you that you said that the next time you try to sneak out in the middle of the night and leave me behind because you're worried about a pesky felony or six."

"Didier made me promise not to go anywhere by myself under threat of punishment." Fab grimaced.

I squeezed my eyes closed. "If this is about your sex life, I don't want to hear it. And for heaven's sake, don't let Didier share whatever deviancy he dreams up with Creole."

Fab hit the key fob. "Probably make me go without." She shuddered. "I hate that." She slid behind the wheel. "What's that look?"

"Sympathy."

Fab threw her head back and laughed.

Chapter 7

As Fab turned the corner to The Cottages, I pointed through the windshield. "What's that?"

"Some skinny old woman humping a hose." Fab slowed.

I rolled the window down, hanging my head out. "Knock it off," I bellowed.

The painfully thin woman in spandex shorts and red stilettos was in the same age range as Mother, perhaps, but life hadn't been kind. Her face was leathered and lined, a blondish-grey bun was pinned to the nape of her neck, and her bugged eyes made one wonder about her mental competency. She blocked the entrance to the driveway, spraying water everywhere as she danced in a lewd fashion with the hose between her legs. When I shouted at her, her face turned bright red and she could barely contain her anger, yelling back at us as Fab backed her down the driveway with the bumper of the SUV. She jumped the hose and turned the nozzle on the Hummer, blasting a jet of water through the passenger window. I ducked in time to keep from getting a face full of water, which at that setting would have felt like an assault, instead ending up with water shooting down my back, soaking my top.

"If Mac gave her permission to move in, she's fired," I barked, shaking the water from my t-shirt.

Fab hit the windshield wipers as the woman continued to batter the Hummer. She revved the engine, the woman jumped to the side, and Fab slid into a parking space. "That's an empty threat. Who the hell else would you hire that enjoys dealing with these people the way she does?"

Fab and I watched as Mac flew across the driveway, hollering at the woman. "What in the hell?" She shook her fist in the woman's direction.

In return, the woman's middle finger shot in the air.

Mac drew her Beretta.

I jumped from the SUV and ran to her side. "Calm down." I put my hand on her shoulder.

"Bitch." Mac stalked towards the woman in her soaked shorts and plaid button-down shirt and yelled at the woman. "I already warned you about trespassing. This is the last one you get; next time, I'm calling the sheriff and banning you from the property."

The woman whipped out her cell phone. "I'm calling them and having you arrested for threatening my life."

"That would piss me off," Fab growled, stepping between her and Mac. "You want to wake up tomorrow in Kentucky, you make that call."

"Besides, it's your word against the three of us." I smiled at her.

She mumbled something under her breath and started to stomp away, tripped, and kicked her heels off, sending them airborne, one after the other landing on the sidewalk.

"Put your gun away," I whispered to Mac. I nodded to Fab, and she flanked Mac's other side as we escorted her back to the office.

"What the hell was that all about?" I asked as soon as the office door closed behind us.

The unshuttered windows kept the soft green room from feeling claustrophobic. When open, as they were now, they made it easy to monitor coming and goings in the neighborhood. Fab sat in her reserved place on the couch and did just that; I settled in one of the two brown leather chairs in front of the bamboo desk.

Mac slid around the far side of the desk, retrieved her jean jumper, and pulled it over her head, covering her down to her shorts, then plopped into her chair. She picked up the wad of bubble gum she'd left on a notepad and stuck it back in her mouth. "You thought I rented to her, didn't you?"

The door flew open, and Shirl bounced in and threw herself in the only available chair. "I didn't miss anything good, did I?" she huffed breathlessly.

Shirl, an overly endowed female, sported short shorts and a bright-yellow t-shirt and matching flip-flops. She lived directly across the driveway from the office, and whenever she saw the Hummer parked in front, she hustled over to get the latest news. "Better firsthand," she'd explained once. "Good stuff always gets left out in the retell."

"Madison stopped me from shooting that Starletta cretin." Mac beamed at me.

"Why don't I get any credit for sticking up for you?" Fab grouched. She stretched out on the couch and pushed a couple of pillows under her head.

"I'm always available to return the favor." Mac smiled at Fab.

I knew that if Fab called, Mac would do any ridiculous thing she asked and enjoy it.

Mac continued after banging her hot-pink high-tops on the desk and brushing the dirt off the toes. "Starletta pranced in here one day, her Impala stuffed to the gills, demanding to rent a cottage. I laughed and told her that she scored high on my loon radar; she looked confused, so I explained. Turns out, she doesn't have a sense of humor. She threw a hissy fit, strung together several variations on the F-word that I found impressive. When she was done, I told her to hit the bricks. Just my luck, they had a vacancy next door, and she must have had cash because she moved in that day."

The windows started reverberating with the sound of drums punctuated by the crashing of cymbals. Fab sat up, readjusting a shutter to look out. "Party across the street. Setting up for a live band on the porch. The drummer and his sidekick are the only ones out there."

Shirl tossed one of her flip-flops in the air, catching it on her toes. "The property management company rented to a single man: showed up in a suit, said he owned a tech company."

"How did you find all that out?" Fab asked.

"I knocked on the door, told them I was from the neighborhood welcome committee. That's how I found out that what actually moved in was four party boys in their early twenties."

"We need to use that story?" I asked Fab. "'My cat's missing' is getting old. Better to say dog anyway. The cat story irritates some people."

Mac snorted. "E-v-e-r-y night they ratchet up the noise; cars fill the street, blocking driveways; and a deputy drops by at least twice before the party breaks up. I heard the sheriff's department gave the rental company notice to clean up the problem."

"Isn't it part of their job to check these people out?" I asked.

Mac kicked back in her chair, tussling with her top to get the girls covered and continued. "Turns out the guy who did the renting had set up an extensive phony profile. When their phones started burning up with complaint calls, the property manager hired another company to run a check. What came back was a detailed report showing that all the information belonged to an eighty-year-old man, not a twenty-something. Makes me think the rental company never does a thorough job, hence all the ass clowns that occupy the place. References were rechecked and the phone numbers went to an answering service that read a prepared speech. Whoever set the scam up wasn't stupid, and when more inquiries started coming in, they disconnected the phones."

"All that work to rent a house. That tells me that if a real check were done, no one would rent to them. Except for pay-by-the-week places." I turned up my nose. "Call in a noise complaint," I said to Mac. "We're not going to be forced to give refunds to our guests. Party boys can take it inside and close the door."

"With our luck, Kevin will show up," Fab grumbled.

"Last night, when I got home from my

shift at the hospital, Kevin was tramping across the street barefoot, big hole in the butt of his jeans. I waited for him to walk under the streetlight for a better look." Shirl licked her lips. "Still too dark."

"Focus." Fab snapped her fingers. "What happened next?"

"Kevin went in, the music went off, and he left. On his way back, several guys and a girl flipped him the bird. When he reached the driveway, they screamed 'FU' in unison, laughed, and ran inside. Kevin never broke stride."

"All the good things happen when I'm not around. Thank goodness," I mumbled. "Aren't you Head of Security?" I stretched out my leg, kicking Fab's shoe. "You go take of the problem."

"Oh darn," Fab said sarcastically. "The police just rolled up."

The three of us jumped up, trying to squeeze in around the window.

"Sit back down," Fab ordered. "If anything good happens, I'll let you know. It's not like you have far to go. I get irritable when I'm crowded."

The door blew open as if hit by a hurricane and banged into the wall. "I need you, nursey," Crum whistled, out of breath.

I grimaced at the sight of him in a cut-off muscle shirt and very large boxers over his tighty-whities. It made me wonder if once you reached a certain level of intelligence, it got its revenge by eating your brain.

"You poke a hole in my wall, and you will pay for the repairs. You won't get off with one of your do-it-yourself jobs." I pointed to his face. "Aren't you a little old for a fistfight? Have a seat. Nursey can you check you out, and we'll watch."

Shirl jumped up. "Don't say one word until I get back." She raced out the door.

I had a hard-and-fast rule—no renting to locals. It had turned out to be a stupid rule since my brother and Mac, and occasionally myself, did it anyway. Shirl was one of the first to show up after the rule was instituted. She was only supposed to stay for a couple of nights, but drama broke out and she showed off her talents, bandaging the scrapes. She also had people skills; men in particular loved her chairside manner.

"You got a good story?" Mac opened the refrigerator, handing him a cold bottle of water. "If the only thing you can come up with is contact with a doorknob, save your breath."

Shirl burst back through the door, black bag in hand. "What did I miss?"

"We're waiting for the professor here to come up with a good story," I said.

Shirl gave the black eye a cursory glance, patting his hand as she took out her stethoscope and thermometer. No wonder the people around here loved her. She went beyond the "suck it up" advice Fab would dispense, giving them her full attention.

"A couple of days ago, Scooch jumped out from behind the hedge at the end of the block," Crum grumbled. "Clocked me with a flat object and knocked me on my ass. The little bastard laughed and ran off before I could get back on my feet." He gazed at Shirl in adoration. "I wouldn't tell this to anyone but you, but I got dizzy and had a hard time getting home."

"What does that sweet story have to do with how you got that black eye?" I asked.

"We got into an argument over a woman at Custer's—you know: who saw her first. While we were trading well-thought-out observations about each other's parentage, the object of our affection slipped out the back." He shifted forward, trying to sneak a peak down Shirl's top, which everyone saw. "Scooch hit me with his fist, and I kneed his nuts in return."

Mac sucked in a loud breath.

"No one would ever believe your background. I know I have a hard time remembering. If you lie in wait and start the next fight, he'll call the sheriff. Then what?" I demanded.

"Scooch is a bitch and a grudge-carrier," Crum grumbled.

"No damage." Shirl patted his knee. "Ice

it—that'll make it feel better."

Fab pitched her empty water bottle in the direction of the trash; the bottle bounced off the wall, landing on the floor. "Why does Scooch have a hate-on for you?"

"We… um… " He paused. "We used the same girl for sexual services, and apparently she told him mine was bigger." His cheeks turned red, and he looked away. "He shouldn't have asked."

Mac hooted, kicking her feet on the desk.

I stared down, my shoulders shaking with laughter. "Paying for sex can get your booking photo published in the throw-away. You know the police log is the only thing people read in that waste of paper."

"Honey," Crum purred to Fab. "*You* could make Scooch go away."

Mac, Shirl, and I stared in shock. "Honey?" I mouthed. No one said a word.

Fab trotted out her evil smile. "That would mean you would owe me, and when I collect—no whining."

"That smile—" Crum shuddered theatrically, "—makes my hair stand on end. It will work on Scooch, unless he's more of an imbecile than I think."

Fab turned to me. "Do we know this Scooch fellow?"

"Heard of… by weirdo reputation." I knocked on the bottom of Mac's shoes. "Got an address?"

"I can draw you a map and give you a good description of the building." Mac looked between Fab and I. "You two be careful, no matter what time of the day or night you go there; it's a well-known squat house."

"Let's get something straight." I leveled a stare at Crum. "If I go along with Girl Wonder, you'll also owe me. Smart man that you are, you'll realize that equals two favors." I lifted my skirt to my thigh so my holster was visible. "The boyfriend gave me a handgun, and I haven't shot anyone… yet. Putting a bullet in your behind would qualify as my first."

Crum stood and executed a sweeping bow. "You ladies can count on me." He mumbled "thanks" in Shirl's direction, his cheeks turning pink, and beat it out the door.

"I love it when I come home from a hard day nursing the sick and your SUV is parked in a space. I know that, whatever is going on, I don't want to miss out," Shirl said. "How's the BF?"

"When I left, Creole had decided his attendance was required at a meeting in Miami. He could barely hobble to the bathroom. I called out a chirpy 'Have a nice day' and slammed the door."

Shirl snapped her doctor's bag closed. "Bruised ribs hurt like the devil. He won't be wanting to do a lot of moving around. I'd be surprised if he made it out the door. Who knows, though; he's stubborn. He's like my Stephan that way."

I raised my eyebrows at the mention of her boyfriend. "How is your insurance salesman?" Stephan was Creole's partner, and I wanted to ask a thousand questions but had to walk a fine line in order to keep my promise not to expose what I knew about the man.

Shirl's cheeks flushed. "He's great." She looked at her watch. "I have to make a phone call. Dinner later?" she asked Mac, who nodded. "Call if you need anything." She waved goodbye.

"Time to go." Fab stood and flipped the back of my hair.

"Sit down, sister." Mac shook her finger at the couch. "There's something I think you should know. Something Shirl told me. I'm trusting you to keep it to yourself."

"What already?" Fab snapped.

"Stephan," Mac whispered, "is an undercover cop."

It was unclear to me whether Stephan was his real name, though if there were a bet involved, I'd put my money on negative. Creole had told me that "Help" was his street name, but I suspected that was also phony and reserved only for me and unexpected trouble when I couldn't reach Creole.

"Why are Madison and I the last to know

these things?" Fab asked indignantly.

I turned and rolled my eyes at Fab, zipping my lips, then turned back to Mac. "Is Shirl sure?"

"While he was in the shower, she rifled through his briefcase and found identification. She turned, and he was standing in the doorway, uh… naked, and he was pissed." Mac paused. "They got into a huge fight, followed by the longest make-up sex she said she'd ever had." She pushed her chair back, standing. "When are you two going to fix me up with someone?"

Chapter 8

I tiptoed into the kitchen of Creole's beach house, certain he'd never made it out of the house; his truck hadn't moved an inch.

Creole had bought a beachfront house far off the main road, tucked away at the end of a dead-end road, his nearest neighbor a half-mile away. He'd hired a contractor to remodel the outside, and gutted the interior himself, turning it into a large, comfortable living space.

"If you're a burglar," Creole called from the bedroom area, "bring me a cold drink."

Not looking at him, I slid onto a stool, tossing my keys on the counter and dumping my bag next to them, then laid my face down on the cool travertine and contemplated whether I should still be annoyed.

"You were right," he yelled.

I smiled. Who didn't like hearing those three little words? I crossed to the refrigerator and opened it, the cool air feeling good on this sweaty Florida day. My hand gripping the neck of a beer bottle, I leaned around the refrigerator door, catching his eye. "Did you take aspirin recently?"

"Yeah, and I need two more," he said, his voice strained.

I put the beer back and grabbed two bottles of water, then found the aspirin in the bottom of my purse. "You got something to trade? My good will doesn't come free," I said, kicking off my shoes and crossing the room.

He half-laughed. "Will you extend me credit?"

I leaned down and brushed his lips, then uncapped the smaller bottle, shook the contents into my hand, and handed the pills to him along with the water. "The interest will be steep."

He stared while I stripped down to my lace cheekies and bra and slid onto the cool sheets next to him. We lay side by side, sharing a pillow. I looked up at the ceiling. "How do you feel?" I asked.

"Like someone who's been kicked in the ribs. Called the boss and told him I was taking the week off. He commiserated and told me to take as much time as I needed."

"That's good news." I rolled over, resting my head on his shoulder.

"Is there bad news?" Creole kissed the top of my head.

"Fab has a car retrieval job for Brick; she needs a getaway driver." I shifted, curving my body into his.

"Is he withholding details again?"

"He made it clear today that I'm an

irritant and he only wants Fab working for him. That was hurtful."

"He's such an ungrateful bastard. I vote for never working for him again, but that would leave Fab hanging and you'd never do that." He played with the ends of my hair. "If you scoot up so we're nose to nose, I could take advantage of your lips."

"One of the reasons I love you: you listen." I wiggled my way up. "I don't want you to stay by yourself." I slipped one hand under his t-shirt and ran my fingers down his chest. "Think about moving to my house tomorrow."

"I've got something else on my mind." He leered.

"First groan on your part, and the fun stuff is over." I tapped the end of his nose.

Our lips had barely touched when my phone started ringing.

"Do you hear that noise?" he asked.

"No." I hooked my leg over his hip. I knew from the ringtone that it was Fab. She knew that I was with Creole, so that meant it was an "emergency." I looked up at Creole, making a face when it started ringing again. "I told Fab I wasn't working tonight. She must have ignored me." My phone had barely stopped ringing when Creole's vibrated on the nightstand. "You know it's Fab. Hand it to me, and I'll take care of her." I held out my hand.

He shook his head. "What do you want?"

he growled into the phone. "She's busy." His shoulders started shaking with laughter and he held the phone away from his ear. Fab was calling him a litany of names, one that I recognized—her favorite: Neanderthal—coming through loud and clear.

I shrugged at him and mouthed, "What?"

"Brick wants the car picked up tonight, and she's yammering on that she doesn't want to go by herself. I think she should use Didier."

My eyebrows shot up, and I shook my head. "That's not a good idea. I can't imagine him shooting someone."

Once again, my phone started ringing. "I think she hung up on you."

Creole looked at his screen. "Yep."

I slid off the bed on my stomach until my feet hit the floor and went in the direction of the irritating noise, retrieving my phone off the counter. Before I could push the "return call" button, it beeped with a message: *You promised.*

I texted back: *Be home soon.*

Creole sat up on the side of the bed, huffing from the exertion of something that normally wouldn't be any effort at all. "Will you help me dress?"

I squeezed my eyes shut, shaking my head. "Damn her."

* * *

"You're a piece of work," I grouched at Fab as she veered off the Turnpike to Ft.

Lauderdale in pursuit of a missing Lamborghini driven by a drug dealer's girlfriend. *What could go wrong?* We'd ridden most of the way without talking. I had her phone and was trying to figure out the app she'd managed to get downloaded with the help of someone she refused to name, which had me suspecting one of her more scurrilous acquaintances and hoping they hadn't come to the house.

"I got a call from Brick earlier."

She paused for too long, which had me worried. "Just blurt it out."

"Brick wants us to call as soon as we pick up that car. He'll call Briscoe. We're to keep an eye on the girlfriend until he shows up. Under no circumstance is she to up and disappear on her own."

"I guess I don't have to feel bad about leaving her with no ride, then. I missed the part during the job pitch about dealing with Briscoe." My stomach formed a hard knot.

Fab muttered, "I mentioned the same thing to Brick; he tripled our fee. He did say he would remind Briscoe that we better come out of this job unscathed."

"If anything goes awry, we bail. The hell with this job." I sighed in frustration.

"Find Miss Corn yet?" Fab asked.

"She's this little dot right here." I pointed at the screen.

"That's so helpful," she said, her voice

laced with sarcasm. "Did you happen to notice that it's dark outside, and also inside, this car?"

"Hmm..." I shook the phone, tapping the screen. "The screen lights up."

"Do you have an actual address?" she barked.

I smiled sweetly. "Atlantic Boulevard, right past the Hilton on the left, is the best I can do. It would be good to have a plan about now."

"Shouldn't be hard to locate a bright red quarter-of-a-million-dollar sports car once we get in the vicinity. If whatshername is driving, we'll follow until she stops. At some point, she's going to need gas, food, something. I'll jump in and drive off. You stay and do surveillance; make sure she can't see you. I'll stash the car and come back. After I told Brick I'd bill extra for hotwiring skills, he messengered a set of keys he'd forgotten to give us."

"I hope it's as easy as you just mapped out," I said. "You should use word association to help you remember names. For Tracy Corn—think peas. Or vegetables."

Fab eyed me as if certain I'd suffered a head injury. "And you look so normal. Life is short, some smart person said for a reason. No shots fired," she stressed. "That would set Briscoe off for sure. I'm certain he wouldn't appreciate us maiming his girlfriend."

"Let's hope we don't see her pic on the news in a few days, deader than a doorstop.

Hopefully, Briscoe doesn't want her back just to kill her."

"There's the car." Fab pointed excitedly.

The Lamborghini sat at a metered parking spot along the beach. The time to replenish it with quarters had long expired. Two surfer types were drooling over the car, bent at the waist and leaning in the driver's side window; a quick swipe of the Hummer to the right and they'd be butt-less.

"Now what, hot shot?"

"Don't get surly." Fab pulled over and rested her head against the steering wheel. "We wait. The more I think about this job... We can do it sans guns. No need. If she runs, we'll message Brick with her last location and go home, make it his problem. This case shouldn't be that difficult. She's young; we're hardened private investigators."

I bent over, face in my lap, and laughed. Once recovered, I said, "There's only one of us with a license, and that would be you."

There had been a time when I wanted a license, wanted to be cool like my best friend. But it entailed working for Brick on a "snap of his fingers" basis. We didn't have the same rapport as he and Fab. In fact, based on our last discussion, he was as tired of me as I was of him.

"Don't sweat the little details." Fab's reassurance fell short.

"I don't like this--"

"If this is where you tell me the hair on your neck is standing on end, I don't want to hear about it." Fab stuck her fingers in her ears.

I punched her shoulder.

"At some point, Corncob will be on the move, we'll follow and I'll snatch the car with a friendly wave out the window as I drive off. You stick around to see where she goes. It's not like she can call the cops."

"You have to stop with the charming nicknames." I shook my finger at her. "I never liked the cob part; Mother always cut my corn off the cob or I wouldn't eat it. To this day, it doesn't taste good unless she's the one to do it."

"Don't look at me. Do you think my mother would allow any food to be served that is eaten with one's fingers?" she asked in mock horror.

I'd never met the Merceau family, and considering their non-existent relationship with their daughter, I probably never would. In addition to being unforgiving of their daughter's lifestyle choices, they weren't the touchy-feely, warm sort, from what I gathered in conversation with Fab.

"I'll cut your corn." I beamed at her.

"You're so weird. I don't eat things that stick in my teeth," Fab said haughtily. "Lookie." She pointed. "Corncob is on the move."

"Got to give Corncob credit—she's sticking to the speed limit, probably trying not to attract any more attention than the car itself already garners."

The Lamborghini signaled and pulled into a liquor store.

"Why does every town have the requisite pink liquor store, a flamingo or two in front?" I asked.

"Get ready," Fab ordered and opened her door. "Once she parks and gets out, I'm jumping behind the wheel."

"Not so fast." I reached across and grabbed the back of her shirt. "This is a drive-thru. Let's hope she's not going to drink and drive."

The Lamborghini curved around the side of the building, pulling up to the order window. Fab yanked her door shut, made a U-turn, and pulled to the curb just off the exit.

Minutes later, the sports car exited the parking lot, pulling out onto the busy boulevard, and we followed. In less than a mile, she signaled and turned into a beach parking lot, pulling into a space that gave her a front-row view of the ocean. Or what little you could see of it with only a quarter moon. There were a handful of cars in the lot, parked and empty. We pulled into a space one row behind her.

Fab bounced impatiently in her seat. "How long have we been here?"

"A minute, maybe two. She has to know Brick's looking for the car; maybe she's afraid to leave it." I rolled down the window, eager for a big breath of ocean air.

"I say we confront her while she's in the car. We'll give her options: get out or we'll call the cops. If all else fails, we put a bullet in one of the tires." Fab scowled over the steering wheel.

"You ever notice that Brick never calls his cop brother in on any of these cases? Casio could have issued an APB on the car, and it would already be back in Brick's clutches. And Casio could've personally delivered Corncob."

Fab ignored me. "Let's get this over with." She jumped out of the SUV.

I lagged behind, making sure to stay in Corncob's blind spot.

Fab's idea of a one-on-one chat might have succeeded, except for one minor detail. When she walked up, the driver's door flew open, and Corncob stepped out and pointed a gun in Fab's face. An unidentifiable stench wafted from the inside of the car, and the interior light illuminated junk food trash littering the floor, clothing flung across the passenger seat, her purse open with wads of money sticking out the top, and a blanket and pillow partially stuffed behind the headrest.

"Don't move." Finger on the trigger, Corncob wagged the gun back and forth. "Might be fun to shoot you. Get over here." She pointed the gun at me. "You two are lame; I saw you following me."

"Don't do anything stupid," I said, taking a deep breath and moving slowly, not giving her the provocation she felt she needed to shoot. "We're not here to start trouble; we're only here to pick up the car. If you kill us, at the very least you'll sit in a prison cell the rest of your life. Ever been to jail?"

"I'll make headlines, be on the six o'clock news, go out in a blaze of glory, be a household name." She gave us a wide smile, wobbling on her feet. "If Briscoe gets his hands on me, it will be like I never sucked a breath. Not even a decent funeral; my body will never be found."

"Apparently, Briscoe has a soft spot for you. He told Brick that he misses you and wants you back in one piece," I said. Who knew what the man's exact words were, but my interpretation sounded good.

"Give us the car, and we'll give you cash." Fab took a step back.

"Don't move," Corncob barked, shaking the gun in a wild gesture.

Fab held her hands out in surrender. "You can go anywhere you want. Brick doesn't want any trouble, just his car back."

"You're just a little too pretty. I can remedy that." Corncob didn't appear drunk, but her pupils were dilated, leaving only a small ring of color around the outside. She was high all right, but on what?

Stupid girl! I'd had enough of her.

"No, she's not; look at her. Sadly, no personality either." I leaped in Corncob's direction, planning to bring her to the ground. She shrieked at the top of her lungs, moving away. Fab's long leg flew out, making contact with her arm and sending both the handgun and the woman skidding across the pavement.

I took two steps in her direction, but a muscled arm wrapped around my middle, pulling me against a hard chest. At the sound of the woofed-out growl, I stopped my elbow just before it would have made contact with Creole's ribs.

"You get up off the ground, and I'll shoot you," Creole said to Corncob, loosening his grip on me only slightly.

Didier grabbed Fab, pushing her behind him and stepping on the woman's arm. "Don't even try it." He pointed a gun at her.

I pulled my phone out of my pocket and called Brick. After handing it to Fab, I rested my face against Creole's chest until I heard him hiss. "I'm sorry," I whispered. "I forgot you were wounded."

"Ms. Corn wanted to kill me," Fab huffed into the phone. "What do you want done now? Hurry up and decide; there's a cop here, and he's glaring at me."

"Which one of you is the cop?" Corncob asked. She lifted her top, showing her small protrusions, and focused on Didier. "You're pretty hot." She blew him a kiss.

"Not interested," Didier said in disgust.

Fab handed my phone back and turned to Corncob. "You're staying right where you are until your ride gets here. And we're babysitting the car until the flatbed gets here; I refuse to go near it."

I walked over to the SUV and returned with a pair of cuffs looped over my finger. I held them out to Didier. "Here you go, officer."

Fab stepped in front of him and grabbed them. "Let me," she snarled. She flipped Ms. Corn to her stomach in a slick move and tightened the cuffs before she could get out a second yelp. Didier tugged on Fab's arm, whispering in her ear. She helped Corncob to a sitting position. "If you're not quiet," Fab threatened, "instead of getting a free pass, you can go to jail."

"You okay?" I turned and ran my hands lightly down Creole's torso. "I don't know where you came from, but thank goodness."

I looked around and saw that the drama we'd created had gone unnoticed. The cars that were parked there before hadn't gone anywhere. Scanning the beach, I saw a few people snuggled under blankets on the sand.

Instead of answering, Creole nuzzled my hair, kissing the top of my head.

"Come on. You need to sit down." I put my arm around Creole and walked him over to the SUV. "You got to ride in the Mercedes. I've never been invited."

He laughed. "I want to drive that sweet Porsche of Fab's."

"Good luck wrestling the keys out of her hand, and if you do, you'd better take me along for the joyride." I smiled up at him. "I hope I didn't add to your bruising when I banged into your chest."

"You're worth it." He tightened his hold. "I'll be milking it for more attention later." He cocked his head. "What's up with the Lambo?"

"She completely trashed the inside, and the smell is excruciating." I turned up my nose. "This isn't the first car that we've returned thrashed. I wonder what Brick does with them?"

"It'll be gone in a couple of days. Give it a good cleaning and discount it; he won't lose any money," he said in disgust. "If it smells as bad as you say, the first hot day parked in the sun and the owner will be cursing the seller. Brick's smart enough to use a straw seller, though, so the buyer can't come kick his teeth out. I wish you'd quit accepting jobs from that a-hole."

"I'm thinking seriously about doing just that."

Fab waved me over and let me know that, after a second call from Brick, Briscoe had sent word to hold Corncob until he showed and picked up his dirty-word-spewing girlfriend. She had flung herself back on the pavement, twitching around and uttering every curse word she could think of while staring at the partial moon overhead. At one point, Fab threatened to gag her if she said another word, and she went silent, but not for long.

I mouthed "Briscoe" to Fab, reminding her with a look that we didn't want to get on the man's bad side, and thought uncuffing her before he arrived would be a good idea. I was worried that a Miami police squad car would pull into the parking lot at any moment; Corncob wouldn't be the only one in cuffs then. We had the legal right to repo the car, but it wasn't just murky where Corncob was concerned; it was called kidnapping. Creole would make good on his promise to kill Brick if he had to watch his girlfriend be taken into custody.

A custom, double-sized badass black Lincoln Navigator with limo-tinted windows rolled into the parking lot, slowed, and turned in our direction. This was one drug dealer who apparently didn't dip into his profits by snorting or sniffing his products.

A burly man exited the passenger side: the infamous Briscoe. If he hadn't passed his football prime, any team would have welcomed him based on his sheer size.

Briscoe surveyed the scene with a menacing glare, and the scowl on his face deepened. "I said hold her here," he barked and stomped over to where his girlfriend lay. “Not manhandle her.” He pulled her up and patted her head. “Get those off her.” He pointed to the cuffs, looking at each of us, unsure whom to direct his order at.

“He’s a cop.” Corncob tossed her head in Didier’s direction.

Fab, key in hand, whipped the cuffs off.

Corncob pouted, rubbing her wrists.

Briscoe held his arms out, and she ran into them. “I wanted to come home but was afraid you were mad at me,” she whimpered.

Didier straightened and stepped forward. “If this wasn’t being done as a favor for Brick, then your friend here would be on her way to jail for attempted murder and a handful of firearms charges. And let’s not forget that it’s a felony in this state to not return a rental car.”

I stopped myself from glancing over my shoulder. I knew Creole was sitting in the SUV, the window down so he could hear every word, probably with a gun in his hand. One of Briscoe’s men stepped out of the back of the Escalade, and the tension raised my neck hair.

Hands on my hips, thrusting out my chin, I stepped forward. “I’m going to tell my step-dad-dee that you were mean to us.” Where the whiny little-girl voice came from, I wasn’t sure, but I needed to remember it so I could trot it out again if necessary.

Briscoe sneered. “I don’t give a shit who

your kin is. And who told you that you could speak anyway?"

"Ha, a dirty word." I could feel Didier's smile, as he was a stickler about bad language and had his work cut out for him at times. Noting that Briscoe had run out of patience and thrust his hand into his pocket, I blurted out, "Jimmy Spoon," before the man could shoot me.

Briscoe's steely glare ran over me from head to toe. "You're a liar; he's not married." He smirked, calling my bluff. "Call him."

He looked surprised when I took out my phone. It rang twice.

"You in trouble?" Spoon asked.

"Hi, step-daddy," I drawled. "I'm here with what I'm sure is only an acquaintance of yours—Briscoe—and he's being mean."

"Hand him the phone," Spoon barked.

"Here you go." I held it out.

He took it and turned away, grabbing Corncob's hair and dragging her along with him.

The conversation lasted longer than the few seconds I'd imagined it would.

When he returned, Briscoe said, "We'll put this matter behind us as though it never happened." He handed me back my phone, then dismissed me with another once-over. He bent slightly, picking up his girlfriend and tossing her over his shoulder, and marched back to his Escalade, the other man holding the back passenger door open.

To my surprise, Corncob didn't so much as squeak, only fisted her hand in the back of his shirt. I ran to the Hummer and slid into the back next to Creole. I'd been right about the gun, which he was now shoving in the back of his pants.

I clapped when Didier climbed in. "Well done. I was impressed."

"It was fun impersonating a cop." He laughed.

"Technically, you never identified yourself as such; you can't help the conclusions someone jumps to," I said.

"That is so weasely." Creole snorted. He'd adjusted the seat and leaned back.

Fab leaned over and kissed Didier. "Thanks, love. Really happy to see you, as always."

"Yes," I said, "thank you, Creole *and* Didier."

"I meant him too." Fab squealed out of the parking lot.

Chapter 9

I left the front door open for Fab, who lagged behind me, talking on her phone… to Didier, I think, which was an easy guess on my part, as she was speaking in French. We'd left the house early that morning. I'd gotten a call that the fire alarm at Jake's was going off—luckily, it was a false alarm—and we stopped for coffee on the way back.

"Mother?" She stood on the other side of the island, a grubby thirty-something jammed against her side. An uneasy feeling swept up my spine. I didn't appreciate the strained look on her face. I focused on the man. "Who are you?"

"Your mama's new boyfriend," he said in a gravelly voice, smiling at me, then at Mother, as though she were his prey.

"Congratulations," I said with phony exuberance. "When did this happen? I feel bad I haven't talked to you lately. Happy to meet you…"

He paused, then nodded. "Bob." He stuck out his hand, which I didn't take.

"The four of us should have dinner together soon." Mother moved slightly, and Bob tugged her back to his side. She rocked on her feet, unsteady.

I glanced down, needing to wipe the glare off my face.

"Who are you?" Fab bellowed, slamming the front door.

In a subtle motion, I lifted the back of my shirt, tucking it behind the handle of my gun, certain Fab would see the movement. "This is our mama's new boyfriend," I said to Fab, not taking my eyes off Mother. "Hmm... Bob, wasn't it?" He nodded. "I was just saying that we should stay in better touch."

"I didn't know you had two daughters, sweetheart." Bob nuzzled Mother's neck. He didn't appear to notice the slight shudder that went through her.

Fab sidled up next to me, patting my gun.

Message received.

"Remember the doctor's bag from the flea market?" Mother squirmed, and Bob tightened his hold. "I came to pick it up."

"I haven't gotten the lock changed for you yet," Fab said. "I wanted to find someone with expertise in lock picking, who won't ruin the value if it turns out to be an antique."

I almost laughed, knowing that Fab thought it was a piece of junk and something she could open in three seconds flat; no outside expert needed. At least we'd communicated to Mother that we had her back. She appeared less frightened than when I walked in.

"That's even better. Would you get it? We're in a hurry," Mother said.

"It's out in the garage." Fab skirted around me.

"Change of plans." Bob whipped a gun out from behind Mother's back, waving it between Fab and I. "You two go first; we'll follow. Won't we, honey?" He leaned in to kiss her cheek, and she jumped back.

"You can have the damn bag," Fab said evenly and strode to the door leading out to the garage. Fab's domain. She loved my aunt's old tools; the first thing she'd done upon moving in was reorganize them to her liking. If you wanted something, it was better to ask her to get it than risk grouchy comments about poking around, messing things up.

If Fab didn't use her fancy footwork on his face by the count of three, I planned to shoot him between the eyes. So much for my shoot-to-maim policy. I smiled as Fab reached for the doorknob, whirled around, and planted her foot in his chest. Bob went flying. He needed to learn you don't bring a gun to whatever this was—a robbery? It was clear that he didn't have any experience with firearms.

"Love you girls," Mother said, then turned her attention to Bob, who had landed on his back, moaning. She lifted her foot and jammed it down in the vicinity of his lower friend, and from the screeching, she'd hit her mark or close enough. "You bastard."

"Watch him," Fab ordered and tore out into the garage.

Stupid Bob must have missed that my handgun was pointed at him; rolling to his side, he pulled his body across the tile in Mother's direction. I pulled the trigger, and he screamed like a banshee, twitching on the floor.

That was close. I smiled broadly. The bullet had whizzed past him and lodged in the door of the seldom-used pot and pan cupboard.

"You move an inch, and my next shot won't miss." I pointed my gun at his face. "You get over here," I said softly to Mother, wrapping my arm around her and squeezing until she grunted. "You're going to need a shower; he touched you." I glared in Bob's direction.

Fab came through the door, a gloating look on her face and a fistful of zip-ties in her hand. She shoved Bob over on his stomach and secured his hands, then his feet.

"We need a class." Mother nodded to me, watching wide-eyed over the island.

After the success of Fab's first seminar, which was on lock picking, we continually badgered her to teach us other useful skills.

"Really, Mother." I caught myself from rolling my eyes. "Who are you going to practice on?"

She was actually giving the question

serious thought. "Maybe we could rent someone for an hour or two."

"Only a drunk would do that, and with our luck, he'd die," I said.

"Get him to sign a release," Fab said.

I flashed her a dirty look. "I'll run it by my lawyer."

"Killjoy." Fab laughed at me. She jerked Bob to a sitting position, his back against the door. "Okay, you wormy little piece, let's see what's in the bag." From her back pocket, she whipped out a lockpick, along with her gun.

"Bob, your big mistake? Mother would never hook up with the likes of you, even if she was desperate for a man, which she is not." I held up my Five-SeveN and smiled at it. "This is now my favorite handgun; I've gotten plenty of practice time at the firing range, but I've yet to shoot anyone." I frowned. "If you don't start talking by the time my sister over there has that lock popped, you'll be my first."

"Look." Fab fiddled with the lock and pulled the bag open wide.

"No, no," Bob howled, trying to scoot away. "What do you want to know?" he asked in desperation.

"Relax, take a breath, Bob. We'll hear Mother's version of events, and then you'll get your turn." I pulled out a stool from the island.

"I was in the garden working on my roses this morning, when Bob here—" She glared at him, "—snuck up behind me, poked me in the back of the head with his gun, and told me to keep the 'F' quiet. I had something of his, he said; he wanted it, and if I cooperated, he'd leave and no one would get hurt."

"Are you okay?" I reached out and ran my hand gently across the back of her head.

Mother nodded. "Bob demanded the bag. I told him I didn't have it; I'd left it at my daughter's. He shoved me at gunpoint back into the house, where he tied me to a chair and rooted through the house. I guess he finally believed me when he couldn't find the damn thing. He did steal the cash from my purse."

Fab kicked him in the side, sending him sliding along the floor. "You piece of… You're lucky my sister never lets me shoot anyone." She flashed her evil smile at him, and he shivered.

Mother blinked and stared in awe. "He had to untie me for our 'little car ride.' I had planned to get away once we got out to the driveway, but he hit me in the back with that stupid gun of his and told me: 'Don't do anything stupid. Blood wouldn't look good on your white pants.'" She shuddered and briefly closed her eyes.

Fab moved behind Mother, lifting her top and lightly running her hand down her back. "You're damn lucky," she barked at Bob, "that she doesn't have any bruising. I'd give you a backache you'd never forget."

Mother patted Fab's arm. "I assured him I'd cooperate and that if anything happened to me, he'd never get his stinking bag. I was relieved when we got on the road, despite the fact that his gun remained trained on me. I knew you two would make stew of him. You both make me so proud." She beamed at us.

Fab searched the bag on the counter and examined every corner, quickly finding what she was looking for: a secret compartment at the bottom. She removed the cover and held up a handful of cash. "How much money is here?" She retrieved several bundles of money, fanning through them; they were all hundred-dollar bills.

Leaning across the island and glaring at Bob, I growled, "Your turn. Get to the good part—really fast."

"Keep your panties on—it's all counterfeit." He stared at the money like it was a long-lost friend. "My partner—if he knew I lost the bag, he'd kill me. I didn't pay my storage bill, and all the stuff got sold to that flea junker. I tried to stop the sale with some of the bills I had stashed, but the guy ran one of them special marker pens over them and threatened to call the police." Bob shot Mother a dirty look. "If only the old broad had cooperated, I'd already be back on the road and no one the wiser."

"You're treading on thin ice. Insult my mother one more time, and I'll do something I have on my bucket list: shoot your little friend off." I leveled my most hair-raising glare. "Explain to me how you ended up on my mother's doorstep."

"I had to pony up a twenty for the buyer information on my storage unit. Found out from the neighbor that they had a regular booth at the flea market. I slept outside their house and followed them."

I shook my head. Some neighbors didn't know when to keep their mouths shut.

"A million people around and you, what, poked a gun in their faces?" Fab rolled her eyes.

"No, I planned to buy it back. After a search of their tables didn't turn it up, I approached them and gave them a story about being an undercover cop and that there was evidence inside the bag pertaining to a crime." Bob looked pleased with himself.

"You? Impersonated a cop?" I asked in shock.

Fab laughed at him, not believing his story.

"I showed them my badge and identification, and they were very cooperative. Your old lady, I mean mother—" his eyes flitted between me and Fab, "—left her phone number for something else she wanted, I don't remember what; I didn't care. A hacker friend owed me a favor and got me the address."

Well, that explained that. *Now what do we*

do with him?

I slid my phone out of my pocket. "Got a problem that needs your expertise," I said when Spoon answered.

"This is getting to be a habit." He let out a growly laugh. "You now owe me. Where are you?"

"Home and don't dilly-dally." I shoved my phone back in my pocket.

"We can make a win-win deal. Cops don't need to be involved. I'll even apologize." Bob flashed a greasy smile.

"What was your big plan? Kill our mama?" Fab asked.

"No…no," Bob stuttered. "I've never shot anyone; not about to start now. I'd never get out of jail. It's bad enough when you know you've got an eventual release date, but to never have one…." He shuddered.

"If you get the bag back, then what?" I asked.

"I'll disappear. I promise," Bob whined. "I won't say a word to anyone. You'll never see me again. Just let me go." He crossed his heart.

* * *

Tired of listening to Bob, Fab ordered him to shut his trap. I moved to the kitchen sink and stared out the garden window, reaching out to pluck a couple of dead leaves off my baby-pink African violet. Didier's Mercedes blew by our driveway and parked in the driveway across the street. The neighbors used the house as a second home and liked that we gave it a lived-in appearance when they weren't around. Just then, Spoon's truck screeched up to the curb. Creole and Didier had crossed the street and now waited in the driveway for him. After a brief exchange of words, the trio ran into the house, the door slamming behind them.

"What the hell is going on? And who's that?" Creole roared, pointing at Bob, who attempted to shrink against the wall.

The kitchen seemed smaller with all of the testosterone from the three newcomers.

Didier rushed to Fab's side, whirling her around and checking her over from head to toe.

Creole jerked me back against his chest. "Umph!" He whooshed out a breath, clutching his ribs.

Spoon pulled Mother into his arms. She sighed and snuggled up against him, then smiled shyly at him, her cheeks turning pink. "Someone needs to start talking," he ordered.

Mother and I simultaneously pointed to Fab.

She snarled in return before reciting the details in the briefest form possible.

Creole fingered the money. Taking the paper band off a packet of bills, he chose ones from the front and back and held them up to the light. "These are crap. No one would ever take one of these bills." He turned on Bob. "You're not getting the chance to find out. Since you're so stupid, greedy, or both, you'll be spending time in prison."

I reached out and flicked a bill from between Creole's fingers. "I want one as a souvenir."

"Wait..." Bob begged. "No police. What do you want?"

"Shut it!" Spoon roared.

"You want me to call Kevin?" Didier asked.

I groaned.

"No cops," Spoon said, adamant. "I'll take care of this. It's been difficult enough on Madeline." He hugged Mother to his side, smiling down at her, then glared at Bob. "You're damn lucky there's not a scratch on this woman." He appealed to Creole: "This will make the news, names will get out, and I can't always be around to protect her."

I'd never seen Spoon do a modern day version of a caveman, and Mother was enjoying every moment of his attention. Remembering Mother's foot to Bob's lower region, I mumbled, "She's got you bamboozled."

Fab nodded in agreement.

"If Bob here turns up dead, you'll be arrested," Creole warned. "I won't turn a blind eye to murder, even for a little pissant like him."

"I can offer redemption and the same to his partner." Spoon looked at Bob. "Give me the man's name. As of right now, you two are no longer in business, and you'll be relocated for a second chance to do something non-felonious, which you'll accept if you have a brain between the two of you."

"I can't give you his name; he'll kill me," Bob whimpered.

"That's your choice, but one way or another—" Spoon cracked his knuckles. "—you're going to tell me the name. *Capisce*?"

Creole squirmed again, his face drawn. Mother turned her attention to him, staring him down. "What's wrong with you?"

I cut off any response he might have made. "Oh, nothing, Mother," I said sarcastically. "Black-and-blue ribs, some faded to yellowy spots here and there, but don't baby him or suggest he get off his feet and rest a little, like a certain registered nurse told him to do." I looked up at Creole. "Go ahead and lie to her. Tell her it's nothing and how great you feel; leave off the part where you suck in your breath at every other movement."

"Why am I the last to know you got hurt?" Mother demanded.

Creole broke eye contact and turned to Didier. "Isn't this where you say something about the weather?"

Didier held up his hands as if to say, *Sorry, pal*. But he did change the subject. "What about the money?"

"Burn it," Spoon said. He pulled Mother aside.

Fab and I strained to hear. The gist was that he was going to deal with Bob and his friend and Mother needed to stay put until he came back for her; he didn't want Bob to even breathe in her direction.

"Mother can come with us to Jake's. We've got a staff meeting in a little while," I said, not bothering to hide the fact that I'd been listening.

"I'm staying here with Didier. You can fill me in later," Fab informed me.

I tried to hide my annoyance but failed. "Okay. Fine."

"Sorry, love." Didier put his arm around Fab. "I promised to drive Creole to… somewhere. I'll tell you when I get back."

"I guess I'm going," Fab sulked.

"That's a nice offer, but no thanks," I said to Fab.

"Now I know you're up to something, and I'm going." Her militant expression amused me.

Spoon kissed Mother, then flipped out a knife, advancing on Bob, who squealed. The big man laughed and bent down, sliced the zip ties around his lower legs off, and jerked him upright. "Let's go for a ride." He hooked his hand under Bob's forearm and propelled the man, who struggled to stay upright, out of the kitchen and out to his truck.

"Do you think you can stay out of trouble the rest of the day, Mama?" I shook my finger at her.

"Once the two of you showed up, it was fun because I knew you'd make toast out of him. He's getting off awfully easy."

"Spoon's probably right," I said. "Whoever Bob and his partner were peddling their phony cash to might not have been happy to read about it in the news and might have taken it out on us, you in particular. We get in enough trouble without inviting it to the front door. Or the back."

"You doing okay?" Mother asked Creole.

"He gets no sympathy," I said. "He hurt my feelings, blew off my nursey skills; he doesn't get to have you fawning all over him, making him your famous homemade chicken soup."

Creole enveloped me in his arms. "When I don't feel so hot, I'm irritable," he confessed. "I'll make it up to you. You wouldn't happen to have a tight-fitting nurse's uniform, would you?"

Mother coughed. "We'll bring dinner back; speak now if you've got a preference."

"You need to call Brad and tell him what happened," I told Fab. My brother and I had agreed after experiencing being the last to know too many times--no more secret keeping.

"I don't like to deliver bad news. Well, sometimes. But not in this case. Probably a good idea if Julie doesn't find out about today anyway; then it doesn't put her in an awkward place with her brother. Kevin wouldn't appreciate that we disposed of the problem ourselves," Fab said.

Chapter 10

Judging by the parking lot, Jake's regulars must have gone to another dive bar to drink their beer today. I had acquired it from its namesake owner, who was on the run from the kind of debt collectors that made house calls rather than harassing people on the phone. He could never come back to the Cove; these folks had long memories.

As we pulled in and the two guys I'd hired to do maintenance came into view, I bit my lip, waiting for the fireworks. Fab screeched to a halt; lowering the window, she hung her head out. I didn't remind her that she loathed it when other people did that—said it always made her think of a dog.

"What in the..." Fab yelped, bumping her head, which earned me a double glare as she stared at *her* lighthouse getting a bath.

"I'm over you waffling over whether you're going to use your new offices or not. You've barely looked at that gorgeous old lighthouse since you had it trucked here as though it was stolen." I'd discarded that idea since plenty of sheriff's deputies had parked behind it to eat or chase speeders.

"When I asked you about the lighthouse—" Mother punched Fab's shoulder. "—your story was such a pitiful lie, I didn't know whether to laugh or be mad."

"What's your aversion to it being cleaned? Do you plan on ever using it as office space?" I asked. "Since I met you, the only client of yours I've met is Brick, and he won't come down here. The rest of your clients thus far are just voices on the phone."

The lighthouse was original and not some pre-fab knock off. Fab and I had talked about that location for her offices, and I'd pictured an old house renovated for her use, but her vague reasoning for the lighthouse was that she couldn't let the hot deal pass her by.

"You never did tell me how you got it delivered and off-loaded in the middle of the night."

"Friend of a friend who moves mobile homes for a living. Just because some of my clients pay in trade doesn't mean it's stolen." Fab sniffed. "No one wants to go in there. A few potential clients have complained it smells like a dead body; it's not like I can tell them it's dead animals and mold."

"Didn't you call that crime scene cleaner dude? He always leaves the jobs he's done for me smell-free."

She shook her head. "He hung up on me

after reminding me that I'd pulled a gun on him and then told him he was weird. I almost called him back and told him it was his own damn fault for sneaking up behind me."

Mother looked at her open-mouthed and then laughed.

Fab glared out the windshield in silence.

"Let's make a deal on the lighthouse," I suggested. "Joint custody. You can use Jake's anytime you want."

"You want to turn it into a stupid gift store." Fab careened up in front of Jake's, slowing and finding an empty space next to the kitchen door. "What kind of deal does Phil have?"

"I'm not asking you to pay rent," I huffed. "Here's my offer—no store, but I do get to have it repainted and give it curb appeal. I'm in the process of giving the property a makeover: a little strip mall with character. A bunch of run-down buildings doesn't work for me." Jake's had been first on my list. The outside renovations had recently been completed. It got a new paint job, copper roof, and plenty of outdoor lighting, and I'd supervised the planting of some new palms, both small and large, wrapping the trunks in white lights.

"You should have asked me." Fab sniffed.

"Like you did before it arrived? Have a little trust; a powerwashing isn't going to hurt its charm." I'd known she would hate my surprise, which was why I'd decided to spring the first part of the process on her… after the fact.

"No damn gift shop." She got out of the SUV and slammed the door.

That went pretty well. She's not stomping across the lot with her gun drawn, scaring the workers.

Mother turned and looked at me. "Could've been worse." She laughed again.

The block was no longer the eyesore it had once been. The gas station had been turned into a garden antique store. I'd partnered with Junker, and he'd hired his wife, "The Mrs."—a no-nonsense slip of a woman, barely five feet, with waist-length grey-black hair and enough character lines on her face for several lifetimes—to run the place. It gave me a place to drag the occasional roadside find that I had to threaten Fab into pulling over to retrieve.

The *Twinkie Princesses* lime-and-yellow mobile kitchen had been parked parallel to the road since before I owned the property. Their slogan was "We fry anything." The only problem was that they were never open. The two women paid their rent on time and, so far, had no arrests. I'd sent them an email saying that the place was a bit seedy-looking and could they spruce it up. I never received a response, but a few days later, a work crew had showed up, cleaned the place, and given it a fresh coat of paint, which spurred my plans for the lighthouse.

Fab ignored me as she went into Jake's, settling out on the deck with phone in hand. Mother spotted her cigar vendor and went to meet him.

I looked around the large open area; besides a couple of familiar faces at the bar, the place was empty. I craned my neck to look out on the deck, and with the exception of Fab, it appeared empty as well. Too subdued for me; I flipped the switch on the back of the jukebox as I crossed the room to kneel on a barstool, acknowledging Phil with a smile and leaning forward, trying to keep my voice from carrying as I whispered hoarsely, "You can make this happen?"

"Consider it done. Just remember: I get details." Phil poured a shot of whiskey and slid it down the bar.

"What do you need done?" Fab, who had ended her phone call—most likely with Didier, because if it was business, she'd be jerking on my sleeve—appeared out of nowhere, sliding onto the barstool next to me.

I gave her a blank stare, then nodded at two regular customers who had just walked through the door. "The meeting has been moved from outside to here at the bar; Phil's attendance is mandatory."

When I bought Jake's, I'd thought about a "Name the bar" contest but discarded it as a bad idea. I'd shuddered at the thought of telling some drunk I refused his name idea and having a full-scale fight break out. Now I couldn't imagine it being named anything else.

I'd made several changes to the interior, starting with a floor-to-ceiling cleaning, then turned it into a popular place to come drink, watch sports on the big-screen televisions, and have fun. An arcade basketball machine, a recent flea market find, now sat in the same corner as the pool tables.

Mother came in and slipped behind the bar, stashing cigar samples under the bar. She poured a sparkling water, added a lime wedge, and gave it to Fab, then made one for herself.

"I need your help," I told Mother while Phil busied herself at the other end of the bar. "Phil's birthday is coming up, and she doesn't want the party I'd planned to throw for her here."

"So much for the surprise." Mother snorted.

"When I find out who told her, I'm going to tell their ass off."

Fab put her glass back on the bar with a thump, garnering everyone's attention. Of the three men and one woman in the place, none would object to a tussle between two women.

Phil finished ringing up a customer and came back to stand next to Mother.

"The dead guy. Did you get anything

good?" I asked Phil.

"Couldn't find anyone who wanted him dead. According to neighbors, he always said hello but kept to himself. No one had anything bad to say or any clue why anyone would shoot him and ditch his body in the trash. The only thing missing is his car, which hasn't turned up. He had a little money, but it goes to a grandchild when the boy turns thirty."

"Random?" Mother raised her brows. "Wrong place and time?"

"Those are impossible to solve unless the killer slips up and talks." Fab pushed her glass across the bar to Mother. "I'll take a refill."

"You might consider a sign for the trash bin: 'Dump your dead bodies elsewhere.'" Phil smiled.

"Or 'Dead bodies get dumped around the corner' and an arrow," Fab said.

I grimaced. "Neither of you are funny."

"You're no fun." Phil laughed.

"One of us has to be the stable one, and today it's me." I poked my chest.

"Maybe your funeral friends have some information. Surely the coroner takes *their* calls," Mother suggested, spiraling Fab's drink back to her and frowning when it almost tipped over.

Fab and I had become good friends with the local funeral directors, who had hid us on a couple of occasions; when they needed help, we returned the favor.

A commotion at the front door had us all turning our heads.

"Everyone stay seated," Kevin barked as he crossed the threshold, several deputies behind him.

"What now?" I grumbled.

"Be nice," Mother whispered. "He might be family one day. Hopefully, he won't be so tight-assed when that day comes."

I gave her a toothy grin and blew her a kiss.

"He's headed this way," Phil whispered.

"Everyone take a seat out on the deck." Kevin pointed to the patio door. "We'll call you back inside one at a time. Try to leave, and you'll be arrested and taken to jail, where you can answer questions in custody."

He shuffled over to where the four of us were all still standing at the bar. "You're no exception: out to the deck." He laughed. "First The Cottages, now Jake's. You need to find a better place to dump the bodies if you don't want to be a suspect."

"What are you talking about?" I asked.

"We got a call—dead body in the dumpster out back. And look: here you all are." He snickered.

"You can wipe that smug smile off your face," Mother said, hands on her hips. "Have you ever arrested my daughter for murder? Or anything else? No, you haven't. Because you've never had cause and never will."

Kevin glared back at her.

Phil stepped over next to Mother. "They have the legal right not to answer your questions without an attorney present."

"You graduated law school yet?" he asked.

"I learned about people's rights in the first semester. You really should inform the people on the deck that it's their right not to say jack." Phil glared back at him. "Are you informing them that anything they say can be used against them in a court of law?"

"When I want legal advice, I'll get it from a real lawyer."

"Do you have a name or picture of the deceased?" I asked Kevin. "We might know him or her." I tugged on Fab's arm. "She'll be happy to identify whoever it is, if she knows him; she knows everyone we do. The rest of us will stay here."

Fab was perfect for the viewing, considering her all-around fascination with dead people, including taking their pictures. This way, she wouldn't have to sneak out to get a picture and risk arrest.

Kevin whistled to a fellow officer, meeting him in the middle of the dance floor that was used mostly when drunks wanted to show off their uncoordinated moves. He snapped his fingers at Fab, waving her over.

"Unleash your charm," I whispered.

She joined the two deputies without hesitation.

"Last time I'm going to say this—" Kevin pointed to the patio door. "—out."

"You need to do some more digging," I said to Phil. "Why has my property become so popular for dumping bodies? Why not drop them off at the funeral home? At least they know what to do with them. I hope one doesn't turn up at my house." I shuddered, linking my arm with Mother's.

"We'll split up, question the patrons, see who knows what," Mother said in a low voice.

"No need. They're all regulars. Phil can grill them next time they come in. Don't forget to offer them free beer." I nodded to Phil. We both knew free drinks were a conversation starter. None of those here today would kill someone unless it was an accident, and they were all smart enough to dump the evidence in a swamp.

My private table on the patio had been commandeered. I changed direction and headed to the far end of the deck, thinking Mother was right behind me. It was all I could do to contain my annoyance when I heard one of the deputies tell her, "Stop with the questions or I'll arrest you." I settled back, leveled the "behave" stare that she'd used frequently on Brad and me as kids at her, and motioned for her to come and sit in the chair next to me.

Phil ended her conversation with a regular, laughing at something he said and patting him on the back, then joined Mother and me.

Kevin stomped over.

I held up my hand. "I'll cut to the chase for you—all employees and guests were inside and knew nothing about a dead body or that the sheriff's office had been called. If you think any of us are murderers, you're wrong." I kept *as usual* to myself.

"Jake's is closed until further notice," he snapped. "You'll be informed when you can reopen."

Fab burst through the door with a smile on her face that disappeared when Kevin turned in her direction. She casually slid her phone into her back pocket. "Never saw him before," she blurted. "Hasn't been dead long. He's not bloated and doesn't smell, even though it's a warm day."

I made a retching noise.

Mother tugged on my hair.

"Do we need to get a new dumpster?" I asked Kevin. "Are you taking it with you?"

"I'll be sure to tell your trash company to bring it back once we're done," Kevin said with amusement.

"Oh no," Fab interjected. "We want a new one. I'm certain dead people carry cooties." Fab and Phil broke out in laughter and knuckle-bumped.

Mother snorted and laid her head on my shoulder; I'd bet she was also laughing.

"Can the regulars finish their drinks?" I asked. "They *did* pay for them."

Kevin glared at each of us in turn. "Yours isn't the only dive bar in town; they can go to one of the other ones."

"Since the crime scene is outside, any reason we can't lock up now?" Phil asked Kevin.

"We're not done processing this place, and it'll be a while. Don't look to re-open for another few days." Another officer called Kevin and he left.

"I'll stay until they're done," Phil offered. "I'm sure the body is hot gossip by now. We'll have them lined up at the door as soon as we re-open. Nothing like murder to bring in the business. Only thing better would be if it happened inside; then we get big crowds wanting to stand in the exact spot."

Fab shook her head. "When that guy got shot in here, you painted an X on the floor. How are you going to top that?"

"I made good money off that idea. If we can, we need to keep the current dumpster, but any beat-up one will do; I'll tell a little lie and say that it was *the* one. You—" She pointed at Fab. "—forward me pics of the dead guy. Oh, stop with the innocent face; I know you got them."

Fab retrieved her phone from her back pocket. I glared at her, hoping she wouldn't pass it around.

"Then what?" Mother asked in total fascination.

"Nothing, Mother. We can do a tasteful memorial plaque or something," I said.

"Boo," Fab hissed. "I want to hear Phil's idea."

"I'll take one of the pictures, blow it up to poster size, and tape it up on the outside of the bin. The best part—are you ready?—a one-dollar charge to peek inside," Phil said, thoroughly proud of her impromptu idea.

"It's frightening that, one day soon, you're going to be a lawyer." I pursed my lips in a frown. "You hang your shingle locally, and you'll have a head start on understanding your clients, especially if they come from around here."

"Who votes for the poster?" Fab raised her hand.

Mother and Phil's hands shot up.

"Don't get excited. The owner has five votes; motion denied," I said.

But I knew it wouldn't matter if I had a hundred votes. The poster would go up, and the bar would be standing room only once again.

Chapter 11

Fab came down the stairs in a pair of form-fitting blue jeans and a silky royal blue camisole. She jumped off the bottom step, a pleased-with-herself look on her face.

"Aren't you going to change?" I eyed Fab up and down.

"What's the big deal?" She eyed me with suspicion. "It's just the four of us for dinner. And why you wouldn't let Didier do the cooking, I don't know. You'll feel bad if one of us gets sick from your culinary 'skills.'"

"First off," I growled, my fists going up in a fighting stance, "just because I don't cook doesn't mean I can't."

Fab laughed and smacked my hands down, smiling indulgently. "Calm down. I'm sure whatever it is, it will be… delicious."

I scowled, not buying her pitiful excuse for an apology. "Just so you won't worry your pretty head about it, dinner is being barbequed by your boyfriend." Fab skirted around me, and before she could go to the patio, I added, "I have a little surprise for you. Tonight, I'm going to show you how much our relationship means to me and that I do listen to you."

"Something going on that I don't know about?" She scrutinized me closely.

"I hope you'll be pleased. In the spirit of friendship and all." I smiled and disappeared into the kitchen.

I had left a cellophane-wrapped bouquet of variously colored roses, which I'd picked up from the outdoor market in town, sitting in a pitcher of water. I took five small, square glass vases from the cabinet and dumped a handful of shells in the bottom of each. Then, shortening each stem, I divided the flowers, arranged three blooms in each vase, and put them on a tray, interspersed with starfish, to use as a centerpiece.

Walking through the French doors, I heard Fab tell Didier, "She's up to something."

Didier stepped away from the barbeque, wrapping his arm around Fab and pulling her to his side. "When is Creole getting here?"

I turned slightly, taking a breath to calm my nerves. "This is a special night." The doorbell sounded louder than usual to me. "Ooh, there's my date."

Didier's brows knitted together. "Since when does Creole ring the doorbell?"

"Two kinds of people do that—those that want to shoot us and solicitors. I hope you have your gun," Fab called out.

"I'm counting on the two of you. Be nice."

I hurried inside and threw open the front door, not sure what to expect; I hoped that Phil had come through with someone believable.

The tall man with messy blond hair grinned down at me, surfer dude written all over him. I admired his tan silk shorts and tropical shirt; they reeked "designer" if I knew my men's clothing, and I did.

"Madison, I presume." He took my hand, running his lips across the back of it in a kiss. "Phil texted me a picture so I wouldn't mess up before I got in the door."

"Ross Dugan." I smiled in welcome, holding out my arm and ushering him inside. "Thanks for doing this." I leaned in and whispered, "The story is that we just met, so we won't be expected to know each other's life story."

His eyes ran over my white, scoop-neck handkerchief dress with gold rope shoulder straps, matching belt, and low-heeled slides that showed off my tanned legs. "I wouldn't mind going out on a date for real."

"Rules for tonight: We need to look as though we're in the first throes of lust, but don't go overboard. I'm partial to the boyfriend I already have. My hope is that if you play your part, I won't have to listen to any more snotty comments about the love of my life from my roommate."

Ross drew my arm through his. "Gotcha.

I'm looking forward to this dinner." He huffed out a low laugh.

I pointed the way, and he led me out to the patio. "Fab, Didier, this is Ross." I whispered hoarsely to Fab, "You're always telling me how I can do better than Creole, so I took your advice and decided it was time to look around, interview replacements."

Didier's mouth dropped open, and even Fab looked shocked.

"I mean really, who wants to date a Neanderthal?" I directed my question at Fab.

Didier didn't skip a beat; he extended his hand to shake Ross's and offered him a drink. But while he was getting the requested beer, he shot me a disgusted glare, the first he'd ever given me.

Ross silently perused every inch of Fab from head to toe. "Madison told me you're her best friend and that you're both little crime fighters."

Damn – I should have set up a video camera.

"Funny, Madison has never mentioned your name," Fab shot back.

"Ross is great. I know you're going to love him. Aren't you happy that I listen to your suggestions?" I asked in a challenging tone.

Ross ignored the awkward silence. Cupping the back of my neck, he swooped down, kissing my cheek. He held up the beer Didier had handed him. "To new beginnings."

He clinked bottles with Didier, but Fab ignored him. "I hear you're an underwear model." He gave Didier a once-over. "What's that like: trotting around in your undies, you know, everything on display?"

Didier shot him a glacial stare. "That's the way my career started out. I've made a name for myself and now work exclusively for high-end designers.

Fab growled.

Ross's brows arched. "I think your girlie is hungry." He hugged me to his side. "I can hear her stomach from here. So skinny, she could use seconds."

I pinched my thigh, concentrating on not laughing. I did feel some sympathy for Didier, who was not amused and looked like he wanted to take a swing at Ross. But he couldn't learn that this was payback or Fab would find out. Didier excused himself and went inside.

Ross tightened his hold, looking down. "You're not one of those bird eaters, are you?"

"I love good food. And even more when there's leftovers." I beamed at him.

"How did you two meet?" Fab asked, eyeing him with suspicion, her tone ice cold.

"Early one morning, before Jake's opened, I came up the back steps and there sat Madison, on the deck at what she informed me was her favorite table." Ross squeezed my shoulder.

"You there to rob the place?" Fab asked.

"Fabiana!" I hissed.

Didier returned from the kitchen, platter in hand, in time to hear Fab. He smirked. "I'm putting the grouper on the grill. Dinner should be ready soon." He'd apparently decided to hurry the evening along. No chitchat and drinks by the pool.

Brad had delivered several pieces of cleaned fish after he returned from his last run. I stuffed a couple with a crab filling and cleaned and chopped vegetables for grilling. Good thing everyone in the family liked all types of seafood; with my brother being a commercial fisherman, he kept the freezer stocked.

"You little French things are all spit and fire, aren't you?" Ross looked at Fab in amusement. "I certainly wanted to steal Madison away that morning." He nodded in Didier's direction. "He's pretty and can cook too. Nice. You need some help?" he called.

"I'll help him," Fab said in disgust and stalked away.

"She can cook? Now that's a package."

I knew Fab had heard by the way her shoulders stiffened, but she didn't turn around.

I grabbed Ross's arm and pulled him to the opposite side of the pool, checking to make sure Fab hadn't doubled back to listen. "Good job." I muffled my laugh against his chest.

"We can do better." He pushed me into the corner, covered my body with his, and bent his head to mine. "Can you see around my shoulder without them noticing?"

"They're both glaring. Do not kiss me—my boyfriend won't forgive any indiscretions, and frankly, I wouldn't forgive him either. We don't share. Even if it *is* to teach my friend not to trash talk my boyfriend."

"Does the boyfriend know what you're up to?"

"Not yet. I decided that telling him after was better." Ross quirked his brow. "What's your story?" I asked. "You're a looker; I imagine the women are lined up."

He bowed, his eyes twinkling. "Just a friend of Philippa's, willing to help her boss out. If it sounds like fun, I'm in."

It felt awkward to ask the usual get-to-know-you questions, but I was saved by Fab's shrill whistle that dinner was almost ready. I was tempted to whistle back, but hard as I tried, I'd never mastered whistling, and now wasn't the time to embarrass myself by showing off my lack of skill.

Ross took my hand. "Do I dine and dash or what?"

"The way those two are acting, I'm thinking that after dinner is going to be even more awkward than it's been so far. We should see how it goes."

Ross and I returned to the table, where he sat across from the grim-faced Fab. I joined

Didier at the grill, feeling guilty that I hadn't been more help.

"Thank you," I said to him, pointing to the risotto he'd cooked on a side burner.

"We have everything?" he asked, not looking at me. "Funny thing, Creole never mentioned your relationship being over."

"For dessert, I got your favorite: gelato." My stomach was already a mass of nerves; I'd be lucky if I could eat anything. "I'll tell Creole later." I turned and walked back to the table.

Fab stabbed her fork into the grouper. "You know, Madison bought this already prepared from the store. Or begged it off her brother. He fishes."

My eyes narrowed; she made it sound like my brother took his fishing pole to some creek. I kicked her under the table. "At least I *can* cook."

Fab ignored me, instead focused on interrogating Ross. "So you're auditioning for the new boyfriend position? Who does that?"

He puffed out his chest and said arrogantly, "A man who knows he can blow away any competition."

"What exactly is it that do you do—you know, for a living?" Fab looked down her finely chiseled nose.

I glanced at Didier; the smug look on his face told me he had no intention of reining in his girlfriend.

"As a member of the idle rich, nothing as exciting as prancing around in my underwear." Ross matched her condescending stare.

I reached out and covered his hand, squeezing it in a warning that would probably be lost on him. He didn't know that my volatile friend might well upend the table and leave us both wearing our dinner.

Fab pushed her chair back and glowered at Ross. "Get your foot off me. You've got the wrong leg."

I quirked my head down in time to see Ross jerk his leg back.

"Sorry," he said, clearly not. "I'll double-check next time."

Didier put his arm around Fab and joined her in grilling Ross. "What do you do to workout - run, bike?"

Fab snorted, giving Ross the once-over; her face let him know he came up short.

Ross pretended not to notice. "I've got a trainer that comes to the house three days a week, and on the off-days, I shoot hoops, play volleyball, anything I can do at the beach, even bowl once in a while. You two should come out with Madison and me one night."

"I like to bowl," I said. "But I'm not very good." Turning to Fab and Didier, I added, "It would be fun, don't you think?"

"I'll buy the beer," Ross said. "The alley doesn't stock these fancy European beers." He held up his bottle. "Plenty of American ones, though. Even have that one that's five dollars a case on tap."

"One of my tenants drinks that." I shuddered. The beer aficionados in the family would never speak to me if I bought that.

Silence descended on the table. No one seemed inclined to speak up, and we ate without saying a word. The others finished their dinner while I pushed mine around on the plate. Ross squeezed my knee; looking at him, I saw it didn't bother him and was able to relax.

Eventually, I'd had enough and stood. "Ross and I are going to do dishes since Didier barbequed."

Without bothering to ask if they were finished, Ross reached across the table and relieved Fab and Didier of their dinner plates, handing them to me. He ignored their dirty looks and swept the silverware off the table, piling it on top of the plates. "Come on, hon." He steered me back into the house, saying over his shoulder, "We'll be back."

Once we reached the kitchen, Ross turned to make sure we hadn't been followed, then took the plates, setting them in the sink. "I thought undie boy was going to slug me when I passed the dishes off to you. Nice touch, don't you think? Makes me even more obnoxious."

"My face hurts from holding back the laughter."

Ross hopped up on the counter and waved to Didier and Fab. "I'll supervise while you show me how dishes get clean."

"Do you think they'll wait until we get back outside to sneak off?" I laughed.

"Escape plans are in the works. Neither of them likes me." He grinned. "Fab would have stomped off in a huff already if it weren't for her boyfriend. You know, she has this hair-raising look—scared me a couple of times. Didier doesn't look like he can handle her, but he must." He shook his head, obviously finding it hard to believe.

"A lot of arguing in French seems to do it for them."

"If you've got any more applicants standing by, you need to give them a warning about her. Did you see when she locked eyes with me and licked the tip of her knife? My boy parts shriveled." He shuddered. "They can hear us laughing; probably wondering what you find so interesting."

Didier stepped inside the French doors. "Fab and I are going for a walk on the beach. Nice meeting you."

Ross waved. "You want to work out sometime, give me a call." He waited until the two of them left through the fence, then hopped off the counter. "I think they're gone." He walked to the patio and peered out. "They were sure in a hurry to disappear." He chuckled. "You need me to stay? I warn you, though; I'm about out of obnoxious."

"Thank you. You ever need a favor, call. Next girlfriend, send over her name; we'll run a background check. She goes psycho; we'll relocate her for you. Free food and drinks anytime at Jake's."

"This was fun." He walked with me to the front door and kissed my cheek.

I scanned the kitchen to see that everything was cleaned up, then raced out to the patio, wiping down the table and taking the centerpieces inside to the garden window. Once everything was put away and cleaned up, I texted Creole: "Confession. No one hurt. No bullets," and hopped up the stairs to my bedroom before Fab and Didier got back.

* * *

Rugged hands ran down both sides of my body, wrenching me from a sweet dream that I struggled to hang onto. Recognizing the barking growl that permeated my consciousness, I murmured, "You're annoying."

Creole flipped me over on my stomach, running his hands down my back and legs, then smacking my bottom.

"Ouchie," I grumbled.

"Just making sure that you don't have so much as a scratch on you. What the heck happened tonight? Another job for that dick, Brick?" He nuzzled my neck.

"That rhymes." I giggled. "Just take off your clothes, slide under the sheets, and be open-minded."

He groaned and dumped his clothes in a pile on the floor.

"I love you."

Creole eyed me suspiciously. "Jump to the good part," he said gruffly.

I snuggled up to his side. "That's not a good idea. Starting from the beginning would be better." And I related every detail, beginning with why and ending with running up to my bedroom.

"I think, under the snarky attitude, Fab likes me a little." He chuckled. "We've worked well together on a couple of cases."

"I'm hoping that, after she gets a taste of what it would be like if I chose someone neither of them liked, she'll have a new appreciation for you." I laughed. "Ross was great. If only I had video."

"Is this the end of my replacement search?" He watched as I scrunched up my nose. "Didier will clue me in on it tonight. What do I say?"

"I've got one more date, which will be the last. I need Didier's disgust to be real. My last resort is to beat the stuffing out of Fab, and I'll probably get hurt."

"All this for me?" He moved closer and kissed me. "Don't do anything that might get you hurt. Not even a little bit," he grouched. "If you think you're going to replace me, all I can say is: poor guy. I'll warn him that I know where the hungriest alligators live."

"I've always wanted to know if alligators will eat a whole body."

"Alligators don't chew like humans. A while back, Fish and Wildlife had it on good authority that a particular alligator had eaten a man—well, parts of him. They captured the gator and found the man's leg and shoe inside."

"I suppose that's why the signs say: Don't feed or pet the gators."

"Young lady." He bit the tip of my nose. "This is horrible foreplay."

I pressed my face against his neck and laughed.

Chapter 12

I lay sprawled on a double chaise positioned to overlook the pool and the rest of the backyard. Past experience had taught me to always sit where I could watch the comings and goings in my vicinity. Over the top of my book, I spied Fab standing in the doorway, staring in my direction with a wary look on her face. I pointed to the pitcher of iced tea and extra glass, motioning for her to come sit on the chaise next to me.

Fab filled a glass with ice and an orange slice, pouring tea for herself and refilling mine before sitting. "We've got a job."

I already knew but asked anyway. "Who's the client?"

"It's Brick." She held up her hand. "And since I know your next question, it's a skip on a bond."

"Bail jumper?" I wrinkled my nose. "No, thanks. I can give you a list of ways this job could wrong... fast. Starting with the fact that the person is a criminal, or a suspected one anyway, and running out on a bond makes him or her look... hmm... guilty!"

"It's just backup." Her voice rose, headed into a full-blown snit.

"When do I ever say no to you? Never. This time I am. You know that sixth sense I have? It's telling me—no, screaming—that this one is a bad idea." I waved my hand, cutting her off before she launched into defense mode. "If you don't tell Brick to shove the job up his rear, then I'm going to tell on you."

Fab crossed her arms and glared for a long moment before saying, "You wouldn't."

"Oh. Yes. I. Would. If something were to happen to you, where would I find a new best friend?" Trying to lessen the tension, I said, "I would compare them all to you, and they'd come up… well, lacking. Please…" I sighed at the familiar shifty, sneaky look, knowing she was about to spew forth the comforting words I wanted to hear and not mean a one of them.

But Fab changed course, offering no justifications and instead shrugging. "I'm not committed, so I'll think about it. And you do the same. We have a couple of days to decide."

Translation: The job starts tomorrow. Who's going to wait days to track someone on the run?

Fab and I engaged in a mini stare-off.

My phone beeped, announcing the arrival of a text. "Hideaway—lunch time."

"Oh! Ross." I giggled at the screen. "He wants to meet for lunch. I'll be back in a couple of hours." I jumped up. "If you're not here or not answering your phone, I'll have Creole's boss put out an APB on you."

"I'll be here." She refilled her glass, checking her watch. "I'm waiting on a call from another client. You know, he's not so bad."

"Ross? You like him?" I pasted on a smile, trying to appear pleased.

"Creole. Free advice, which you know I never give: Don't mess up your relationship with Creole for the likes of Ross. He's not the guy for you."

I tugged on one of her long curls. "Don't get in any trouble while I'm gone."

She raised her glass in a salute.

* * *

The Overseas Highway headed south was quiet, my SUV and a few cars sharing the four-lane highway that connected the Keys to the mainland. The drive to Key West never got old, passing the blue-green waters of the gulf, which glittered from the sun dancing across the small white caps, the palm trees swaying in a gentle breeze.

I patted the steering wheel and asked, "Do you remember me?" Fab drove my car more than I did, despite having a fancy sports car of her own.

The exit approaching up ahead appeared to most people to be just a turnaround in a desolate area, a way to get back on the northbound side of the highway. To the right, there was one side street. The pavement ended after several hundred feet, and the road wove through a bank of trees and wound around to a secluded street running along the beach that boasted five houses a half-mile apart from each other.

The lie to Fab about Ross nagged at me; it had slipped too easily from my lips. I owed her a trip to the high-end boutiques she liked that, much to my disgust, rarely had a sales rack. And I'd have to do it without a grumble. But no matter how guilty I felt, I drew the line at the six-inch stilettos she kept insisting I buy.

I squeezed the SUV in next to Creole's oversized truck, leaving just enough room to get the door open. An eight-foot fence ran across the front of the property and down the side. Creole had recently installed a keypad, and I entered my code and slipped in, securing the gate behind me. The front of the house had no windows, but the back had a solid wall of pocket doors running from one end to the other with an amazing view of the Gulf.

The door opened before I could insert my key. I paused, then—remembering that Creole's ribs had finally healed—launched myself into his open arms. He bent, putting one arm under my knees, and lifted me, carrying me to the king-size bed and dumping me in the center.

I wiggled backward.

"Where do you think you're going?" He

latched onto my ankle, dragging me closer.

"I need an expedited super favor." I tried to shift away. We needed to talk before his one-track mind put the conversation on hold.

"You and I—" He wagged his finger. "—we don't have a need for favors. You ask and I do. You're overdressed," he scolded. "Let me help you off with your clothes while you tell me what it is you need."

He pulled me into a sitting position, dragged my top over my head, sending it flying across the room, and shoved me gently on my back.

I launched into a recitation about the bail jumper job and my worry that something could and would likely go wrong. I didn't point out that our track record substantiated that comment. "Would you call Brick and tell him to find someone else, or else? I think he's a little afraid of you anyway. And don't tell Fab."

Creole sent my skirt airborne. Picking up my leg, he lightly massaged my calf, nibbling on my big toe. "I'm so proud of you. You recognized a dangerous job and said no to her. Cops get shot all the time rounding up those bastards."

I sighed as he rubbed my arch with his knuckles.

"Feel good?" He grinned. "I'll take care of Brick this afternoon. It will be my pleasure."

"Pleasure, I love that word." I lifted my

legs and wrapped them around his waist.

Chapter 13

On my way back from my afternoon tryst with Creole, I got a phone call from Mac that Miss January had gone missing. No one had seen her since that morning, including her drunken boyfriend, Score. According to Mac, he was still drunk from the previous night, passed out in a chair out by the pool. He'd tumbled out of the chair, which he took with him; it'd ended up straddling his body, but he never moved. I sighed with relief when Mac assured me he was still breathing and luckily hadn't rolled into the water.

The beanpole-thin man didn't look a day over one hundred but claimed to be a bit younger. He'd found himself a girlfriend who was less than half his age, although she didn't look it—looks-wise, they were a matched pair. You'd think they could both sober up and enjoy more than smoking and drinking.

I called Fab and asked if she wanted to ride along; although she didn't like to deal with the problems at The Cottages she hated to be left out. She was waiting in the driveway when I pulled up; marching to the driver's side, she glared when I suggested that I wanted to drive, so I moved to my assigned seat to keep the peace.

"I suppose you're going to insist we find Miss January?" Fab snarked.

"You know damn well that you'd feel bad if something happened to her." I turned away and stared out the window. "Mac called all Miss January's usual haunts, and she's not at a one of them. Damn that friend of hers for showing her how to use the trolley. She could be anywhere."

"Doesn't she have a cell phone?"

"Dead. She can't remember to charge it and only knows how to use it the five minutes a day she's awake and sober. Probably a good thing. If she ever discovers drunk dialing, she'll never get off the phone. And guaranteed the sheriff's department would somehow get involved."

Fab half-laughed. "That could be entertaining."

"Over there." I pointed and swiveled in my seat, keeping an eye on the truck we'd just passed.

"Don't screech," Fab said irritably. "That racket hurts my ears. What am I looking at?" She looked in the rearview mirror.

"Slow down, pull over, something. You need to get back behind that pickup you just careened around. I'm pretty sure that was Miss January hanging onto the tailgate. Whatever you do, don't scare the driver; he brakes suddenly and the woman might fall off."

Fab eased to the side of the road a block ahead of the old battered Dodge truck. When it passed us, she pulled back out behind it. We both recognized Miss January, sitting on the edge of the truck bed, one hand clutching the spring. At that moment, the driver swerved—must have not been paying attention, as there was no other reasonable explanation—and Miss January rocked back and forth.

"Do something," I squealed. "We'll run over her if she falls off."

"I'm going to pull alongside. You yell to him and give him a reason to pull over; car problems or something."

I rolled down the window and leaned out, waving to the man behind the wheel. I cupped my hands around my mouth, pointed, and yelled, "Tire."

The scruffy-faced man looked at me in confusion, then nodded, slowed, and pulled to the curb. Fab parked several feet farther down the road, and I jumped from the SUV and ran back. "There's nothing wrong with your tire," I assured the guy, who was getting out of the truck. "I just needed you to pull over. If that woman falls off the back of your truck and is killed, you could do a serious amount of prison time. I'll take her with me, and next time you offer someone a ride, they ride in the cab with you; anywhere else is illegal."

His face glowed beet red. "If you think I'm going to let some scrawny bitch barf in my truck, you're crazy," he yelled, waving his arms. "She's not going anywhere." He shoved Miss January back and slammed the tailgate. "She made a deal with me: if I drop her off at the corner up a ways, Junior gets sucked."

The man stumbled forward—propelled by an expertly placed kick to his backside, courtesy of Fab—throwing his arms out to catch his fall. "She's coming with us." Fab stepped around him and snapped the gate back down, reaching out a hand to Miss January, who huddled in the corner. Over her shoulder, she said to the man, "You're going to keep your mouth shut. Do you want to know why? You say one word, and I'll shoot you." She lifted her shirt, showing off her firearm.

The man grumbled but managed to stay silent.

"Hi, honey," Miss January slurred, crawling out of the truck on her hands and knees. "Sweet man, got me almost all the way home. Forgot his name," she rasped.

Until both of her feet were flat on the ground, I maintained an iron grip on her bony arm, happy that she'd chosen tennis shoes for her latest adventure. I led her to the driver side of the SUV, helped her into the back seat, and ran around and slid in after her, shuddering at the thought of her getting sick. She leaned her head against the window and, judging by the slight snore, instantly fell asleep.

I watched out the rear window as money exchanged hands between the man and Fab. They must have made up; he waved before he got back in his truck and shot back onto the road in a blast of black smoke.

"If she gets sick," Fab said, looking over the seat as she climbed in, "can the crime scene cleaner dude get the smell out?"

"He works wonders with dead-people odor." No one else in the neighborhood could boast having such a contact on speed dial.

* * *

Fab eased up in front of Miss January's cottage. I shook her shoulder, and she mumbled something indecipherable, barely moving.

Fab got out and came around to jerk open the passenger door. "I'll grab her ankles and drag her out."

I fisted my hands in an enormous amount of fabric from her overly large tent dress so she wouldn't fall out.

"Where did you find her?" Mac yelled as she wandered over, not one to watch from a discreet distance. "Don't let go of her. We'll slide her across, and from there, it's only a few steps up and we can dump her on the couch."

Mac slipped her arms under Miss January and hoisted her to her feet, walking her up the steps like an oversized rag doll, and got her to the bedroom in one piece. I removed her shoes, and Mac covered her with a blanket. Score was hogging the couch, snoring. Kitty lay on the floor at an odd angle. Score had no patience for the dead animal and had to be threatened to make sure that the cat didn't disappear. I used his shirt, which was lying on the floor near the cat, to pick up Kitty and climbed on a chair to put her on the top of the bookcase.

Kitty had been dead for an unknown number of years, certainly ever since I inherited The Cottages. I'd had to have her re-stuffed twice. It was still unclear to me whether Miss January knew that the cat had moved on to its next life, and it was a question I avoided, pretending all was normal.

Back out in the driveway, I turned my face to the sun and soaked up the warm rays. "I know that the doctors long ago wrote off Miss January and Joseph for dead, but I realized today, when I saw her hanging precariously from the back of that truck, that I'm not prepared for their demise." Both of them had terminal cancer but kept chugging along. I admired their tenacity, that they flipped life the bird and did as they pleased, self-medicating with liquor and cigarettes, and in Joseph's case, medical weed in a state where it wasn't legal. I'd pointed that out once, and he flounced into his cottage and slammed the door.

Mac patted me on the back. "You have more patience for unusual crap than anyone. Ever. I'd hug you, if it weren't for your no-touch policy."

"Thanks for the… compliment?" My phobia had more to do with handshaking. I thought Miss Manners should review her policy and change it. A hand stuck in my face had me wondering where the heck it had been previously. "When she wakes up, you need to have a talk with her; disappearing episodes will not be tolerated. Ground her or something. You be the tough one, and I can be the nice one."

"And if she tells me to piss up a rope? Reminds me she's an adult and can do what she wants?"

Fab burst out laughing. "That I'd like to see."

A bright-red short bus pulled into the driveway, bringing the conversation to a halt. The driver cut the engine, and the doors opened.

"Welcome!" Mac waved. "This bunch is here for two weeks," she informed me. "We're being invaded by your lawyer's extended family members again. First timers."

"How many family members does Cruz have?" There must nine hundred people in his family, and it seemed like we'd entertained at least half of them.

Cruz Campion—lawyer extraordinaire, or so he boasted—and I had made a deal. In exchange for free legal advice and occasional representation, I'd agreed to entertain his out-of-town relations. I hadn't known at the time how many of them there were.

"The Cottages is the hottest ticket in the Cruz family." Mac gestured for me to follow. "Every one of them can afford to go someplace better."

I pulled a face, and Mac rolled her eyes in return.

"They come for the entertainment, and we better deliver." Mac puffed up her chest in her white button-down, which strained at the seams, and smoothed her gaucho skirt.

I wanted to ask if her feet were swimming in sweat in the fur-lined black ankle boots but decided it was one of those things I didn't need to know.

"They talk amongst themselves. Compare notes," Mac said. "If one group gets a shooting or fight, the next expects the same, or something else a classy joint wouldn't offer."

Fab had lagged behind, but something must have changed her mind because she ran to catch up. "They're not satisfied with the tours you set up, the reservations at restaurants where they never have to wait? Surely you don't have problems every time they visit?"

"Perti-near." *Mac's folksy way of saying "yes" made me smile.*

It took longer than I thought it would

before the six adults and three kids disembarked from the bus.

"Don't worry, I've got the entertainment covered," Mac said. "I've got a couple of drunks on standby to stage a good fight. Hopefully, they don't beat the spit out of one another and end up getting the police called. Though that could be a perk—I'd get a twofer."

Before I could tell her "no way," she went to greet the guests and help sort out the luggage.

The stack of luggage grew higher on the other side the driveway. "We need someone to schlep bags. Need my help?" I asked.

"Show time." Mac rubbed her hands together. "I'll check them in; you escort them to their door. I don't have to tell you to say something friendly, like I would her." She squinted at Fab. "I'm a great baggage schlepper, and it pays good. Besides, I've got it covered." Mac flexed her muscles.

A scraping noise behind me caught my attention. I turned and saw Joseph, a cigarette dangling from his lips, dragging a beach chair with one hand, his other arm wrapped around his girlfriend, Svetlana's, waist.

"I'll run and tell him to get his ass back inside," Fab said.

Mac grabbed her arm. "No, you won't. I already paid for his help, and I won't get my money back. Before he'd shake, he made 'no refunds' part of the deal."

Joseph unfolded his chair in his parking space, plopped Svet down, and crossed her legs. "Got to keep an eye on my girl," he said and nodded as his cigarette bobbed up and down. He headed to the shed and came back out with the industrial-weight wagon for the luggage.

Mac nodded to Joseph, giving him a thumbs up. She spoke to each guest and motioned for me to follow. Fab had already disappeared inside the office and claimed her seat on the couch.

"I'll give you the key; you call out the number to Joseph and show the people where they're staying," Mac instructed. "The luggage will be right behind you."

Mac impressed me with her organization—she had the paperwork prepared and ready to sign and quickly ran their credit cards. I escorted each family group, introducing myself and saying something nice about Cruz as I tried to figure out where they fit in the familial food chain.

Chapter 14

The morning sun streamed through my bedroom window. I stood by the window, finishing my cup of coffee as I looked down at the crystal-blue pool. When I moved in after my aunt's death, the pool had been surrounded by a slab of concrete lined in identical terra cotta flowerpots and chaise lounges topped with faded cushions. The concrete had endured a facelift, and I surrounded the entire area with more flowers in an array of colorful pots and seashell mulch. Most people thought I was nuts when I said the shells kept the bugs from procreating, but I was right. With family entertainment on my mind, I'd added a cooking space with storage, comfortable chairs, chaises, and an oblong table that sat twelve. I was proud of the way the backyard had turned out.

Fab and I had no plans for the day, and I intended to indulge myself by sitting by the pool with another cup of coffee and a book. I upended a shopping bag on my bed, and a hot-pink two-piece fell out. In the store, it had been so bright that I blinked when I saw it hanging on the rack. The saleswoman had insisted I try it on—something about my coloring and the suit were a good match, flattering style, la, la—I tuned her out, thinking she said the same thing to every customer. Under pressure, I disappeared into the dressing room, having already decided on a tangerine suit. Instead, I left the store with both suits and two cover-ups.

I grabbed a book and my phone, slid down the stairs, and followed Fab and Didier's voices into the kitchen. "Good morning." I reached for my coffee mix to make a second cup of my favorite vanilla-flavored brew.

Fab grunted and Didier ignored me. No more sexy "bonjours" from him since my "date" with Ross. A girl could have a plan go south on her once in a while; I was already rethinking this one and needed a fast exit plan. I made a mental note to cancel the next date.

I put my coffee mixture into the microwave, a long-running joke since the other two drank designer brew out of the coffee maker only the two of them knew how to work. Even Creole had his own pot. Fab had told him in no uncertain terms that he was not to comingle his pedestrian brand with theirs. I'd teased her about coffee not walking and gotten a glare for my efforts.

The kitchen was quiet; three people and no one had anything to say. I kept my back turned, deciding to blurt out the truth about my so-called dating before I was the one to end the relationship between the four of us. But when I turned, Fab looked ready to combust into flames, her face angrier than I'd ever seen it. Didier shuffled through the pages in his black leather portfolio, not looking at her. Whatever they were fighting about must be a doozy. Now wasn't the time for a confession. Thankfully, Didier's phone rang at the same moment my coffee was ready; I grabbed it and forced myself to walk, not run, out to the patio.

I sat on the top step of the pool, kicking the water, sipping my coffee, and daydreaming about starting every morning like this; I wondered if I'd enjoy it as much if it happened all the time.

"How dare you!" Fab hollered.

I looked over my shoulder. Seeing her standing in the doorway, I was surprised to realize it was only her and me in the backyard. "What's wrong?" I stepped out of the pool, reaching for a beach towel and wrapping it around my waist.

"You know my account with Brick is an important one, but you went behind my back and got me fired off a job. More correctly, your boyfriend, who has one foot out the door, threatened him," she continued at a yell. "Does he know you're boyfriend shopping?"

Good thing the neighbor's hard of hearing. Fab had never been really mad at me before, and I didn't like it.

"I was worried for your safety," I said, filled with dread and unsure how this would work out.

"In case you haven't noticed, I can make my own decisions. I've been on my own for a damn lot longer than you have!"

"Do you think you could stop yelling?" *Oops! That was the wrong thing to say. I should have stressed the safety issue instead.*

"No. I. Could. Not." She paced a few steps and turned back, lowering her voice. "He's my biggest client. What happens if he decides to stop using me?"

Now wasn't the time to tell her I thought that would be the best thing that could happen. "You don't need the money. That worthless ex-husband of yours left you plenty."

"What do you want me to do? Sit around all day and dangle my feet in the pool?"

"I suppose not." My friend had a ton of energy and always liked to be on the go, preferably to the next case. "I'll call Brick and smooth the waters."

"I'll do it myself. You stay out of it," she snapped and flounced back into the house.

I trailed behind her, and when she picked her bag up off the couch, I said, "Don't leave like this." I swiped a tear off my face when, without a word or a glance, she slammed out the front door. I ran to the garden window, flinching at the sound of tires squealing out of the driveway and all the way to the corner. She'd taken off in the Porsche; that wasn't a good sign. Thank goodness the street was clear.

I went back outside to the patio and retrieved my phone, texting Creole, "Didn't you tell Brick to keep his mouth shut?"

A minute later, it rang. I answered and said a quiet, "Hi."

"I did," Creole huffed into the phone. "What happened?"

"The bastard told her, and now she's livid. She slammed out of here, and I'm not sure she's going to forgive me."

"I'm going to make this up to you. Are you crying?"

"No." I sniffed. "This isn't your fault; Brick's the a-hole. Him and his stupid jobs."

"I'm going to break his nose," Creole barked.

I huffed a laugh. "Can you take a picture?"

"What are you doing?"

"Sitting here in my new bathing suit that shows off my assets in a flattering way." I still felt sulky, but it lightened my mood to tease him.

"We need to have a moonlight swim at my house; there, we can leave the bathing suits on the side of the pool."

"Sneak into my bed later."

His growly laugh sent tingles up my

spine.

I lay back on the chaise, texting Brick, "I quit. And you can tell Fab." Blocking his number had me smiling at the screen.

Chapter 15

Fab and Didier stayed away for two days. After the first night, I called and found she'd turned off her phone. When I called Didier, he didn't pick up but texted that he and Fab had gone to Naples for a getaway.

Creole called and asked to meet at Jake's, which was a first. He had called the bar and reserved the game room. I tried to wheedle the details out of him, but he only fended off my questions with more questions. The only thing he *would* tell me was that he had the food taken care of but had forgotten to order a salad.

I yelled and waved to Cook as I swept in the back door, noticing the orders on the wheel. I wrapped a bib apron around my skirt and button-down shirt and reached for a stainless steel bowl, setting it on the sideboard, and grabbed the lettuce mix out of the refrigerator, chopping the greens into a reasonable size. Looking over my choices, I tossed in tomatoes, olives, and other items that I knew Creole liked.

I'd just finished when he slid up behind me, turned me to face him, bent me back towards the counter top, and devoured my lips.

"Isn't it weird that you're kissing me and dating other guys?"

"That was a silly game. I haven't told them yet, but it's over. Next time Fab calls you a name, I'll hit her from behind and run. Besides, we can smooch it up; no one is here but you and me. Well, Cook, but he's not paying attention." I took his hands in mine. "What's this?" Holding up his right hand, I kissed the white gauze. "Are you not playing nice again?"

"Bruised my knuckles." He raised them prizefighter style. "But well worth it."

I frowned at him, not missing the slight wince.

"I brought pizza from our favorite place," he said, leading me into the game room, where the boxes were already on the table. "Got the fancy vegetable one for Didier and Fab and the grilled shrimp for the two of us."

"Don't let Cook find out you snubbed his cooking," I whispered. "How can you be sure the twosome will show up? They're out of town."

"They're back. They'll be here in a few minutes. I deliberately cut her off at the signal, blowing by her and making sure she got stuck at a red light."

"I bet she cursed you in two languages. I'll set up the room." I raced back to the kitchen and gathered up dishes and silverware, putting everything on a small cart along with the salad, choosing the dressings that I knew each person liked; it took my mind off waiting to see if Fab was still furious.

To my surprise, the game room had never been a popular draw, but part of that had to do with Mother discouraging its use by other patrons. She justified it by reminding me that she'd single-handedly turned it into a moneymaker, using it for her friends to play poker. I flipped on the ceiling fans and threw open the double doors to the patio. If I'd arrived earlier, I could have gone into the bar and worked out my jitters playing arcade basketball.

Fab's and Didier's voices wafted in from the hall ahead of them. Creole followed a few steps behind with a tray holding beer, a mixed drink, and bottled water.

Fab quirked her brow at Creole. "What's that?" She pointed to the martini glass.

"An appletini."

"I don't drink those anymore." Fab sniffed.

"Fabiana," Didier hissed.

Creole picked up the martini glass, took a couple of steps, and heaved the contents over the railing. "Bar's over there." He waved. "Go get what you want."

No chance of harming the wildlife, as the water that ran by the deck was murky at best, but the mosquitos could get their drunk on.

She flounced over to the soda machine

and pulled out a bottle of water, ignoring the one Creole had brought her. She unscrewed the top, took a swig, recapped it, and slammed it down hard on the table. "What are we doing here?" she demanded.

At least, if the damn thing springs a leak, it's only water.

Didier reached out to Fab, but she skidded out of his reach.

"I thought we'd eat first." Creole flashed Fab a smirk. "Look." He lifted the lid on the pizza box. "Your favorite, and a salad lovingly made by Madison."

"Why don't we do two things at once?" Fab suggested in a less snarky tone.

Didier glared at her from across the table—men on one side, women on the other.

I leaned across the table and dragged the pizza box closer. I ripped off a slice, slapped it down on a plate, then added a tongful of salad, making sure to get some of the fun stuff and not just a mouthful of lettuce. I set the plate down forcefully in front of Fab, then wiggled my finger at Didier and Creole until they handed me their plates and did the same for them.

"Let's take a vote," Creole suggested. Eyebrows went up around the table. "Raise your hand if you like Fab's suggestion that we get down to business."

The vote was 4-0, all of our hands shooting into the air, followed by laughter that sliced through the uncomfortable atmosphere that had permeated the room.

Creole sat back in his chair, taking a long swig of his beer. "Try not to interrupt me in mid-sentence; wait until I take a breath and then butt in." He eyed the backup beers he'd brought for himself and Didier. "Two might not be enough."

"Don't worry. We don't have to go far for more," Didier said.

"Good thing." Creole nodded in Fab's and my direction. "There's two of them, and we both know that's a dangerous combination."

I cut the crust off my pizza and cut it into smaller pieces.

Fab wrinkled up her nose. "Pick up the slice with your fingers, eat until you get to the crust, then toss it aside." She put on a show and tell.

I leaned in her direction and whispered hoarsely, "I missed you."

Creole finished off his beer and looked at Fab. "I probably shouldn't have interfered in your business with Brick-ass, but Madison was worried, and I knew she'd end up going with you, and that wasn't going to happen. I'd like to say I'd never do it again, but that would be a lie." He held up his hand. "Before you rip my head off, let me give you a little update."

Fab stayed silent, which surprised me.

"Whatever it is will be news to me too," I said to her. "I didn't get a preview, although I did try."

Creole cleared his throat. "Did you know the fugitive you were to bring in had his bond revoked because he killed a man, a witness to his other crimes, while out on bail? Another so-called friend is in the hospital. Did your friend Brick happen to mention any of this to you?" he asked in disgust.

Fab shook her head.

Didier banged his fist on the table and said in an almost-yell, "You made it sound a whole lot different than what Creole just described."

"Brick is almost always vague on the details," I said in Fab's defense.

"What did you suspect that Fab didn't? Why get Creole involved?" Didier rattled off the questions and, not waiting for a response, glared at Fab. "Do you just not give a damn about your safety?"

I covered Fab's hand with mine and squeezed. "From time to time, I get an uneasy feeling that makes the hair on the back on my neck stand on end. This was one of those occasions."

Creole flicked Didier's shoulder, motioning for him to hand over another beer. "It gets better." He popped the top, taking a swig. "Before asking you to do the job, Brick hired a well-known bounty hunter in the area. He got shot for his efforts. He's still in the hospital, but at least he's not going to die—too big and mean."

I turned to Fab in shock. "That could have been you."

"Is the guy in custody?" Didier asked.

"Bail jumper is at the coroner's office. The cops got a tip that he was hiding out at a friend's house; when they arrived on scene, he took a shot at the cops and thankfully didn't hit anyone. They returned fire," Creole said.

Silence descended over the table.

"I'll never forgive you if you get yourself killed," Didier said to Fab in an even tone.

Fab hung her head, and I heard a sniff. I wasn't the only one.

"Not to defend the man…" I winced, knowing I was doing just that. "But I really believe that Brick thinks Fab is invincible. And he only thinks about himself."

"If the reason you work for that odious man is that you get a free car," Didier said. "I'll buy you any model you want. It's not like you drive yours anyway. Your name will be on the title, and no one will be able to take it from you."

"It's about friendship. He's had my back since I first came to town." Fab jumped up, almost upending her chair, ran around the table to Didier, and jumped in his lap. "I promise you that he didn't disclose the background of the perp." She whispered something in French. Didier and Creole both nodded.

"Just great." I threw up my hands. "Even you know what she said. I feel left out." I sulked.

"She told him she didn't need the car." Creole laughed. "I do need to disclose something that all of you should know. I ran into Brick after finding out all of this, and the meeting didn't go well."

I lowered my gaze to his gauze-wrapped hand. "Did you get pictures?"

Didier banged his spoon on the table. "Is it agreed that we're all made up?"

Everyone nodded.

Creole stood and collected the plates, silverware, and trash, placing them on the cart. "Does anyone want anything before we start the second part of the meeting?"

Fab stood and mouthed "water." I nodded.

Creole opened the door. Standing in the hall, he yelled, "Hey," and held up two fingers, then motioned with his arm. He took the cart to the kitchen, and when he came back, waited at the door until Phil appeared with a tray of beer and bottled water. Creole swept out his hand, ushering her inside and closing the door behind her.

He sat down next to me, laying his arm across my shoulder, ending the "boys on one side, girls on the other" thing. "Next part of this meeting: Phil is going to update us on dead John Doe number two."

"New client?" I winked at Phil.

"Once Creole assured me it wouldn't be freebie work, I agreed to a trial run."

"This is our information girl," Creole introduced Phil for Didier's benefit. "Her identity must remain a secret. She's a law school student who bartends, no other explanation needed. If anyone takes an abnormal interest in her, I want to know." He bowed slightly and waved Phil toward the table. "The floor is yours."

Phil sat at the head of the table. "Law enforcement is keeping the details on a need-to-know basis. At first, all I could get was that the only common denominator between these unlucky fellows was that they were found dead, with no apparent reason for anyone to kill them. They were also both shot in the back multiple times. In both cases, the first bullet most likely killed them; the rest were gratuitous. Neither was killed in the location where they were found. The second body was that of sixty-three-year-old Rodney Wheeler. Rodney was just getting ready to retire from the post office. Owned a small house in Marathon. He had no identification on him, but a missing-person report made it easy to identify him. When the deputies went to his house, they found it had been ransacked. The burned-out shell of his car was found before he turned up."

"Did he have family?" I asked.

"Two grown children. Your funeral friends took good care of him," Phil assured me. "Dickie and Raul came in the other night; I seated them at the reserved table, which I told them was for family and friends, and comped their check over their objections. They got a little tipsy and loud playing pool; it was fun to watch."

"And Dead Doe number one?" Creole asked.

"Denton Newlin, a fifty-year-old fisherman, last seen about a week before his body was found, when he left his house to go on a trip for which he didn't show up. Denton was a loner, lived in a run-down efficiency in the seedier part of the docks. He didn't own a car or much in the way of personal belongings."

"Any link between the two men?" Creole asked.

"Nothing that my investigation has turned up. The cops are playing it off as two separate incidents, but they're fairly certain it's the same shooter. You know they never disclose their full hand to anybody, holding back a choice tidbit or two; well, this one is a doozy. Both men's genitalia were mutilated post mortem." She smiled.

Both Creole and Didier flinched.

"Yikes," I hissed and exchanged a "what the hell" look with Fab. "Least they were dead."

"When I take my final dance, I want this

body in pristine shape." Creole ran his hands over his t-shirt.

Everyone laughed. I watched in amusement as he flexed his muscles for me.

"The press hasn't reported this one yet," Phil added, "but another body was found in Alligator Alley inside another torched car. I only got sketchy details.

"Will you follow up?" Creole asked.

Phil looked at me. "I'll consider this a freebie if you get me an introduction to the funeral boys as more than a bartender and put in a good word."

I pointed at Fab. "She's the one they like the most. And she'd be happy to make that happen. Wouldn't you?"

"What's in it for me?" Fab squinted at me.

"Really?" I squealed back.

Creole and Didier threw their heads back and laughed.

"Choose a time, and the three of us will go to the funeral home," Fab offered. "I'd be surprised if they didn't have more info, since Dickie primped one of the bodies. They complain that they don't have any friends, but somehow they manage to know everything that goes on in town."

"Fab can give you a tour; she knows where all the bodies are stashed," I said.

"We took a tour of the coroner's office for one of my classes; I thought it was interesting,"

Phil said. "A couple of my fellow students lost their lunch. Didn't bother me."

I shook my head, happy that I'd missed that tour. "I have a question before we adjourn. The bodies were dumped on my properties—did you find a connection to me? I swear I've never seen them before and their names aren't familiar."

"I showed their pictures to the other bartenders, and no one remembers seeing either of them in here. The only property left is your house, so I'd keep an eye out."

"Yikes." I whooshed out a breath. Damn, hopefully that would not happen. "I, for one, am hoping for a quick arrest. In the meantime, I suggest that neither Fab nor I stay at the house alone."

"I agree with that." Didier glared at Fab.

Chapter 16

Fab and I had made up, our friendship no longer in danger of exploding in pieces, never to be resurrected. She hadn't decided about her working relationship with Brick but told me she was mulling over her options.

"Are you going to stare out the window the whole ride?" Fab grumped. "Don't tell me you're mad because you wanted to spend more time at the beach?"

I turned from staring out the window at traffic. "Didn't I graciously say yes to my best friend when she asked for my help?"

She honked at another driver as both of them merged onto the Turnpike, trading finger sign language.

It surprised me when she pulled into the less-congested, "slow" lane, but that didn't last long. She jammed on the gas and took off, leaving the other car in the dust.

"You were light on the details," I said. "Why don't you spill them now? I'll let you know if you need to drop me for an iced coffee and come back when you're done."

"You sound like your damn boyfriend,"

she huffed.

"The same 'damn' one that possibly saved your life?" I returned angrily. "Do you really dislike Creole that much, or is it just easy to make fun of him?"

"I said thank you. I know I don't sound grateful, but I am. It has me seriously thinking I need to be choosier about the jobs I take in the future. Didier and I are happy that the two of you are back together. Why ruin a good thing when our foursome works?"

It bugged me that she hadn't answered the Creole question, but I decided to tackle that subject after we got home. "Is this a Brick job?" I asked.

"No, this one is from an old client I haven't worked for in years. He moved to D.C. for a while, but now he's back in Florida."

"He called out of the blue? 'Hey how are you? Got a job for you.'? That's odd."

Fab ignored my comment. "Edward Lewis is someone high-powered people hire to clean up messy situations they want to have go away rather than make headlines. His client cheated on his wife, and now the girlfriend is refusing to take cash to keep her mouth shut and go away. Instead, she plans to release some 'up close and personal' photos, under the delusion that it will make the man want to leave his wife and set up house with her."

"So her plan for a happy life is

blackmail?" I shook my head. "Let me guess, your client wants the pictures. How are we going to find them?"

"I've already searched every inch of her condo—twice. Last time, I planted a bug and a couple of cameras and hired an IT tech through Phil to monitor the devices. Her connections are far more reliable than mine. I didn't want to get screwed and have someone I hired compound the blackmail situation. Thanks to my bugs, I now know where the drive is. Clever girl, she used your trick and put the USB drive inside a safe built into a piece of furniture. Damned if I didn't miss it."

After I moved into my house, I'd bought a safe and had a box made that fit over the top and disguised it as a side table. Only Fab and I knew about the hiding place.

"Stating the obvious…" I looked over at her. "It's the middle of the day, and it's highly likely we will be seen by someone."

"In-and-out job. Kimber won't be home; she has a standing appointment at Oasis to get her hair and nails done."

I rolled my eyes. "What am I doing, guarding the parking lot while you pick the lock, run in, and snatch and grab?"

"*You* are going to take the flower box in the back seat and stand in the hallway, out of sight of the door. She shows up, you ring the bell. Here's the problem: the only way out is through the door you'll be guarding. And no good hiding places inside."

"You want me to distract her so you can pole vault out the window?"

"Twentieth floor." Fab made a face. "I need to get in better shape. I found this new gym in Marathon run by ex-military men. They teach survival skills and have an awesome climbing wall."

Better shape. I made a gagging noise. Someone needed to smack her.

"This plan of yours stinks." I wrinkled my nose. "If I stand in the hallway and Kimber shows, you can't get out. It would be better if I knew what she looked like and the kind of car she drives; then I can station myself between the lobby door and underground parking and call you if she shows."

Fab handed me her phone. "Check out the pictures."

"Or Plan B: Stake out the hallway. She shows, I force her inside the condo, we tie her up, and run like hell. Then wait for the cops to show up and drag our butts to jail. Kidnapping gets you twenty years, doesn't it? And co-conspirators go to different prisons."

"Don't be so dramatic," Fab grumbled.

"If you get arrested, will your cleaner client step up and make the charges go away? If he doesn't, I'll blab everything I know."

"That wouldn't be a good idea."

Before getting out of the car, I texted the address to Creole. He was going to be furious. I hoped I'd get off with just a lecture. Sometimes, when he was really mad, he didn't show up for a couple of days.

I swept my hair up in a ponytail and stuffed most of it under a baseball cap, donning dark-tinted sunglasses that covered half my face. The florist box was a stupid idea, and I left it on the back seat. I got into position, pacing the area between the lobby and the security gate to the garage. I had several opportunities to sneak into the underground parking lot for a peak around, but past experience reminded me that getting out might not be as easy as getting in.

My phone dinged, alerting me to a message, and my stomach dropped. "She's back. Under the bed." The air sucked itself out of my lungs. How had she gotten past me?

What the hell do I do now?

I ran back to the SUV and grabbed the flowers. I rejected texting Creole. He'd tell me to leave, his rationale being that both of us didn't need to get booked and fingerprinted. Getting into the lobby was a piece of cake with my lockpick. I kept my head down in case the security cameras picked up the unusual activity. Riding up in the elevator, I improvised a gutsy plan.

Taking a deep breath, I shoved my sunglasses into my bra before knocking on the door. The picture on Fab's phone didn't do the petite blonde who answered justice; early twenties, she reminded me of a college cheerleader.

"Flowers for Kimber Reed." I thrust the box forward.

"Ohhh." She flashed a megawatt smile. "Wait here, and I'll get you a tip."

Kimber crossed into the living room and retrieved her purse off a chair. She turned back around, cash in hand, and yelped.

I had stepped inside, closing the door softly behind me. The condo was small, furnished in blue and cream with put-it-together-yourself furniture, but lots of light shone through the windows.

"Don't scream." I held eye contact, trying for a reassuring smile. "This isn't what it looks like. Just want to talk. I promise, I have no intention of hurting you."

Kimber began hyperventilating. Unable to catch her breath, she gasped, "Inhaler," and gestured to her purse.

I forced her down on the couch and grabbed her bag, upending the contents on the floor, grabbing up the medication, and putting it in her hands. Unsure what to do, I sat down next to her, rubbing circles in her back. If she died under these circumstances, it would be murder for sure.

"Anything else I can get you?" From the

corner of my eye, I saw Fab standing in the bedroom door; I motioned for her to leave.

Kimber shook her head and started to breathe more normally.

"I'm Susan; this is Mary." I gestured to Fab, since she'd ignored my directions and moved over behind me. "We just want to talk about your blackmail scheme. Come up with a resolution that is acceptable to all parties."

"Did Marco send you?" Kimber hugged herself and started to cry.

"Kleenex," I mouthed to Fab. Assuming he was the married husband, I said, "Yes."

Fab came back with a roll of toilet paper. Kimber blew her nose, sounding like a foghorn. "I just want to be with Marco," she cried. "I love him."

"I don't want to be unkind, but once you chose to blackmail your lover, the relationship was over," I said.

"Not to mention you'll ruin his career," Fab pointed out.

I looked at Fab quizzically; clearly she'd left out a few details.

"Marco was just re-elected to a four-year term," Kimber said. "By the time elections come around again, people will have forgotten." She blew her nose again. "You don't understand. Even the kids like me better than Isabel. I demanded five million, and when he pays, we won't need her money and can be together."

Five million! I sat back and took a breath. *Marco and Isabel Villa? The congressman from the local district?* So much for the photos of the perfect family his office peddled to the press.

"I hate to be the bearer of bad news," Fab said, though judging by the tone of her voice, she'd like to administer a slap-down. "He doesn't have money of his own; he'll have to beg it off his wife. Why would she pay for a husband who's not sticking around?" she asked in disgust.

Kimber shot Fab an angry glare. "Damn Isabel and her money. We're in love."

I closed my eyes for a second, taking a breath. Love? Maybe for little Marco. "You're asking him to jeopardize his career in order to be with you. The scandal will kick up again come reelection time, and if it doesn't, his opponent will remind the voters. What about the kids you say you love?"

"From the first day I went to work as the children's nanny, there was this connection. I will be a better mother than Isabel has ever been. This will work; I know it will," Kimber persisted like a willful child.

Fab jerked her head towards the door, flashing a thumb drive she'd taken out of her pocket and lifting her shirt to show an oversized envelope tucked in her waistband.

I shot her a dirty look. "The affair is over, and Marco regrets that he has hurt you," I said lamely. *Probably sorry he got caught.*

Kimber jumped up, crossed to the kitchen, and returned with a gun in her hand. "You bitches! Marco's sleeping with one or both of you." Gone was sweet Kimber. Her face had transformed into a vicious sneer; nothing nice about this side of her.

I eyed the .22 that fit in the palm of her hand. Not a Glock, my personal favorite, but still deadly if she knew how to shoot, and at close range, the odds were high she'd hit one of us even if she didn't.

Kimber waved the gun at Fab, directing her to sit on the couch next to me, and paced, grumbling in an irate tone. She grabbed her phone off the table. "He'll take my call now," she yelled at the screen. "Mary? What's your last name?" she asked Fab.

Fab looked confused.

"French," I blurted. "Mary French."

Kimber identified herself as such when someone answered the phone; after a short wait, she exploded and threw the phone across the room. "I'm calling the cops. I'll have you two arrested for breaking in, and I'll come across as sympathetic when I identify myself as the Villas' nanny."

Fab patted my back, and I knew she was about to pull her weapon. If it ended with the two women pointing guns at one another, I had no doubt Kimber would pull the trigger.

I began to stealthily reach for the gun in the back of my waistband, but Kimber turned her gun in my direction, her eyes glued on me. "Oh," I yelled and crossed my legs. "I'm peeing on myself."

I jumped up and heard Fab gasp. Not having the graceful kick that Fab had perfected, I launched myself at Kimber's mid-section in the moment of confusion, knocking her arm upwards and the gun out of her hand.

Kimber fought back and landed a couple of punches before Fab dragged her off me by her hair, dumping her against the wall. "Don't even think about moving." Fab took a couple of steps and kicked the woman's gun under the couch. "The bathroom is that way," she told me, smirking and pointing down the hall.

I threw myself back on the couch.

"Listen up." Fab stood over Kimber, hands on her hips. "Your relationship, or whatever it is, with Marco is over. What will it take for you to go away? You expose this tawdry mess, and you'll be the loser; you'll be a tabloid sensation, then fade into obscurity. Good luck getting a decent man after your reputation gets dragged through the mud, and it will."

"I want to talk to him." Kimber started to cry.

"How much?" Fab demanded. "Name a price. Do it now. Once we leave, you can fend for yourself, and trust me, you'll hate the next negotiator that shows up."

I smiled at my friend—Fab was perfect for a game of hardball—though I shuddered at that last comment. Kimber wouldn't be the first person to disappear at the direction of a politician. I didn't know Fab's fixer friend or what he was capable of; in fact, I'd had no idea such a job even existed except as an interesting plot twist for television.

Fab took her phone out of her back pocket. "In addition to the money, you get a first-class ticket to anywhere you want to go. There are a lot of beautiful places in the world—choose one."

Kimber dried her eyes and underwent another personality transformation. Calming down, she spoke in a soft, little-girl voice: "Five million."

"One." Fab held up her index finger.

"Three million and that's a good deal." Kimber sucked on her bottom lip in a full-blown pout.

Fab reversed the direction of negotiations: "Half-mill."

"One." Kimber number one was back and demanded in a hard tone: "Cash. Los Angeles; at least it's warm out there."

"Don't be ridiculous. The money will be wired to an account of your choice." Fab turned her back and walked away, making a call. "When can you leave?" She looked over her shoulder.

"When I get the money," Kimber snapped.

I kept both eyes on Kimber, ready for another roll on the floor if necessary. Her expression changed constantly; she needed to work on her poker face. I was suspicious of her change of attitude. The Villas needed to be careful. If she went quietly to the west coast, I'd be surprised. I didn't care; I was only thinking about myself. I wanted to go home, bullet-free and without a detour through the local jail. I wasn't sure, if this wild story came out, that Fab and I could get bail.

"Here." Fab closed the space between them, handing Kimber the phone.

Kimber mimicked Fab, turning her back.

Fab half-laughed, "amateur" written on her face. She picked up the pieces of Kimber's phone, which had smashed against the wall, removing the SIM card and setting the rest on the table. At least we'd have a head start before the cops showed up if she decided to call and report us.

Kimber stalked over, slapping Fab's phone into her outstretched hand. "Get out," she hissed.

She didn't have to tell me twice. I bolted for the door and forced myself to walk sedately to the elevator. I held the door open, waiting for Fab, who still stood in the hallway. I'd just started to tap my foot when she turned and hustled in my direction.

As soon as the elevator doors closed, I said, "Let's hope we've heard the last of her."

"Not our problem. Edward has a man in the parking lot who'll shadow her every move." Fab gave me a once-over.

"What?" I wrinkled my nose.

"Peeing?" she said in horror.

I laughed all the way back to the SUV.

Chapter 17

Emotionally drained from the events of Fab's latest job, I told her very succinctly the next day that I wouldn't be accompanying her on another job for her cleaner client. Fab informed me that Kimber had been whisked off to an unknown location when she'd flipped out in an inconsolable crying jag and it was either that or end up in a mental ward; either way, she assured me, Kimber wouldn't end up dead. I stayed home long enough to pack an overnight bag, then left for Creole's without a word. After texting him, I made my way to his bed, slipped between the cool sheets, and fell asleep.

Creole made a quick appearance and listened while I related the details; to say he wasn't happy would be an understatement. Instead of unleashing an angry lecture, however, he held me until I fell asleep again. I woke to find a note in the space where his body should have been, with "I love you" written on it and a crude drawing of an oversized head, hair sticking on end, labeled "self-portrait."

For two days, I hid out at his house, trying to overcome my guilt at how the Kimber situation had ended. Once again, a client had failed to inform us how unstable the subject of an investigation was. I caught up on my sleep and lay on the patio reading the days away. Creole showed up for short periods, offering brief distractions. He didn't bring up Kimber and neither did I, but I was certain the subject wasn't closed.

I finally dragged myself back home for date night. I'd suggested to Creole in a short phone call that we call in sick, but he reminded me we'd already agreed to go.

Mother had been bragging about a new restaurant, The Reef, that had opened in Islamorada, a short drive south through The Keys. It took serious effort to convince Fab to go to the place. I went on their website and printed out the reviews that mentioned that the dress code was casual-dressy and a menu that didn't list a single hamburger; even the kids' menu had seafood dishes.

I barked at her, "Do I have to remind you that Creole and I rarely object to any snooty restaurant that you choose, and we manage to go without attitude? Mostly, anyway."

Didier's eyebrows rose as Fab grumbled in French; when she was done, she gave me a tight smile and said, "Fine."

When I made the reservation, I'd remembered Mother's claim that she knew the owner and dropped his name into the conversation before requesting a window table. The surly woman who answered the phone informed me that we would need to be on time, or she wouldn't hold the table and left unsaid, *I don't give a damn who you know.*

We arrived without a minute to spare, thanks to Fab, who swore she couldn't leave the house unless she looked perfect. Her black, above-the-knee halter dress hugged her frame, showing off her sculpted arms and legs, and she was wearing the requisite stilettos. At my insistence, Didier stopped at the main entrance, and Fab and I hopped out.

Creole had a last-minute meeting but had sworn he wouldn't be late and would meet us at the restaurant.

The Reef was a U-shaped restaurant built on stilts, part of it sitting on land and the rest hanging out over the water. Through a wall of pocket doors that stood open, the dining area extended out onto the glass-enclosed deck that faced the ocean. The tables were elegantly set with white tablecloths, silver, and crystal, and each had a small hurricane lantern in the center, filled with shells and electric lighting.

The hostess pointed to the bar area, telling me it would be a few minutes before our table was ready.

As Fab stopped to take a phone call, the server came by. I ordered a glass of wine and a martini and told her that there were two others in the party, arriving momentarily.

"Is this seat taken?" a male voice asked. Without waiting for an answer, he pulled out the chair and sat, setting his drink down. The dark-haired fifty-something looked a bit rumpled and scruffy around the edges.

"Apparently so." I thought about putting my foot into the underside of his chair, sending him to the floor.

"Let me get you a drink?" He started to raise his hand.

"No, thank you. I've already ordered, and I'm expecting my boyfriend and another couple."

He winked as though I wasn't telling the truth and this was some kind of flirting.

Fab appeared at the table. "Who are you?" she demanded.

"He's with me," another lizard announced. He slithered up and pulled out a chair for Fab and one for himself, plunking his behind down. The men simultaneously produced business cards, slapping them on the table in front of us.

I swept mine to the floor. "You need to leave," I said, out of patience with this bumbling duo's idea of a come-on.

"I'm Dill, by the way." Lizard number two stuck his hand out. "That's Butch." He jerked his head to indicate the other man. "Get to know us; we'll show you and your friend a real good time." He winked.

I ignored him, leaving my hands in my lap. His slimy smile made my skin crawl.

"Tell me about yourself." Butch patted Fab's hand.

She jerked it away and blasted him in French.

Butch laughed and said, "I enjoy a little fire in my women."

Fab and I engaged in a silent war.

Get rid of them, I telegraphed. *Now!*

You do it, she glared back.

Oh hell, where are Creole and Didier?

Fab nodded at the bar. Creole and Didier stood on the opposite end, stupid smiles on their faces, toasting us with their beer. Didier looked at his watch and said something to Creole, and they both laughed.

Game on. I glowered at them.

I settled back in my chair. "I need to relax," I purred. "Just got out of prison." I smoothed my hand down the front of my black and pink, spaghetti-strap tropical sheath dress. "It's been an adjustment, no longer wearing that scratchy orange uniform and eating that hideous food."

"Really?" Dill flashed me a lopsided smile. "What did a pretty little thing like you do?"

Neither looked terribly shocked.

"I never get tired of hearing this story,"

Fab said, kicking me under the table. "Oh, let me!" She held up her hand as if asking permission. "She shot her boyfriend."

"I only grazed his inner thigh," I protested. "The judge believed that I never intended to shoot off his… well, you know."

"I never bought that story, but she did get a shortened sentence." Fab signaled the server for another drink.

The lizards looked a little paler, but they were still gamely hanging on.

Creole didn't like it when I brought my gun on a date. I usually figured that what he didn't know wouldn't hurt him, but I had reached the end of my tolerance with these two and saw an opportunity to get rid of them *and* irritate my boyfriend. I opened my clutch and slid out my Five-SeveN. Giving new meaning to the word "crazy," I licked the barrel, maintaining eye contact with Butch. From the corner of my eye, I saw Fab's Sig Sauer make a split-second appearance from under the table. Thigh holster, I guessed; either Didier had no rule about not wearing a gun on date night, or Fab ignored it, just like I did.

Fab leaned sideways, and Butch jerked upward, a strangled sound erupting from his lips. The look of surprise on his face made me want to peek under the table to see exactly what she'd done with that gun.

I gave Butch the scary look that I

practiced regularly in the mirror and gave the Five-SeveN a long smooch. "It was an accident," I said in a dead tone and sighed.

Dill and Butch paled again under their phony orange suntans. They shoved their chairs back and leapt up, Dill mumbling something that sounded like an excuse about an appointment they'd just remembered, and practically ran out the door.

Fab and I knuckle-bumped. "That was fun." Fab reholstered her gun. "Something to remember for the next time a man doesn't heed our 'get lost'—I just found out that a nice hard tap to his inner thigh will do the trick."

"I don't recall you telling them to get lost." My lips quirked.

Creole and Didier had come around the bar and now stood over us, grinning and clapping.

The hostess appeared. "Your table is ready." She smiled at Didier, which elicited a growl from Fab.

"Happy you two enjoyed the show. Enjoy your walk home," I said huffily and started toward the door.

Creole grabbed me around the waist, holding me in an iron grip. "Order drinks," he said to Didier. "A double margarita. We'll be right over." He propelled me outside and off to one side of the building.

"You could have at least gotten rid of

those two cretins," I yelled at him.

He cupped my face in his hands. "Oh, but it was so much fun to watch. Impressive. You two dispensed with them in under five minutes. So 'hot mess' of you to lick your gun. If I didn't know you, I would have run too."

"I have to disinfect my tongue and the inside of my mouth." I sniffed.

"Here, I'll do it." He tilted my face and lowered his head, brushing my lips with a kiss that was both rough and sweet. "If it had looked for even a second like you didn't have the situation under control, I would've whipped on my cape, swooped over, and dragged their asses out by the scruff of the neck."

He kissed me again, and I found myself melting against him when I knew I should have been putting up much more of a protest. He whispered against my lips, "Let's go inside. We're attracting attention. A couple of the people who heard you scream at me are milling around to see what happens next."

"Just great." I laughed and banged my head on his chest.

Chapter 18

Fab slowed for the large tortoise that had half a foot to go to make it across the busy highway in one piece. “I can’t believe that you were going to leave without me.”

I’d seen the tortoise from a block away and held my breath at his slow pace; I let it out now, happy that he’d made it and hadn’t ended up dead with a badly cracked shell. Once, my brother, being a good guy, had pulled off the road and picked one up, helping it across the road, and got bit as a thank you.

“Just being a good friend,” I said. “I thought I’d spare you the drama at The Cottages, knowing you have no tolerance for other people’s problems.”

“We each have our talents. That’s what makes us work.” She flashed me a cheesy smile.

“Uh oh.” I pointed as Fab careened around the corner. Police cars were blocking the street and driveway to The Cottages. From our vantage point, it was hard to tell whose property rated all the attention.

Fab slowed, scooting up in her seat to look over the steering wheel. “We can park on the side of the property, but that's next to *that* dumpster," she whined.

"First off, the sheriff's department took the first one as evidence and the one there now is a replacement. And second, did you forget that it's in an enclosed, fenced-off area, so you can't drive through there anyway?"

Fab swung around the block and parked. We jumped out, cut through the fence that ran along the side of the pool, and followed the sidewalk along the back of several cottages to the office. Mac was kneeling on the couch under the window, looking out, her jean-skirted butt sticking up in the air. She shot a glance over her shoulder and waved us forward. "The deputies aren't here for us for a change."

I stood next to Mac and scanned the street. "What now?"

Fab took Mac's seat behind the desk and opened the drawers, rifling through them as she went.

"Big bust at the yellow house. They've lined up the all-night partiers." Mac pointed to eight people sitting in the street, a couple of them leaning on each other. "Not sure if they'll whip out the cuffs. So far, none of the four that rented the place have been rousted out yet, so they're either still inside or they ran out the back. My money's on them having run out."

I half-laughed. Quickly growing bored, I went to sit in a chair across from Fab. Mac was almost certainly right about the neighbors doing a runner. That was an often-used escape route, as most of the houses didn't have fencing around them, which wouldn't be a deterrent in any case, as most people deemed jail a sufficient incentive to scale any enclosure. I'd seen it done more than a few times at The Cottages: people scaling the back fence. Once they hit the beach, they were much more difficult to track.

"Miss January wants to talk to you," Mac said over her shoulder. "She just started drinking for the day, so you better hurry if you want her to be sober enough to carry on a conversation."

"Do I get a clue?" I asked.

"All I heard was: 'blah, blah, blah.'" Mac gave a good imitation of a drunk Miss January. "I gave her a couple of 'oh, okays,' and raced to the end of the driveway, wanting a front-row seat for the drama across the street. I hadn't gotten far when Kevin stepped out from behind the first cottage and ordered me to go inside or he'd arrest me. I told him his threat was illegal, that this was private property. Bastard smirked and said, 'Tell it to the judge.'"

"If you're done snooping through everything, want to come with me?" I asked Fab.

"I'll wait here. I haven't gotten to this cupboard over here." Fab pointed.

I dragged myself out of my chair, not in a hurry to cross the driveway. Miss January had never asked to see me before, and I didn't want to hear any bad news—especially not that death was imminent and, unlike all the other declarations from her doctors, they were positive this time. One of these times, they'd get it right, and I needed more time to get used to the thought. I sighed and detoured to check out the situation at the yellow house.

I'd just made it to the end of the driveway when a deputy I didn't recognize approached. *Could work in my favor.*

"Go back inside," he ordered.

Pasting a pleasant look on my face, I ignored his order and said, "I'm the owner here and was wondering what was going on. I have out-of-town vacationers and would like to tell them something."

"We'll be out of here soon." His lips formed a straight line. "Tell them to use the side exit; they wouldn't want to get arrested due to a mistaken identification."

Seeing no other option, I flinched first and ended the stare-down. "Thank you, uh…" *For being no help at all.*

Getting no response, I turned to ferret out Miss January. I didn't have to go far; she was sitting on her front porch, sucking down vodka straight from the bottle, Kitty on her lap. Judging by the small amount left, she was finishing off yesterday's bottle. Today's delivery hadn't been made yet.

"Hi, sweetie," she slurred. "Have a seat."

Since there was only one chair, I assumed she meant the steps. "I'll stand." I smiled, debated whether to ask after the boyfriend, and voted for ignorance. I didn't want to hear how they were perfect for one another because they "drank and banged." In that order, I presumed. When she used the "B" word, I had to remind myself she wasn't the eighty she looked but half that age. The downside to hard living, though I'm not sure she'd agree.

Hearing footsteps behind me, I turned in time to see two twentyish males make a dash down the driveway. Before they could cut to the right and disappear, the deputy yelled, "Stop," already hot on their trail.

Too late, I thought.

The deputy reappeared empty-handed. "Is there a back gate? A shortcut?" He glared angrily.

I shook my head and kept my mouth shut. He ran back to the street, heading for the corner. The two males, besides being in good shape, had to be locals and knew that, once over the fence, they could blend in with the beachgoers. It had been a while since we had a police chase through the property. Bet Fab wished she were out here now.

"Nice asses." Miss January giggled, liquid dribbling down her chin.

"You wanted to talk to me?"

"As much as my doctors warn of doom and death..." She made a strangling noise, laughing at herself. "It will happen one day. Nothing has changed regarding my health; they still predict death any day now." She cackled. "Will you promise to take Kitty?"

An already dead cat!

"Wouldn't you like to be buried with her?"

"Oh, no." She frowned, looking sad. It took her a minute to regain her train of thought. "That wouldn't be fair. I'm asking because I know you'll take good care of her."

I guess that answered my question about whether Miss January knew that Kitty was dead. Apparently not.

"Don't worry. She'll be well taken care of and there are plenty of people to spoil her," I reassured her. This was another reason Mac was never allowed to quit. She'd make sure nothing happened to the deceased animal.

"I knew I could count on you." Miss January fumbled in her pocket, produced a cigarette, and stuffed it between her lips, flipping it around in a nervous jig. She turned both her pockets inside out. "Where the hell did my matches go?"

I glanced down, spotting them under her chair, and said, "Let me look around." I bent down, quickly picked them up, and shoved them into my pocket. She didn't need to be playing with fire. "Don't see anything." I shrugged.

Her cigarette fell out of her mouth, landing in her lap with the rest of the pack, but she didn't appear to notice. "Would you like to lie down for a while?" I held my breath as I gently retrieved them for safekeeping.

"Hold Kitty." She thrust it at me.

I leaned back, almost falling off the step. I had never touched it without gloves on. In one swift move, I jerked my top over my head, leaving me in a skirt and sports bra. I wrapped the shirt around Kitty, holding her away from my body, and followed Miss January into her cottage. The question of where Score was… was answered by the chainsaw snoring coming from the bedroom.

Miss January pitched herself onto the couch, kicking her shoes up in the air. I waited for her to settle, then shoved Kitty in the only vacant space, the wide window ledge. "She can see outside," I said lamely.

"I knew you were the right choice." She closed her eyes and continued to mumble to herself.

I hooked my shirt up with the tip of my index finger from the chair where I'd tossed it, happy that it wasn't one of my favorites. "Do you want anything before I leave?"

Miss January shook her head and rolled over.

Before I left, I tossed a thin blanket over her bony frame. I said, "You behave yourself," as I left, closing the door.

Kevin was waiting for me at the bottom of the steps. "Did you see two young men run by here?"

"Miss January and I both saw their backsides. The two-woman consensus: nice."

"You wouldn't aid in their getaway, would you?"

I didn't break eye contact. "This sounds like a conversation for my lawyer." I withdrew my phone from my pocket. "He'll want to know if I'm under arrest."

"You're going to get your wish," he grumbled. "I'm moving out of this hellhole and taking Julie and Liam with me."

"What is it my grandmother used to say: 'Don't let the door hit your ass on the way out'? You and I both know that if your sister moves anywhere, it will be in with my brother. You pretend to be protective and attentive, but where were you when she was serious about the last loser she dated? Newsflash: My bro spends more time with your nephew than you do. Don't feel bad about moving out as soon as you can, though. Think of it as more time with your strippers." Knowing I wouldn't get an answer, I stomped towards the office.

The door opened for me, and Mac stood on the threshold. I thrust the cigarettes and matches at her. “Make sure Miss January gets these back when she has a sober moment.”

The deputies must have grown bored with rousting the college kids across the street, according to Mac, who moved back behind her desk. The kids were released when the cops were done tossing the house.

“Miss January is fine, but should one of her doctors prove to be correct and she expires, we are the new parents of Kitty. Mostly you.” I nodded at Mac. “We’ll put it up on the top of the armoire, like a decoration.” I looked up, scrunching my nose.

Mac made a choking noise and mumbled something indecipherable.

“Why are you half-dressed?” Fab asked, checking me over from head to toe from her position stretched out on the couch.

“You don’t want to know.” I waved my shirt in front of her, and she batted it away. “Two of the partygoers got away. Probably not for long; one of their friends will cough up their names. Find out what went down over there, will you Mac? Happy news: Kevin is moving.”

“Don’t get too happy. There’s not much available in the area in his price range.” Mac scribbled notes on her trusty pad. “The Canadian couple that owns the property across the street is done with all the problems, and grapevine has it they want to sell. If so, Shirl and I want to buy.”

"Hmm..." I pushed out my lip. "Shirl moving?" I shook my head, not liking the idea. "But it's only across the street. And that would end the parade of troublesome locals."

"You always say you won't rent to them, then bend the rules for someone," Fab reminded me.

"Anything you need," I told Mac, "call my brother, he's got a long list of contacts and will pave the way. Time to go." I nudged Fab's feet off the couch. "I have an appointment."

I opened the door, Fab and Mac behind me. "What are they doing?" I gasped. Starletta was plastered to Crum's chest, her arms and legs wrapped around him, rubbing up and down as they cavorted around the driveway.

"Don't you know dry humping when you see it?" Mac said, her southern accent more pronounced.

The spectacle was bad, a horribly vulgar display that showed that neither of them knew how to conduct themselves in public. At the opposite end of the driveway, two of Cruz's relatives stepped out of their cottage, beach bags over their shoulders, and jerked to a stop. The beach forgotten, they gawked, watching the show.

Fab shoved me forward. "Your guests came for the show; give them one."

Mac grabbed the waistband of my skirt. "I'll do it. I know what these people expect."

Stepping in front of me, she bellowed, "Professor, your ass is showing, and that's against the rules."

Today the professor was wearing a raggedy elastic-waist woman's skirt that required two big safety pins at the waist to stay up. He often complained about clothing being too restrictive. I'd asked him once if he'd gone naked to his college classes, but he only rolled his eyes and stomped away without a word. He'd been about to say something, I think, but probably remembered I was his landlord.

Crum skidded to a stop, and Starletta slid to the ground. Straightening her beach cover-up, she turned and flipped off Mac. Then she clasped Crum's hand and tugged him towards his cottage. He pulled the back of his skirt out of his waistband, flipped it over his once-white undershorts, and yelled back, "I'll keep it down in the back."

"Got your guns, girls?" I asked.

They both snorted in response.

"That makes two." Mac lifted her top to show her Beretta shoved in her waistband.

"Three," Fab corrected. "Madison's got her handgun; she just wants me to do the dirty work."

I almost had to run to catch up with Crum and shove my foot inside before he could get his door closed. My backup posse was one step behind. "Rule number one: You never give my manager the finger," I barked at the stringbean woman who had her palms cupped over Crum's backside.

"I thought the first one was about not committing felonies," Crum grumbled.

"Aren't you going to introduce us?" I gestured at the woman with choppy pink hair. Gone was the grey bun from the first time I saw her; made me wonder if it was fake. My eyebrows went up at the pairing of royal blue stilettos and rolled-up sweats.

"This is my girlfriend, Starletta Wells, and Madison." He pointed unenthusiastically.

"Crum left off the good part—I'm the owner of this property. You need to apologize to my manager."

"Who's going to make me?" She returned my glare.

"Either you do it, and I mean now, or you're banned from the property and you can get laid in his newest acquisition, that junky old Falcon." The old blue-and-white car had replaced a pickup truck that he claimed was a collector's item, worth big money. I'd responded, *Maybe it if weren't a rusted-out pile.* "Another option would be for Crum here to pack up his treasures and move."

He and I both knew that no landlord would rent to him, as his eccentric reputation preceded him. Since he already knew that he could hoard more when not living in an automobile, he'd be loathe to leave.

Crum held up a finger and grabbed Starletta's arm, hauling her off to one side.

"Oww." She slapped his arm.

The two of them hissed at one another like a couple of old cats. I couldn't make out the words but enjoyed the sound effects.

"As much as those two enjoy banging," Mac whispered from behind me, "his dick is going to lose the vote. Crum likes it here; you'll have to get him out with a forklift."

I turned, hands on my hips.

"I didn't rent to him," Mac blurted before I could say a word. "Do you want to hear more about her or chew me out and then feel bad?"

Fab smacked her arm. "Spill it."

"Starletta is a major pain in the…" Mac pointed to her backside. "She's a S-stirrer, if you know what I mean. According to Crum, she spreads BS around the neighborhood, whipping up hard feelings. You want gossip to ignite like wildfire, she's your woman."

The loving twosome broke their huddle and stumbled over. Starletta straightened and thrust out her meager chest, spitting fire at Mac: "I regret my transgression, flipping you the bird." She stuck up her middle finger. "I didn't realize that you didn't have a sense of humor. But I'll remember for the future."

The laughing behind me was faint, but I knew it was Fab.

"If you should need to apologize again, a simple 'I'm sorry' would sound more sincere," I barked, certain that this wouldn't be the last run-in I had with the woman.

"No hard feelings." Crum wrapped his arm around Starletta and pulled her inside his cottage. "We've got plans for the afternoon!" he yelled and slammed the door.

Mac flinched, said, "S-e-x," and made a clucking noise. "He's too cheap to take her anywhere. A meal at his house consists of whatever the food bank is passing out."

"He takes food from needy people?" I asked.

"I volunteer, and the food banks do a good job of making sure that no one who shows up goes away empty-handed."

"You know something, Macklin Lane—you're amazing," I said and meant every word. The woman had been named after her grandfather, and I'm sure he'd have been very proud of his namesake.

Mac's cheeks turned pink, the first time I'd seen her embarrassed. It made me like her even more, if that was possible.

Cruz's relatives moved past us, calling out a friendly hello as they headed to the beach.

"I kept my eye on those two." Fab nodded at their retreating backs. "They didn't move an inch until the drama was over. Maybe a little, but only to get closer."

"Do you think we can sneak away before any more drama erupts?" I asked.

Chapter 19

Fab threw rafts in the pool, and I set a plastic tray with glasses and a pitcher of iced tea on the side, then jumped in, splashing water all over her, which she deflected by throwing her hands up in front of her face.

"When are you going to work for Brick again?" Fab splashed me back, handing me two glasses while she climbed on her raft.

"He finally told you?" I paddled to her side and put her tea in the drink holder.

"He mentioned it after he was done yelling about how ungrateful you were, considering he let you work under his license. Thinks you should have told him you quit to his face and not in a text."

"He never ever took seriously me wanting to get my own private investigator's license. I'd think he'd be happy; he gets you to all to himself, which he made clear is what he wants. Have you two ever…?" I scissored my index and middle fingers.

Fab made a face. "Oh, heck no. Answer my question."

"Besides the fact that I don't want to work

for the man, I promised Creole I wouldn't agree to another job unless I talked to him first. There'd have to be a really good reason for me to consider working when it would irk my boyfriend. I'm surprised that Brick wants to get within ten feet of me after Creole blacked his eye."

I debated whether or not to tell Fab that I had an appointment with my first client in a couple of hours. Not having a clue what the job was about, I didn't want to humiliate myself if it wasn't corporate espionage or something else exciting. Instead, I changed the subject. "What are your plans for today?"

"Waiting for Didier to finish with a meeting, after which we're walking down the beach for lunch."

Good – she won't notice when I slip away.

* * *

JS Auto Body was located in a seedy part of the docks. There wasn't anything welcoming about the business, with its twelve-foot fencing, rolled barbed wire, and perimeters covered in security cameras. Neighboring businesses included fish markets, a tow yard, and an assortment of businesses that didn't bother with signage. None, apparently, were dependent on walk-in traffic. Spoon operated by appointment only and offered impeccable service. Most automobiles were picked up on a flatbed, serviced, and returned, detailed inside and out, the same way.

It had surprised me when I got a call from the man himself, offering me a job; although light on details, he'd piqued my interest. He made it clear he wanted me and not necessarily my "friend/partner" unless I needed her, and that was my call to make.

I parked the SUV in the only visitor parking space in front of the door. Getting out, I smoothed my hands down the front of my skirt, patted my handgun at the small of my back, reminding myself I wanted more target practice with my new favorite firearm, and shoved my phone in my pocket. I traded my flip-flops for low slides, wanting a more professional look. Finally, I grabbed a small leather portfolio off the seat.

Spoon held the door open, whistling when I stepped inside. "How's my favorite daughter?"

I kissed his cheek. "You've been hanging around Mother too much. Brad and I used the favorite daughter/son thing to drum up sympathy or guilt to get whatever we wanted."

"Have a seat." He gestured to the two black leather chairs in front of his desk. It looked nothing like the waiting area at your local mechanic's. His office was spotless, with no grease odor. A large couch flanked one wall, comfortable seating across from the sixty-inch flat screen; there was a pool table in the center of the room, an old vending machine that held cold drinks, and a small bar tucked in the corner. This was the room where I introduced Mother and Spoon; who could have known, on that fateful day, that when he fulfilled her request for a Jack Daniels on the rocks, it would be the start of a great romance.

"You were my first choice for this job, as you possess the needed skills." He paused to take a folder out of his top desk drawer. "I have a friend, Ruth Monroe, who's getting on years. Her daughter wants to relocate her to Naples to be closer to the family and see her grandchildren more often, but she refuses to go until she can find homes for her animals."

The smile disappeared from my face. I didn't hear his next few words. *An animal case, is that all people think I'm qualified for?*

"...she's eccentric and requires special handling, which is why I thought of you. I'm not asking for a family freebie; I pay good."

Hands in my lap, fingers entwined, I squeezed hard. "Does my mother know?"

He nodded. "We agreed that you were the perfect choice. This is one job that won't require a gun."

"How many animals?" I asked, trying to show an interest. "I don't know anyone looking for a pet at this time. I do have a connection with the local animal shelter—it's no-kill, and I can get their assistance."

"Last time I was there, she had a half-dozen cats and a dog." Spoon passed me a sheet of paper. "Here's all the information, and I drew a rough map of how to get to her house." He flipped the page over to show me. "She lives on a dirt road several miles south, off the Overseas. It's best to drive out there in daylight. Ruth is a friendly woman; she'll be happy for the company. I included her phone number, but she never answers."

I perused the map unenthusiastically. I planned to use it as my excuse to leave immediately, telling him that I'd check the situation out today. Studying it, I knew generally where the area was located: a remote section of the Keys. I stood up. "I think I'll go now, introduce myself, and get a pet count," I said, my voice distant. Ignoring his quizzical look, I headed for the door.

"You have any problems, let me know. Call when the job is done, and I'll get a check to you."

"I'm doing this as a favor because I love animals," I said and held up my hand before he could say anything. "In return, you will not tell *anyone* that you offered me the job." I flashed a lame smile and closed the door.

Check? I thought, settling myself behind the wheel. I'd forgotten, after working for Brick and his crisp hundred-dollar bills, that that was how most people got paid. I would have found the whole thing amusing if my pride weren't stinging.

It was another beautiful day as I drove down the Overseas Highway, taking the turn on the outskirts of Islamorada. There was a small Key in here, but I couldn't remember the name and there was no sign. I continued past a run-down trailer park; there were a lot of cars beside each one, but not a person in sight, only a lone dog snoozing in the middle of the entrance. The paved road turned to dirt and gravel, and if I hadn't been paying attention, I'd have missed the "Keep Out" sign. Weeds grew up knee-high along the side of the road, and tree branches hung down, giving it an eerie feeling.

Spoon was right about coming out here in the daytime; I wouldn't want to be on this road at night. It made a slight curve and came to an abrupt end. Parking in front of a faded purple doublewide, I stared, taking it all in: the weed-filled gravel yard, an old broken-down golf cart parked haphazardly in front of the deck that ran across the front, and at quick glance, two dozen cats lounging about, barely sparing me a glance.

Cats are hard to place, more so than dogs, and I hoped there weren't any more lurking around. I'd barely finished that thought when four dogs of undetermined origin and various sizes rounded the corner, running at me full-tilt, tails wagging. I bent down, holding out my hands to ward off the onslaught, and they barked and licked and jumped for attention.

"Sit," I commanded. They ignored me and continued to dance; then one bit another, and the chase was on across the field behind the house. It was then I noticed the partially fenced-in area that was home to three horses.

An older, grey-haired woman strode out on the deck. Ruth, I assumed. Her bright-yellow sundress would have been cute if it weren't several sizes too big and swallowing up her frame. I did like her Wellies; having a pair myself, I knew them to be genuine.

"Hey, dearie." She waved with a smile. "I don't believe I recognize you. Lost?"

"Name's Madison. I'm a friend of Jimmy Spoon's. I've come to help with your animals."

She tilted her head to the side, checking me over. "You need a cat or a dog, I've got one you can take, or both. Come on in." She gestured for me to follow.

Wishing I had my tennis shoes, I traded my heels for flip-flops and walked carefully, so as not to step on a feline. Of course, not a single one of them moved out of the way. Having a cat, I wasn't offended by their lack of manners.

The smell raced up my nose as I stepped inside the enclosed patio. Another door on the opposite wall stood open to the main part of the house. Controlling my gag reflex took concentration and small breaths. I was extremely sensitive to smell and knew I wouldn't be able to stay inside for long. An almost ceiling-high birdcage filled up most of the living room. Half of it was home to several parrots, and the other side housed smaller birds. Not knowing diddly about birds, I nevertheless knew that the cage had to be custom built; it didn't appear to come from the pet store.

"I've got sweet tea," she called from the strip kitchen.

"I'm good." The counters and table were clear, but the kitchen hadn't been cleaned in a very long time; it had the same dirty, gritty feel as the rest of the place. Every piece of faded and worn furniture had an animal lying on it—dogs on the upholstered furniture, cats on the tables.

"Let's go outside and talk," I suggested, unable to take the stench a minute longer. The only chair outside was an aluminum one leaning against the siding next to the door, the ashtray by the leg filled to the brim with cigarette butts. A minute after settling on the top step, I had two cats vying for space on my lap. I just hoped a fight didn't break out.

Ruth snapped out her chair and slunk down, a cigarette poised between her fingers that she didn't bother to light. "Why are you here again?"

"I'm here to help find homes for the animals. Get you ready for your move to Naples."

"I haven't been there in years." She

started singing off-key, a tune I didn't recognize.

Spoon has a lot to answer for.

"What year is it?" I smiled at her in encouragement. When she didn't answer, I asked, "The president?" I remembered that those were commonly asked questions to determine competency.

Ruth cocked her head to the side, wiggling her nose. "You can take a horse, if you like; I don't ride anymore." She was sober, no sign of drug use, fabulous skin tone; women paid big money to get something in a jar to effect that look. Her cigarette still wobbled, unlit, between her lips. My guess was she had no intention of smoking since she had nothing to light it with. I wanted to close my eyes and open them again to find I'd been dreaming. This wasn't a case of "Free Cats." In my limited opinion, she shouldn't be out here by herself. What was I going to do with cats, dogs, birds, horses, and who knew what else?

I should have one of each delivered to Spoon—that idea made me feel better. I turned at the crunching of tires on the dirt road. Two sheriff's cars blew up in a cloud of the dust, parking alongside my SUV. When Kevin stepped out, I knew that whatever was going on had just gotten more complicated.

"What are you doing here?" he demanded.

"I'm fine, and you?" I turned to Ruth. "Go

inside," I whispered. "I'll handle this."

She leaned forward and patted my cheek. "You're a sweet one." It took her two tries to stand up. She went inside, banging the door

"Where's she going? I'm here to talk to her," Kevin growled.

I blocked the steps. "I can help you."

"I'm here to investigate a complaint of animal abuse."

"You'll be happy to know that the reason I'm here is to relocate all of the animals. There's a plan in place, and they should be gone in a week or two." He didn't need to know that I didn't have a clue how I would relocate all the animals. I would have pushed for extra time if it wouldn't have tipped him off to that fact.

"Get out of my way," Kevin ordered.

The other deputy, who had climbed partway up the fence, jumped down. "The horses are doing fine—munching on weeds. That's about it."

"You need permission to go in, or a warrant, and you don't have the former, so I'd like to see the latter." I held out my hand.

"Can't you for once not be a smart-ass?" Kevin sneered.

I had irritated him faster than usual today. "I'm trying to do the right thing. Give me some time; save the county some money. What are you going to do—round up the animals and have them murdered?"

He appeared to be struggling to be civil. "One week." He held up a finger. "Don't make me regret this and don't make me get a warrant. At that point, I'll have someone with me from Adult Protective Services and take Miss Ruth into custody." He turned and stomped back to his car.

"Thank you," I called.

I waited until they'd disappeared from sight, the dust had settled, and the car engines could no longer be heard. Then I knocked and went inside, leaving the door open. It was time to assess how bad the situation was.

Ruth was curled on her side on the couch, asleep, three cats lined up along the back. A very pregnant cat with big blue eyes meowed up at me from the chair next to where I stood. I reached out to pet her; she reminded me of Jazz, except her long hair was solid white. I had no clue how old she was but somehow knew this wasn't her first time popping out kittens.

I started with the kitchen, opening the cupboards and finding them mostly bare. A medium-size aluminum garbage can under the sink held cat food and was almost empty. Another one had dog food in it and was a little fuller, but not by much. There was another enclosed patio room that ran along the back of the house; peering through the window, I counted six hairy, ankle-biter dogs. The next room, which had once been a bedroom, was now empty except for a dozen cat boxes that hadn't been cleaned; there was no cat sand anywhere to be found. Ruth's bedroom, judging by the tray of jewelry and a few other personal items, had several layers of dirt on the floor, like the rest of the house, but the bed had been made and not a single piece of clothing was lying about. Not even a pair of shoes.

I walked outside, phone in hand. When Spoon answered, I demanded, "When in the hell was the last time you paid your good friend a visit or even talked to her?"

"I admit it's been a while. Ruth's not dead, is she?"

"You need to get her daughter down here to take custody of her; if she doesn't, in one week, Ruth will become a ward of the state." I told him about Kevin's visit. "Got a pen?"

I took his grunt for a yes and listed off the supplies that were needed. *Today*. "You need to send someone over to spend the night in the driveway and keep an eye on her. If they have a strong stomach, they could go inside; she probably wouldn't mind the company. I can find someone starting tomorrow. One more thing: this job is no longer free. I see large donations to shelters in your near future; that is, if you want this taken care of without law enforcement involvement."

"I'll send someone over right away. Will you be there when Billy gets there? Someone else will deliver the horse feed—not sure who yet. I have no clue what they eat, but I guess I'm going to find out."

"Tell Billy to check the Hummer when he gets here. With any luck, I can close my eyes and pretend I'm at the beach." Anything to take my mind off the overwhelming situation.

* * *

Billy Keith lumbered up in a camper that was in good condition. It could sleep two comfortably, but it wouldn't take long before you got on each other's nerves. He looked around, brushing his sun-bleached hair out of his face, before making his way over to me. His demeanor was shy and unassuming, but with this man, it would be a mistake not to look below the surface; he didn't have a mean-as-stink reputation for nothing. "Boss Dude says you need help here. I'm applying." He flashed a crooked smile.

"Don't you already work full-time?" I wasn't exactly sure what he did for Spoon and had never asked. I knew from past experience that he wouldn't answer anyway. He didn't actually say "none of your business," but his attitude spoke for him. All I knew was that Spoon trusted him, and when there was trouble, Spoon sent him. Billy had been assigned to all trouble starting with Madison and Fab a while back, and he showed up and delivered every time we needed help.

"I'm the only one at the shop with the necessary qualifications. I have an old crazy grandma, love animals, and have no sense of smell; six dead people could be inside for all I care. Did I mention extra pay?" His laugh reminded me of a growling dog..

"Whatever money you agreed on, I'll tell Boss Dude he has to pay you three times the amount."

"You've always been my favorite." He grinned.

Since Spoon had obviously been light on the details, I filled Billy in on what I'd learned and the work that would need to be done. I was surrounded by people who thought "the less you know the better," but I didn't happen to subscribe to that mode of operation. "I'm mostly certain that I have horse connections, and hopefully, they can be trucked out of here tomorrow—I'll stress the urgency. I'm feeling very confident about a home for the birds. Before leaving, I need an animal count, and breeds for the dogs would be good."

Billy nodded. "Don't worry, we'll get this done in a week. If the daughter wants to sell, I may know a buyer."

"Spoon knows the daughter, and if a deal can be worked out for the property, it would be less in closing costs and more money in her pocket. Come inside."

Ruth was awake and watching television,

the sound muted. When I made the introductions, she smiled at Billy and pointed to a chair.

Billy apparently hadn't exaggerated about having no sense of smell; he hadn't turned up his nose once. He picked up a dog and settled both himself and the dog back in the chair.

"Do you mind if I take one of the cats?" I asked.

"There's not many left now," Ruth said absently. "I'm sure you'll give it a good home."

"I'll see you both tomorrow. If you need *anything,* call me," I told Billy.

On my way to the door, I stopped and picked up the pregnant cat, who meowed and licked my hand. Earlier, I had got a beach towel out of the back of the Hummer and made a bed in the passenger seat. "You're going to a good home, and we'll find good homes for your babies," I whispered to the white ball of fluff as I put her in the bed.

Chapter 20

Fab hung over the kitchen sink, watching as I passed the garden window the next day. "What is that?" She pointed at the box I was carrying as I kicked the front door closed with a bang.

"What?" I looked down. "Oh this." I held up the cat carrier, dropping the new cat bed on the floor. I'd made a quick stop at the pet store after the vet. "This is Snow, the newest member of our family. Mother will be ecstatic—she's pregnant." I bent down and opened the carrier door.

I'd thought more about naming the feline than who I'd call to find a permanent home for the rest of the animals.

"What about the king here?" Fab had Jazz on the counter, which was forbidden, and was combing his fur with her fingers.

"He welcomed the dog we had for a short time. I think as long as we continue to spoil him, he'll be fine. Not so sure about Snow, but she has babies to get ready for."

"What's up with you? Don't you dare say 'nothing.' You barely said anything to Didier before blowing out the door this morning. Your behavior earned you the raised eyebrow, and in case you didn't know, he's not happy when you get *the look*." She put extra emphasis on that last, her hands on her hips. "Before you give me some made-up story, I overheard you talking about horses and birds. I would've confronted you then, about the phone call and that--Snow, but you ran out of the house." She watched as the feline waddled across the room and lay down in front of the patio doors. She had slept by the patio door the night before, so I took her new bed to that spot and put her blanket in it.

"You and I both know that if you were worried, you would have stalked me out to the driveway. But then how would you explain to Didier that you were eavesdropping? Especially after the big 'behave yourself' talk." I made air quotes.

She glared at me and then softened. "I'm supposed to be working on that. I did warn Didier not to expect overnight change."

I knew she was annoyed that she hadn't learned anything from eavesdropping on my conversation, but she had herself to thank for that. I'd learned how to be secretive from the master.

Fab slid onto a stool while I refilled the bowls of cat food and water, deciding that two of everything might prevent a cat fight.

"The vet gave Snow a clean bill of

health," I told Fab.

She clearly thought I'd lost my mind. It looked like she wanted to say something but stopped herself. We both knew the only animal she had ever liked was Jazz, and the feeling was mutual.

The doctor had done an ultrasound and predicted two kittens, which she determined had to do with Snow being underweight, but I reassured her that that would be remedied now that Snow was staying at my house. I'd sighed with relief, knowing the baby count could have easily been much higher. Snow, as it turned out, was three years old, and this was not her first pregnancy, as I'd predicted. Once the kittens came, I'd make an appointment for a return visit for mother and babies to be fixed.

On the drive home, I'd received calls that two of my connections had come through and were happy to help out. They assured me that the horses and birds would be moved today. I didn't have a single worry about their new homes.

My phone rang, and I looked at it; a behind-the-bar shot of Phil smiled back at me. I smacked Fab's hand before she could answer for me, which most people didn't appreciate as she had a surly phone attitude. "Is this good or bad news?" I asked Phil.

Fab motioned for me to hit the speaker button.

"Another dead man was found last night. Good news: it wasn't on any of your properties, but damn close—he lived at the trailer park your brother unloaded."

"Close enough." I grimaced. The trailer park had once been accessed by a dirt road that ran through the property Jake's sat on. By mutual agreement, that entrance had been blocked by a solid fence, and the trailer park was now accessed from the road around the corner. "Anyone we know?"

"Reed Johns was a long-time local and janitor at the high school. He didn't have a criminal record. He was the only full-time resident of the trailer park, scoring reduced rent in exchange for handyman jobs, and the owners liked him; nothing but good things to say."

"Does this one have a connection to the others?"

"No one's talking. Shots to the back, like the others, and my sources say there are whispers of a serial killer, but the cops want to keep that out of the news as long as they can."

"Any leads?" Fab asked.

"Once again, no. The cops aren't stupid; they may not have a solid lead, but they have a pretty good idea what they're looking for—one person. Crimes by more than one person will never be exactly the same."

"Thanks for the info. Let us know if you find out anything new. Next call, I hope it's to tell us the killer is in custody."

Fab nodded in agreement.

"Hopefully, there will be an arrest before another body turns up. If not, you'll be my first call."

I stared at the phone after disconnecting. "Serial killer." I shuddered, looking at Fab.

"The Cottages, Jake's, and now the trailer park. Coincidence?" Fab wrinkled her nose. "Neither of us believes in those. If there's a personal connection, and not just the luck of the draw, we need to figure out what's going on."

"If someone wants to make me look like a killer, they're doing a poor job. It was clear from the start that the bodies found on my property were dumped there; they didn't bother to hide that fact. There hasn't been a scintilla of evidence that even suggests I had something to do with it."

Chapter 21

I blew into the parking lot of Jake's, parking illegally at the front door. Being the owner had its perks.

"What are you doing here?" Phil demanded, looking up from washing glasses and schmoozing with her regular customers.

"If you must know, I need to drop the receipt reports off at the CPA's tomorrow."

Phil pointed to the clock on the wall. "Did you forget about your date?"

"My date?" I stared in confusion. Suddenly, I remembered the whole "auditioning a boyfriend" thing with a sinking feeling in my chest. I'd had every intention of coming clean about the "dating" thing but kept putting it off. "Oh damn, I forgot about him. I had it on a to-do list somewhere to cancel that." I turned, surveying the bar. "Where is he? I'll tell him I have food poisoning."

The two regulars at the bar belly-laughed. Phil shook her head. "He's either at your house or about to arrive."

My phone rang, and I knew it was Fab; she had her own tone. I held it out to Phil. "You talk to her."

She stepped back. "Hell, no."

It stopped ringing for several seconds, then started up again. This time, I answered. "Hi."

"Your date is here," she growled. "What's your name again," she yelled without moving the phone far enough from her mouth. I winced. "Bart's here. He mentioned dinner, and just know, Didier isn't cooking for this one."

"I'm on my way, and so is dinner. Be nice."

Fab hung up.

"You set me up with Bart…?"

"Watford is the last name. You wanted different, you got it." Phil flashed me a crooked smile.

I fished my car keys out of my pocket. "Put in a big order—you know what we like—with extra for leftovers. Have it sent to my house. Tell Cook there's a big tip in it for him if he steps on it. We got the liquor covered." I ran out the door.

* * *

Fab met me at the door. "I thought this dating business was over with. He says this is a blind date. Who would fix you up with him?"

"I'm sure he's very nice." As I raced home, I had every intention of coming clean about the deception, but one foot inside the door, I lost my nerve.

"Whatever." She snorted and grabbed my arm. "Are you done with Creole? Is this because of me?"

"There you are," Bart interrupted. "Madison, I presume." He spread his arms wide as if to embrace me.

"Back off," Fab told him, stepping in front of me. "She doesn't hug."

I smiled tentatively, trying to place the balding man standing there with his big-boy jeans belted above a slight beer gut. He looked vaguely familiar. A Jake's customer, perhaps? I scooted around Fab, frowning at her. "Would you like something to drink?" I asked, setting my bag on the entryway bench. "Dinner is on its way," I added and skidded into the kitchen.

"The other guy got me a beer." He followed behind me and whispered, "I've been quite obnoxious in your absence."

"Thank you for doing this." I covered my laugh with my hand. I spotted Fab still hovering in the entryway and decided to stop stalling, apologize, and push Bart out the door. Instead, I filled a glass with iced tea, linked my arm in his, and steered him out to the patio, where we joined Didier at the table.

Bart hung his arm across my shoulder, flicking the ends of my hair. To my credit, I didn't jump, but I hoped that was the end of the touchy-feely.

"You and I have something in common,"

Bart said to me. "You love seafood, and I sell bait. I own Bart's Worms, Etc., down on the docks."

I had to bite back laughter.

Didier hadn't said a word; in fact, he had smoke coming out of his ears and kept shooting angry looks at Bart and me.

"Who fixed you two up?" Fab asked, snuggling up to Didier.

Thankfully, I had taken a drink of tea and decided to extend it into a gulp.

"Patsy at the bar, the one who sings along to the jukebox, thought we'd be a good match." Bart curled his hand into a microphone shape, singing a couple of off-key notes through it. "Madison tells me you're a male model. Like, dresses and stuff?" He checked Didier out.

Fab sat up straight, and her fist made contact with the table. "Hardly."

I looked down and sucked my lips together. "I'm sorry," I said to Didier. Bart was a great find, but now was the time to stop this jig before I lost two friends. I twisted my glass around. "I have something to say."

The doorbell rang, and Fab shot out of her seat. "I'll get it."

"If it's the food, I promised a big tip," I called to her receding back. We kept an envelope in the kitchen drawer nearest the door for times like these so we didn't have to run around hunting up cash.

I reached out to pat Didier's hand, but he withdrew it, which only solidified my certainty that I couldn't let this ruse continue. It would have been better to come clean when I first came through the front door, but what they say about hindsight is true.

I peeked over my shoulder to see Cook's wife setting bags of food on the counter and waved at her.

Didier stood. "We'll see you later. Fab and I are going out to dinner."

"Please wait." I reached out again, and he ignored me. "I have something to say, and I'm waiting for Fab to get back. Everything will become much clearer."

"Who are you?"

Recognizing the voice, I tried not to groan, but failed. How many times was someone going to ask that question today? Mother stepped out on the patio in boating clothes, her nose and cheeks pink from the sun. Spoon stood behind Mother, similarly dressed.

Fab skirted back to Didier's side. "Oh please… let me tell her." Fab smirked and threw out her arm in a flourish.

I glared at her.

"This is Bart." She flashed her creepy smile. "I forgot his last name, but you know how I am." She moved next to his chair, patting his shoulder. "He's Madison's date; she kicked Creole to the curb."

That declaration brought an immediate silence. It clearly made everyone uncomfortable; if all eyes hadn't been glued on me, I would've laughed.

"Madison Elizabeth Westin, what the hell is Fab talking about?" Mother yelled. "I recall telling you and Creole that you should never have started dating if you were going to break up. Creole hasn't called me. When did this happen? I thought you two were happy."

"Where have we met?" Spoon looked at Bart like he was a dead bug under a microscope.

"I've seen him at Jake's." Mother turned on me to hiss, "You date the customers?"

This was such a mess, and with more than a few angry faces staring at me, I wanted to run and hide in my room. "This is all Fab's fault," I blurted.

"Me?" Fab screeched. "It most certainly the hell is not." Her pitch went up with each word.

Mother's tone didn't hide her disappointment and irritation. "Quiet, the both of you." We both shut up, and she turned to Didier. "I need a drink."

A sound by the side fence drew everyone's eyes. I knew who it was even before I turned. *Creole.* I ran to his side but refrained from throwing myself in his arms.

"What's all the yelling about?" he asked in amusement. His blue eyes darkened as they flickered around the group.

"You must be her brother." Bart stood, extending his hand.

"And you are?" Creole asked.

"Madison's date," Bart said with a big grin.

Creole, in worn jeans, scuffed boat shoes, and a day-old beard, barked, "This is my girlfriend." His hand whipped out, pushing me aside, and he took a step in Bart's direction.

I scurried in front of Creole. "Everyone take a seat. I can explain."

Creole leaned down and whispered, "Another date? Again?" He laughed in my ear.

I turned, keeping my voice low. "I forgot to cancel."

Creole hung his head, his shoulders shaking.

"Are you two still together or not?" Mother demanded in exasperation, sitting in the chair Spoon pulled out.

"I'd like to know the same damn thing," Fab said in annoyance.

I grasped Creole's hand, motioning everyone to the table. "Everyone. Sit. This is a good story; you won't want to miss out." I wondered how many would speak to me by the time I was done. When I looked around the table, I did a double take. "Where's Bart?"

"Your *date* beat it out the door after Creole barked at him. Nice touch, cracking your knuckles." Spoon laughed.

Creole sat down and pulled me into his lap, clasping his arm around my middle and making sure I had nowhere to run. He knew me so well. He brushed my lips with his, murmuring, "You don't have to justify yourself. I'll tell them we're back together and the rest is none of their business."

"If you two are done," Fab sniped. "I'd like to hear what I have to do with your love life and who you date."

"This ought to be good." Spoon settled back in his chair.

I launched into an explanation of how tired I was with how Creole got treated and the name calling, leaving Fab's name out it, though everyone knew who I was talking about. I told them that I'd decided, after the first date—which caught Mother by surprise and earned me a glare that I was certain it was because I hadn't confided in her—that it wasn't very much fun and planned to cancel this one but forgot. I then announced that Fab had finally admitted to liking Creole and appreciating the times he had her back. I snuggled back into his chest, and his arm tightened. "I love him, and he's not going anywhere."

"That's the sweetest story," Mother cooed. "I'm relieved to know that you're not breaking up and we don't have to suffer through your dating again."

Creole and I laughed.

I banged my glass on the table. "Before we adjourn for dinner, I have another announcement that will make you happy, Mother. You're going to be a grandmother." I pointed towards Snow, curled up asleep on one of the deck chairs.

"What's that?" Mother asked, disappointed.

Fab laughed. "Good. I'm not the only one."

"You and Fab should be embarrassed not to know your animals," I said.

"I had two-footed grandchildren in mind." Mother snorted. "Does it have a name?"

"Snow," I said.

"Hmm—" She shook her head and smiled. "Just because Spoon hired you for the job doesn't mean you had to take one of the cats."

I grimaced; apparently she hadn't gotten the memo that I didn't want anyone to know. "It wasn't a hard decision; Snow and I had instant rapport."

Mother humphed. "I heard the place was overrun with animals; I'm surprised that you didn't take ten of them. I knew you'd be perfect to handle the problem."

"I didn't receive a text about this job." Creole kneaded the back of my neck.

Not knowing what to say, I hesitated.

"Madison had it covered," Fab said. "I wasn't any help. She did it all on her own and did an excellent job."

I sent a silent "thank you" to my friend. "I'm starving," I declared, hoping to end this conversation.

Mother started issuing orders, giving everyone a job: setting the table, making the drinks, heating up the food.

"I'll tell you about it later," I said to Creole. "There was never any danger."

Didier dragged Fab over, an arm around her waist. "If you have another problem with something that you can't get across to Fab, you let me know. I'll explain to her in a way she understands. Won't I?" He looked down at her.

"Yes." She gave him that "I'm drunk on sex" look.

"Better yet, I'll figure out how to explain it myself. It shouldn't be that hard, should it?" I asked her.

"He's okay." Fab nodded at Creole.

Creole winked, and she smiled back.

Chapter 22

Fab and I had just finished arguing over where we'd go for lunch when Mac called, frantic. Someone had broken a window to get into her house, but it didn't appear as though anything was missing, which left her puzzled. She felt certain, however, that it was her ex-husband, getting even with her for the sale of their marital home.

She lived in a blue-and-white bungalow cottage in a small housing tract. I'd noticed the "For Sale" sign on the property and knew she'd recently been given notice to move. Another owner disenchanted with handling rental property. When we pulled into the driveway behind Mac's truck, she came out on the porch, slamming the screen door with her hip.

Fab jumped out of the SUV, pulling out a pair of latex gloves and snapping them over her fingers. "Did you call the cops?" she asked, sidestepping Mac, not waiting for an invitation to go inside.

I loved that she always came prepared.

"Hold on, sister," Mac shouted to Fab and followed her back inside, shaking her head.

"Nothing got stolen. That's why I called you and didn't report the break-in. I figured the cops wouldn't take it seriously."

Fab stopped her snooping and turned to Mac. "I'll have a camera installed in the house, and if your husband comes back, you'll have proof and can have him arrested."

I had already claimed a chair, and Fab sat down across from me.

Mac paced the small living room, which held only a handful of furniture. Soon after the divorce, the ex had taken everything that wasn't nailed down while she was at work. "You know all those favors I've amassed from the two of you over the years? I want to cash them in all at once."

I whipped out my hand, grabbing a handful of Mac's skirt. "Sit," I ordered. "What could be so huge that one favor wouldn't suffice?"

"Lay it out," Fab said gruffly. "Then we'll decide. Don't get all wordy. Keep it simple."

I made a face at Fab. "You know that's not how it works. The favor-holder gets what they request." I patted Mac's shoulder, then glared at Fab. "No whining."

"As I told you, Shirl and I want to buy the place across from The Cottages." Mac wrung her hands. "I followed up on a rumor and contacted the Canadian owners. They blamed me personally for all the riff-raff that The Cottages has attracted. It's apparently also my fault that they rented to the ones we wouldn't. First, I told them that we'd broomed out the undesirables, and when that didn't work, I blamed everything on you, as the owner and all." She beamed at me. "They sputtered an angry tirade and hung up."

"That's damn nervy of them." I sniffed. "I recall offering them a better deal on property management than their current one, and they didn't even respond. Not that we could guarantee problem-free rentals, but the bust that just went down wouldn't have happened. Once we'd discovered the con of 'rent to one and another moves in,' our new eviction service would have quietly relocated them."

"I have yet to hear a favor," Fab griped.

"I'm getting there," Mac huffed. "I don't want to be accused of skimping on the details."

Fab growled at her.

I smacked Fab's arm. "You have to stop doing that; people will think you're unfriendly."

Mac laughed. "I called Beach Realty, which I know is handling that house, and the receptionist said that they had no such listing, but she'd check and get back to me. It was the realtor who called back—Janice Pincher—and when she found out it was me, she told me tough luck; she had a pocket listing and would never sell to me. She's hated my guts ever since I ran over her foot in Custer's parking lot."

Custer's was the biggest rathole bar in town. In addition to serving the cheapest beer, they also boasted the most bar fights and sheriff's department calls. They claimed they shouldn't be held responsible for what went on in the alley to the rear, leaving off the part that the troublemakers drank in the bar first.

"Here's the favor. Get the property for me. A friend of a friend who works in the office says Janice is holding it for an investor due back in town next week, so there isn't much time." Mac flashed puppy dog eyes at us.

"What do you want us to do? Force Janice at gunpoint?" Fab asked in exasperation.

"Fab's right. If she's holding out to sell to her own client, which earns her a double commission, I'm not sure what we can do," I said.

Mac stamped her foot. "If *you* wanted the property, you'd get it."

"She does have a point," Fab said.

"Our only hope is to negotiate with the potential buyer. Major roadblock there: we don't know who that is. I see a felony, right off the top, in trying to get said information." I thought a minute, then asked Mac, "Can your friend get the name of Janice's connection in exchange for a few bucks to ease her conscience for ratting out a co-worker?"

"She says no." Mac frowned.

Fab pulled her phone out. "Do you know

anyone at Beach Realty?" she asked the person on the other end.

I figured out, from Fab's end of the conversation, that she was talking to Phil about any options we might have that didn't include a felony. I held out little hope. "Do you have your money ducks in a row? Financing? Unless we're talking cash?" I asked Mac.

"How much fun would it be to drag in a sack of cash and heave it on the desk and say, 'Yeah, I'll take that'?" Mac smiled big.

I made a face at her.

Fab ended the call. "Here's the deal. It's a violation of the realtor rules for her to hold the listing off the market. Even though it's done all the time. We pay a call on her boss and threaten to file a formal complaint. The last thing they want is to be summoned to a board hearing."

"Let's do it. Keep it legal for once. It will make our boyfriends happy." *Especially mine.* Being law enforcement, he has stressed that he doesn't want a jailbird girlfriend.

"We can pitch this case as helping a friend; they both like Mac," Fab pointed out.

I shook my head at Fab. Her first plan was to run a con on the guys. It never worked.

"We have a business to run," Fab barked. "They have to accept that we can't run every job by them. Even Didier says, 'Meeting in Miami or New York,' or whatever; he doesn't run down the talking points.'"

"You sell that explanation, and I'll be there to lend support and try not to look simple-minded," I said.

Mac's phone rang once. Text message. She looked at it and stood up. "Gotta go. Domestic disturbance at The Cottages."

* * *

Fab and I followed her truck at a discreet distance, arriving minutes behind her. I wanted to stop for a shot of caffeine first, but Fab grumped that she didn't want to miss out on anything.

Mac stood in the driveway, Liam bouncing a basketball next to her. She motioned to us.

"Crum and Starletta are screaming inside his cottage," Liam informed us. "You need to get them to tone it down; Kevin is on his way home." He hesitated. "I'm sorry. This is kind of my fault. I knocked and Starletta flipped out. Apparently, I interrupted them while they were… uh…." He wrinkled his nose.

"This is a job for our Director of Security." I nudged Fab.

Fab crossed her arms. "I quit that job a long time ago."

Mac took her Beretta from her waistband and blew on the barrel, shining it with her skirt. She shot Fab a challenging look. "If you've forgotten, I'll show you how it's done."

Fab grunted at her.

"Don't shoot Crum; I kind of like him." I picked the basketball from Liam's hands and tried for a free throw.

"Yeah, and not before he helps me with my Trig homework," Liam called as they walked away.

"You're so smart." I ruffled his sun-bleached hair. He always sported a just-off-the-beach look. "Let's see how I do at real basketball," I said, laughing at myself. I'd been honing my skills at arcade ball recently, but I was sure to suck at the real thing. Missed.

"I probably shouldn't tell you this, but my uncle is a sneaky one." Liam took his shot and scored. "He didn't keep his promise to give you time to find those animals homes. He saw your car at Jake's, claimed he was worried about the old lady, and headed straight for her trailer, taking backup. I know that you two don't get along, but I thought it was crappy, and he did it to get back at you."

"When was this?" I asked. "What about the animals?"

"A few hours ago. I didn't find out until afterwards, or I would've warned you. Backfired on him, though; she was gone and only a handful of cats and dogs were still there. Boy, was he mad."

"Thank goodness," I whispered.

"Kevin said there were two dumpsters parked in front, one full to the top. He said the property had never looked like anything other than a run-down pile, but now it doesn't look bad, though he said he'd never live out there. Also mentioned some dude with an attitude on guard. You might want to warn him to tone it down."

Billy had called and offered to organize the cleanup after a man from Code Enforcement showed up and threatened to ticket Ruth if he had to come back. I'd readily agreed to his plan—another item Spoon could pay for.

"How did you hear all this?" I asked.

"Eavesdropped." He laughed. "Learned from the best." He pointed in the direction that Fab had disappeared.

"Don't worry about me telling anyone; I can keep a secret," I said, wanting to reassure him.

Liam nodded. "I don't gossip, and I keep stuff to myself. Nothing good comes from babbling everything you know."

"We have that in common. Anytime you need to talk, I'm here to listen." I gave him a quick hug. "Have you seen Brad?"

"He docked early from a fishing trip. One of his regular guys got sick—food poisoning—off fish, I heard."

I grimaced. "I've been sick on seafood before; it's gruesome."

"Here they come." Liam pointed to where Mac and Fab were walking toward us. "A buck says Crum didn't open the door."

"No, thanks. I smell a set-up."

"You're no fun." Liam laughed.

"What happened?" I asked.

"No answer. Not until I threatened to shoot the locks off," Mac related.

Liam elbowed me.

"And that's only if, by answer, you mean pulling that window rag aside, shaking his finger, and yelling, 'I'm busy,'" Fab said in a huff.

Chapter 23

"Let's go," I shouted to Fab, who lay curled up in Didier's arms on the couch. "There's a fire. Gotta see if we can help." I raced out the door and slid into the driver's seat of my SUV.

Looking out the back window, I did a double take when I saw both Fab and Didier race outside. Realizing that I hadn't disclosed the location, I chuckled. *Why tell Didier now?*

As soon as the back door slammed shut, I shot out of the driveway.

"Why are you driving?" Fab demanded.

"Hang on." I ignored her and squealed up to the corner in a perfect imitation of her. Unlike Fab, however, I made a complete stop at the corner and scanned for a speed trap; seeing none, I blew out onto the Overseas, hooking a U-turn to cut across the highway to the opposite side of the Cove.

"I didn't think I'd ever say this..." Fab gripped the sissy bar that she unrelentingly tormented me for using. "But your driving makes me sick. Did you even look before you careened across the highway?"

I needed to slow down before I scared myself. "*You* don't." Glancing in the rearview mirror, I saw that both of them had scowls on their faces and their arms crossed. "I'm slowing down."

Didier, who had been mumbling, barked, "This isn't the way to Jake's."

"What made you think we were going there?"

The last fire truck pulled around the corner just as I made the turn, going in opposite direction. I slowed before turning into the Tropical Slumber Funeral Home.

"What are you up to?" Didier roared.

I wanted to laugh and tell him, "Welcome to my life." When Fab had a job she knew I'd balk at, she waited until we were driving to inform me, with as little detail as possible, where we were headed, knowing I wouldn't jump out into traffic.

"Look, a red carpet." I pointed for Didier's benefit and parked alongside the building, climbing out.

The old hot dog stand had been renovated into a funeral home before Dickie and Raul bought it. They added on living quarters, tripling the size of the building. They offered a wide array of services in their quest to be Tarpon's one-stop shop for funeral needs.

Fab peered out the window and opened the door. "Must be a false alarm. I don't see any smoke."

"I'll wait here," Didier said, arms crossed.

I opened the back passenger door and asked, "Scared? That's what I'll tell Dickie and Raul, rather than that you're too snooty." I pointed to an outbuilding. "That's the garage over there, where the caskets are stored. Want a look?"

Fab held out her hand to Didier. "Don't worry. Except for the guys and their dogs, everyone else is dead."

Raul peeked out the double doors of the funeral home, relaxing and waving when he saw us.

"What happened?" Fab asked, hands on her hips, looking around. Didier slid out, standing behind her.

"The crematorium suffered a little explosion. Out now." Raul brushed his hands together. "The way the smoke billowed from the stack, you would've thought the whole place was burning to the ground." He motioned for us to follow him inside.

Fab made the introductions, then asked, "Was it… ah… occupied?"

"Yes." Raul let out a big sigh. "We need to contact the family and reassure them that the funeral will go forward according to their wishes. The deceased will be transferred up to Miami for final preparations."

Didier hugged me to his side with a jolt.

"You are so going to pay for this."

"How long before you can fire that baby back up?" Fab winked at Raul.

Raul laughed. Closing the space between them, he enveloped her in a hug. "We've missed you around here."

I could tell from Didier's face that the affection the funeral director had for his girlfriend took him by surprise.

Everyone turned at the sound of footsteps coming down the hall. Dickie appeared, platter in hand, their two Dobermans, Astro and Necco, at his side. "We have a few sandwiches left over from when we fed the firemen."

"Leftover funeral food," I answered Didier's raised eyebrows. "They're good, and the guys don't mind if you stick a couple in your pocket."

I couldn't quite picture the elegant Frenchman stuffing his pockets with sandwiches, but the idea had me belly-laughing and skirting out of the reach of his hand.

"Fab," I said, crossing the room ahead of her. "You should give Didier the tour, since you've snooped through every cranny in the place."

Dickie led us into the main viewing room, setting down the platter next to another one filled with assorted fruits and vegetables. An oval bucket at the opposite end of the table was filled with cold drinks.

The dogs followed and lay under the table, watching the room with their heads on their paws and paying particular attention to me. They knew I was a soft touch for a stray sandwich.

Didier and Fab politely declined the food. She tugged his arm, trying to get him to move forward, which succeeded for two steps before he dug in his heels and jerked her back to his side.

I tried to wave her away from the first visitation room when I spotted the card indicating that the room was occupied, most likely by someone propped up to receive their final round of guests. Didier straightened, brushed Fab's hand off his arm, and returned to join us in the main room, Fab trailing behind.

"Didier's a little nervous; first time on a funeral home tour," I whispered to Raul. Didier claimed a seat at the end of a church pew used by guests. "Get ready for new business; he's going to kill me for tricking him into coming." I helped myself to a sandwich and snuck one to each dog. I needed to maintain my status as their favorite guest.

Raul laughed. "Such a stressful morning; it feels good to laugh." Dickie nodded in agreement.

"We've begun offering themed funerals," Raul announced. "The first one is this weekend. The casket arrived this morning." He waved to the front of the room, where it sat surrounded by shopping bags.

"Is that a double-wide casket?" I gaped, wondering if two people were going to be buried together and promptly squeezing my eyes closed, forbidding any imagery to take hold.

"It's a special order: the client requested a double-sized, down-filled mattress, pillows, and high-count cotton sheets—all in white to best display her long, dark hair and pale skin tone."

Fab headed toward the casket. Didier came up off the bench to stop her, but she eluded his grasp and he ended up right behind her by the open casket. Suddenly, Fab nudged him, and he turned and leapt back, the color draining from his face. He blurted out something in French that I was certain contained a bad word. Some words one learns faster than others.

Fab laughed. The rest of us stared, all thinking an unspoken, "What?"

"The dead person just waved," Didier choked out as he reclaimed his seat.

Fab lowered her head, stuck her hand inside the casket, then turned and said, "She's not dead, guys."

"Priscilla!" Raul half-yelled. "How did you get past us?" He stalked to the front.

A very pretty twentyish woman poked her head over the side of the casket. "You were busy with the firemen. I just wanted a test run," she fussed. "I'm happy with the way it came together."

Dickie and Raul each took one of her arms and helped her out, making sure she landed on her feet.

I wanted to get a peek, but only if I could do it without moving from my vantage point. "Is this another case of the dead coming back to life?" I eyed the petite woman from head to toe; she didn't show signs of being a complete nut case. The bling on her wrists and ears appeared to be real diamonds, and she was dressed in a black designer tee, her jeans rolled up above her ankles. She slipped her feet into a pair of red stilettos that I hadn't noticed lying next to the casket.

Priscilla giggled, twisting a lock of her long, dark hair around her finger. "My funeral is tomorrow. I want to know what my friends will say about me."

"Do these friends think you're dead?" I asked.

"They each got a call that I'd expired from natural causes." She threw herself into a fake sobbing fit for several seconds, then looked up and smiled.

"If this is a test of some sort, you might be disappointed. Don't people always say nice things at funerals?" I directed my question to Dickie and Raul.

Dickie let out a low groan. "We've had a few funerals where the mourners showed up to air their grievances, some of them decades old."

Fab appeared at my side. "If I grieved your death and found out it was a hoax, we would never be friends again."

"I would never do that." I didn't see this surprise of Priscilla's ending well. "Mother would kill me."

Didier was silent, his lips pursed in a tight line. Not making eye contact with anyone, he nudged Fab in the back.

Priscilla grabbed a tote bag. "I'll be back later." She waved.

"Is this a new trend?" I asked. "Having a funeral before you're dead?"

Dickie turned his head, looking sheepish. "A customer is a customer." He sighed.

"Our phones have been ringing off the hook since we started advertising our themed funerals," Raul said. "We just got an inquiry about a stripper theme. The deceased was fond of the entertainment."

"I wonder if he was a friend of Brick's?" I mumbled to myself.

Fab patted Raul on the back. "I've got a connection for dancers that can put on a live show, guaranteed not to disappoint. Not sure if the poles are portable, but I can find out." She beamed at him.

"I find it distasteful," Dickie snapped.

He looked sad about the turn of events. I knew how hard he worked on every detail. "It won't diminish the job you do," I said to him. "Your work will be center stage, even more so than before."

He didn't say anything but appeared to be thinking about what I'd said.

"Be sure to get pictures; you can use them for promos," I suggested.

After another nudge from Didier, this one more insistent, Fab concocted an excuse for us to leave. A meeting with a client was always a good one. It could even be true.

We said our good-byes. Fab hugged both Raul and Didier, and I waved to Priscilla, who had returned with a plate of food and sat in the front row, admiring her purchase.

I overheard Didier tell Fab, "You drive. Madison can sit in the backseat with me so that I can strangle her on the way home."

I ran around to the driver side and jumped in, sliding behind the wheel and pushing the lock down.

Chapter 24

I walked through the low tide, kicking the water as I went and sending it flying, giving myself a good drenching as I headed home. When I got parallel with the back of my house, I cut across the white sand and made my way up the steps. The sound of Fab's voice echoing through the opening in the fence caught my attention. Peeking in, I did a double take when I recognized the back of the man sitting with her.

Fab waved over his shoulder, her patented smirk firmly in place, and Brick turned. Sitting on the edge of his chair, poised for flight, he shifted, a reasonably friendly smile pasted on his face.

This is a first. Brick must have wanted something awfully bad to show up at my house. Not sure what to say, I waved and skirted past them.

I was steps away from the patio door when Brick called out, "Madison, I came to talk to both of you."

Blowing out a whoosh of air before turning, I walked back and sat in a chair next to Fab.

"I want Fab to come back to work for me, and she won't without you," Brick stated.

So much for "hi, how are you" small talk. "Let's see if I understand: you'll put up with me to get her back. How nice." I noticed that Fab hadn't offered him anything to drink; translated, that meant she hadn't invited him for this little get-together.

"I didn't mean it like that," he said with no conviction. "Fab and I had a long talk, and she made me realize how important backup is for her safety. For my part, I won't withhold any information in the future, no matter how insignificant."

I should have felt a tad sorry for him, but I didn't. If he could have schmoozed Fab into working without me, he wouldn't be sitting on my patio in a snit. "You worked solo for him before; why not now?" I nudged Fab.

"The guilt would eat at you if something happened to me." She had a point there, and she smirked as though reading my thoughts.

If I were honest with myself, I wanted to tell him to go to hell. I'd be Fab's backup anytime, but I didn't want to work for Brick anymore. "I can't commit until I talk to Creole."

"What, you've got to get the boyfriend's permission to blow your nose?" Brick sneered.

"Don't be rude." I gave him my best contemptuous stare. "If it weren't for Fab, the answer would be no." My gaze flicked over the side of his face; it was healing but still faintly yellow. "How did you get the black eye?"

He growled and ignored me. He didn't dare say, "You should see the other guy," since we both knew that there wasn't a scratch on Creole.

"Where's your snack bowl?" Brick looked around.

"We don't buy junk food," I said snootily, trying not to laugh at the look on his face. "If you want something cold to drink, there's a refrigerator over there." I pointed.

Brick got up and walked over, taking a minute to pull out a beer. "Impressive selection," he said over his shoulder. Instead of returning, he stood in the doorway, checking out the interior of the house. He stared at one corner and pointed. "What's that?"

"They're called cats." I didn't bother to cover up my eye-roll. "If you touch one of them, I'll shoot you. They don't like to be petted." Truthfully, both of them would love it if a human were assigned to pet them for hours on end, but the last thing I wanted was Brick doing it. I kept my cootie comments to myself.

Fab read the look on my face and erupted into laughter. "Just like their mother."

When Snow first arrived, she and Jazz had given each other the sniff over, hissed a few times, then started sleeping together. As soon as Snow had her babies, she was getting fixed, so I wouldn't have to sit her down for the sex talk.

Brick sat back down, and Fab said, "Here's the deal. No withholding information, and that's not negotiable. We find out that you did, and you'll have to find someone new who'll jump when you bark."

"I agree to all that," Brick said, downing his beer.

Fab held up her hand before Brick could stand and escape. "There's more. I also have to run this by Didier. Madison's involvement, along with full disclosure, would seal the deal. Both of our boyfriends think you're a weasel and have run out of patience with your jobs. So no screw-ups."

"I can't guarantee that there won't be problems," Brick said.

"We know that, but in the future, not disclosing that someone is a six-time felon will be a relationship-ender." Fab maintained eye contact.

I enjoyed watching Fab in action. She spelled it out for him in a concise manner, not getting caught up in hurt feelings.

"I've got a case for you," Brick announced. Of course he did. Why else would he be here? He needed Fab and needed her now.

"You might want to hold off; this isn't a done deal," I reminded him.

"I'm not coming back down here," he said adamantly. "Now here's *my* non-negotiable point: in the future, you two come to the office. I'll have all the details at my fingertips."

"Don't leave anything out," Fab ordered.

"I posted bail for this nice young woman," Brick started.

I got up to get a bottle of water and, when I was behind his back, pushed my boobs forward.

When Fab laughed, he shifted in his chair, glaring at me. "Zilla Mirren was charged with the felony burglary of her ex-boyfriend's house. She lacked the ten percent required for the bond amount and, as collateral, offered a several-carat diamond ring that she'd inherited from her mother. I agreed to hold it to give her time to get the cash together." He paused and said to me, "Get me a water."

I glared at him. He got the message and stomped over to the refrigerator to retrieve a bottle himself.

"The case was tossed." He settled back in his chair. "There was some suspicion that the boyfriend had set her up, but no charges were ever filed against him. I contacted Zilla about the outstanding balance on her bail premium, and she gave me the okay to sell the ring, as she didn't have the cash, and refund her the excess. I sent it over to the jeweler, and it came back as cubic zirconia. She'd already blown town."

Fab and I laughed. "You didn't have it appraised ahead of time?" I continued to laugh.

"You should have seen it; it was flawless." Brick sighed. "Thinking the boyfriend might be cooperative, I drove to his house, but found out he'd moved. The neighbor thought they'd reconciled because she'd seen Zilla around and they were all lovey-dovey; her words, not mine. This is what happens when you're a nice guy. I even offered her a job at The Gentleman's Club so she could pay off the debt and keep her mother's ring. I felt bad about selling it."

"You want us to chase her down," I said. "Then what? She doesn't have any money, or did you want the matching necklace?"

Fab and I laughed again.

"You're such a smart—" Brick stopped himself.

"You knew that before you came here."

Brick had clearly had enough of the two us—me, anyway. "Zilla Mirren isn't even her real name. I turned the file over to a skip tracer, but he's avoiding my calls, so I suspect he hasn't turned up anything. My BS detector didn't even ping with the woman. Also, I'm impressed that she somehow managed to craft multiple identities well enough to fool law enforcement."

"So that's why you need us. You want us to track her down… and what? Demand a check? Why bother? It would probably be rubbery. Even if it didn't bounce, you think she's just going to hand it over?" He'd lost his mind, and my stare told him so.

"If she doesn't have the money, you want us to shoot her?" Fab asked.

"I want to know everything there is to know about Zilla Mirren and who in the hell she really is. Then I'll decide," Brick seethed.

"Why not do it yourself? Or even better, write it off as 'distracted by double D's.'" I struggled not to smirk.

"Nobody screws me," Brick practically spit. "And they were only C's." His cheeks flushed.

Fab hit me in the arm. "What do we need?"

"A decent picture of Ms. Zilla, in case she altered her looks in any way. A copy of the proof of identity and application she filled out."

Fab nodded.

Brick stood. "Get back to me first thing tomorrow with an answer. If you need a tip or two about getting your men to say yes, I can help with that."

"No, thanks," Fab said in disgust.

"Tomorrow." He shook his finger at us and went out the side fence.

"How does he know about the misnamed 'secret path'?" I asked.

"I recognized his Range Rover driving by slowly several times, checking out the neighborhood, and for my peace of mind, I went outside to investigate. I brought him in that way, thinking you wouldn't want him inside the house. I know I didn't."

Chapter 25

I stuck my head in the refrigerator, thinking Fab's "divide and conquer" idea was a terrible plan. Creole preferred to get irritating information in a straightforward fashion. If he thought I was using sex to manipulate him... Fireworks. And if the same tactic was used against me, it would provoke a loud, noisy fight.

"Didier and I need some alone time tonight," Fab said to my back.

Jerking a bottled water from the shelf, I turned. She was scrutinizing me for resistance. I sat across the island from her.

Both Jazz and Snow came sauntering in. Snow sat quietly. Jazz, I swear, nudged her, as if to say, "Watch and learn. This is how it's done," then meowed at the top of his lungs. Fab, the enabler, retrieved tuna from the refrigerator and gave them each a spoonful.

"This sneak-ass approach of yours is a bad idea. We should sit them down and present the job as though we have nothing to hide—which, by the way, we don't."

Fab hung over the kitchen sink, surveying the driveway. "Creole is going to know that you're only doing this for me." She turned back; since she didn't whip out her gun, I assumed we were trespasser-free. "I'm serious about not doing jobs without backup. If I had to get a new partner, wouldn't you be jealous?"

"No." I shook my head. "He or she wouldn't be around long. I'd put a bullet in their butt and wave bye-bye."

"It doesn't bother me to try and guilt you, just so you know."

"Is that a trick you learned in convent school?" I smiled sweetly.

"Hardly." Fab snorted. "The sisters knew early on that I needed a watchful eye or I'd inspire chaos. I worked to stay out of trouble and out of the range of the dreaded ruler."

I snapped my fingers at her. "You know Creole likes you and would never want you to be in any danger. He respects your abilities."

Fab raised her eyebrows. "Don't go overboard. Can I call him names once in a while? How about 'Hey you'?"

I gave her the stink eye.

"Oh, okay." Fab pouted. "Only because it hurts your feelings."

"Let's cook them dinner." I opened the refrigerator again, looking for something that wouldn't require much work. We had some leftover Mexican food, but not enough for four, and it would hardly count as home-cooked. "We'll serve it out by the pool."

"Cooking is men's work." Fab humphed. "I hate everything about it, including the dishes, unless it's me and Didier and he makes it sexy time."

I covered my face and said through my fingers, "Stop. You better not be… well, you know, in the kitchen."

"You have Didier to thank for that. He has more restraint than me."

I held out my hand, pulling her to her feet. "Come on, we'll raid the grocery store."

* * *

"What else?" Fab asked from her position on the lounger she was paddling to the side of the pool. She had changed into a black bikini with a little more material than her preferred string-style, but not much.

"No, no, don't stress yourself." I waved my hand, continuing to set the table.

Fab had been a huge help in selecting fresh fruits and vegetables. Didier must be quite instructional, and what surprised me more was that she'd listened. That was the extent of her assistance, though, unless you counted her handing me vegetables one at a time to chop.

"You always set the prettiest tables." Fab climbed out of the pool and crossed to the table. She fingered the shell-embossed dinner plates and stainless bamboo silverware, a recent upgrade because the handles on the wooden ones had begun to snap off.

"Once I began collecting my own dishes, it just became fun. Then there's my need for visual perfection in my surroundings."

"Owning a house suits you. Even the outside looks great, and it was all your hard work. I even like the shell mulch. I'd buy them by the bag rather than stoop down and pick them up off the beach, though. But if you tell anyone, I'll throw them in the trash. I'm more suited to an upscale condo."

I looked up and scowled. "This isn't your way of telling me you're moving, is it?"

"Oh, hell no. When I first barged in on you, I expected to stay a week or two, but now I can't imagine living anywhere else. I didn't think I'd enjoy being part of a family, but I do. Besides, all the good stuff happens in your kitchen. If Didier and I marry, we'll have to stay close by."

"We could build a third story, and the honeymooners could have it all to themselves." I couldn't imagine living by myself. I did it for a few months when I first moved to Florida and didn't like it. Even though unexpected company exhausted me at times, I wouldn't trade the fact that my house was the de facto meeting place for anything. "Just try and leave, and I'll drag your skinny ass back here."

"What, unconscious? Tied up?"

"It's rude to gloat that your ass-kicking skills far exceed mine."

"Someone's home." She shot off the chaise. "Do we have a plan?"

"Eat first. We'll come up with something."

* * *

Didier arrived home first, and Creole came through the front door not long after. Both looked surprised that dinner was ready to be grilled. I'd had the butcher assemble assorted fish and beef skewers. I'd chopped up vegetables for grilling and conjured up some flavored rice that I'd already tasted and gave a "thumbs up" to. I'd passed on a bottle of wine, going with mixed drinks, and put together a tray of garnishes.

During dinner, Didier asked Creole, "Do you know what your girlfriend did to me?"

The tone of his voice suggested I'd committed bodily harm. I tapped Fab's leg under the table and glanced sideways at her, hoping she'd interrupt the conversation and take it in a different direction.

"Pull a gun on you?" He kissed my cheek. "Oh wait, that would be *your* girlfriend."

"How about some brotherly support?" Didier told Creole about the visit to the funeral home. "I didn't appreciate being railroaded."

"If I'd known how sensitive you were, I'd have locked the car door before you got in," I said, giving him a dirty look.

When he got to the part about the corpse

winking, Creole couldn't hold back his laughter. "Sorry." He said it a couple of times, but he continued to laugh. "At least there's never any gunfire at the funeral home."

"There was that one time…" I started.

Fab shook her head, raking a finger across her throat.

"You shot someone!" Didier looked appalled.

"Fab, superstar that she is, did the only thing she could to get a bunch of unruly mourners to calm down; she put a bullet in the ceiling, then ordered them out with instructions not to loiter. I *think* the service was over." I quirked my head in question.

"I suppose you started it," Creole said in amusement.

"Hell, no. Trust me, we were well-behaved and wanted out as soon as possible." I turned on Didier. "Hell, hell, hell—I heard you tsk. You said it, so I thought it was on the exempt list. Unless you operate under a double standard?" The man was such a stickler about bad language, no matter how mild.

"She's got you there. That would be hypocritical, pal." Creole pushed back from the table.

"Are you done laughing at me?" Didier growled.

"Is the entertainment over?" Creole looked around the table in disappointment.

We moved poolside, sharing double chaises.

I fished a quarter out of the top of my bathing suit. "Fab." I held up the coin, ready to toss.

She nodded. "You toss it. I call 'heads.' If it comes up 'tails,' you get to tell them."

"So we *were* being buttered up; I wondered," Creole said, running his hand down one side of my body, then the other. "You're not hurt, are you?"

I shook my head and sent the coin flying in Fab's direction. "You do the honors, and don't touch it until Didier tells us which side is face up. Not that I don't trust you."

She caught the coin and tossed it in the direction of her beach bag. "I'll tell them; it's the least I can do."

"Really?" I mouthed.

"I may need help getting the facts out, so pay attention," she said to me.

At the first mention of Brick's name, Creole and Didier growled in unison, which I wouldn't have thought possible, unless they practiced it.

"You never said that I couldn't work for Brick again. You said that it was my decision," Fab reminded Didier.

"I know you feel a loyalty to that man, but I don't have to like it or him," Didier grouched.

Creole didn't say a word but made his feelings known by wrapping his arms around me as Fab continued to explain.

She detailed the visit and everything we knew about the case, then ran down the new rules she had insisted on and told them she'd informed Brick that if he couldn't or wouldn't agree, she wasn't going to work for him.

Creole's agitated breath blew on the back of my neck. I knew he was waiting to hear how I fit into this new arrangement.

Her next words: "I need Madison as backup," made his arms tighten like iron bands until I whimpered. "Madison quit the bastard already," he said.

I grumbled, and he loosened his hold enough that I could breathe. "Honey." I looked up at him.

"I don't want to hear anything that starts with that word," Creole barked.

Fab grasped Didier's hand in hers. "Madison only agreed because of me. Wouldn't you feel bad if something awful happened to me? Madison would suffer lifelong guilt. Hold it against you."

I wanted to clap. The pouty lip was a nice touch. She must be getting private "guilt inducing" classes from Mother. I'd have to grade her a little lower, though, as she'd used that exact same phrase to motivate me to see things her way.

Didier crossed his arms and exchanged silent communication with Creole, who leaned back against the chaise, taking me with him and wrapping his legs around me.

"I had no plans to go anywhere," I said.

"I know you want to do this for Fab. But we have a few rules of our own, don't we Didier?"

"Before you start this case, you have to have that tracking app installed on your phone," Didier demanded.

I wasn't the only one surprised by Didier's ultimatum. Fab looked at him like he'd grown a second head. She hated any attempts at making her trackable. What really surprised me was that she agreed.

Chapter 26

Fab and I sat in the driveway, her question of, "What next?" going unanswered. My phone beeped, indicating a message, and I mumbled the words as I read.

"You think its fun to drive me crazy? I'm not amused." Fab scowled, holding out her hand for the car keys.

Good friend that I am, I laughed at her frustration over my antics. "According to Phil, she's got the goods on Ms. Zilla." I handed over the keys; she'd been irritated that I grabbed them before she could get to them. "She's in her office; let's go chat."

When we reached Jake's, Fab and I went in through the kitchen. The doors were open and music blaring, lunch prep underway. Cook's son waved. His wife and oldest son took up the slack during peak hours; the dictator himself was inside the walk-in refrigerator. When I hired him, I'd given him complete control over his domain. Our deal was: I wouldn't tell him what to do and he'd put out good food. He had the latitude to sing, dance, watch his telenovelas, talk on the phone, whatever, as long as there were no complaints. There had been a few, but only from the regular complainers looking for something for free.

We stopped at the bar to get drinks, and Phil waved us down from the deck, pointing to a cart she'd set up with bottled water and a pitcher of iced tea.

I nudged Fab out to the patio. "The more information we have on Zilla, the better. Do I need to remind you that the last case of yours, the woman went psycho and pulled a gun? Something about all this sunshine wreaks havoc on mental stability. We need to be careful."

Fab groaned. "Who names their kid Zilla?" she asked.

"Stoners who shouldn't procreate. It could be worse." Fab's astonished face told me she didn't believe me.

Phil had paperwork spread out across the table permanently reserved for family and select friends. Fab and I helped ourselves to a drink, and I flipped on the ceiling fans before sliding into a seat next to her.

"Took you longer than I thought," Phil said, looking at her watch. "I gotta say upfront that this job won't be a freebie because I had to call in an outside contractor."

"There will be no price-quibbling," I assured her. "We'll pass it on to our client, and so far, he's never failed to pay."

Phil nodded, satisfied. "Ms. Zilla is a

clever woman, despite her rap sheet of petty crimes. Unfortunately for her, I loathe unanswered questions. When all leads led to a black hole, I contacted a friend who could run the driver's license pic and see if it got any other hits. Paydirt." Phil smirked, pleased with her find.

"Reassure us that she's not crazy," Fab said.

"Hmm…" Phil paused. "In my professional opinion, she leans that way."

"Another one." I sighed.

"Zilla Mirren lives her more adventurous lifestyle under her pseudonym; her real name is Finn Kennedy, and *that* record doesn't have a blemish on it. I assume because she doesn't want to risk her social status. She's an interesting woman, part of an uber-rich family of overachievers with roots going back a hundred years. Connected, graduated Yale with honors, rich in her own right, courtesy of a trust fund, and heads up a foundation that supports several charities."

I blew out a loud sigh. "She's bored? She's…?"

"Probably addicted to risk-taking." Phil telegraphed her feelings about that: 'what a waste.' "When you get arrested, they run an identity check, so for her fraudulent ID to pass muster, she must have some damn fine connections."

"Wouldn't mind getting those names," Fab murmured.

"Zilla has been arrested several times, but the charges always get dropped. I got more information on her when I ran the name of the longtime boyfriend who accused her of burglary. It would be interesting to know if he knows her real identity. They've never been photographed together, and his name has never been linked to hers, except for the recent arrest."

Fab perked up, finally taking an interest in the conversation. "The neighbor claims they left town together."

"The boyfriend probably put that out there to salve his ego. Zilla doesn't form lasting relationships, for good reason." Phil flicked to another page.

"Do you have a business address?" I asked. "Her office hours?" Fab and I had agreed that this conversation/confrontation would take place in a public place. Her office wasn't ideal and probably not completely private, but it would have to do. Neither of us wanted to pay a visit to her house, which probably had state-of-the-art security.

"The foundation office is in a high-end business park on Corporate Circle in Boca Raton. You've got a long drive. I'll see if I can make you an appointment."

"We don't need an appointment; she'll see us," I said.

Two of the lunch regulars came through the back and seated themselves at the bar, waving.

"This will require dress-up." Fab looked me up and down. "Not your usual business attire of a skirt and flip-flops."

"You know I can break out a pair of low heels when the occasion calls for it." I stood and twirled in my full, black above-the-knee skirt. "How do I look?" I asked Phil, then glared at Fab. "Don't you answer."

"You always look nice; you both do." She laughed. "Time for me to open up, make it official."

Fab stood and grabbed my arm. "I always tell you that you look nice."

"You do? Next time, get my attention first so I don't miss it." I waved to the two men at the bar as we left.

Chapter 27

As Fab flew up the Overseas, headed for home, I stared out the window at the glistening blue-green water. "That meeting took longer than I thought," I said. "Drop yourself at home; I need my car. I'll catch up with you later."

"Where are you going that I can't come?" Fab asked in a whiny tone. "It's the animal case, isn't it? I wanna go… check it out for myself." She paused, wrinkling her nose. "We're not hauling around animals, are we?"

I almost laughed at her. "You worried I'll let them roam wild and get hair all over the SUV?" I twisted around in my seat, waving my hand. "Make a U-turn. That's Mac walking along the road."

Fab honked several times as she pulled up behind her. Mac turned and waved, walking back to the car.

She poked her head in the back door. "Thanks for this." She hoisted herself into the seat. "Normally I could walk it, but not in these damn clogs." She shoved her foot out from under her long jersey skirt, showing off a pair of wooden shoes.

Who knew those were still being made? Were they really even a shoe?

"With the way people drive, you could get run over," Fab lectured.

"You mean drivers like *you*." I nudged her.

"My brakes failed," Mac explained. "Luckily not while I was moving. I had to leave the truck parked at Lucky Dude, the convenience store about a mile back. To make matters worse, my damn wallet is gone out of my purse. I only take it out when I need something and put it right back. I don't know what happened to it." Mac shifted on the back seat, throwing her arm along the seatback. "Where are we going?" she asked as Fab hooked another U-turn.

"Madison has to go check on a job. Unless you want me to drop you here and give you cab fare?" Fab said.

"I'm in," Mac said excitedly. "This will be a girl road trip. Wait till Shirl hears about this."

"Road trip is an overstatement; we're just headed to the next Key down," I turned and said over the seat. "I wouldn't get too worked up. The excitement level will be zero." I nudged Fab's shoulder. "You'll want to change into tennis shoes; it's pretty overgrown." Long ago, we found that it was beneficial to keep a change of clothes and shoes in the back.

"Is this that animal job? I asked everyone

I could think of that could give one a decent home—placed a few, but not many," Mac said.

"I can return the favor right now." I smiled at Mac. "Where do you want your truck towed to?"

"The dealer. And it's up in Homestead," Mac groaned.

I retrieved my phone out of the cup holder and called Spoon; it went to voicemail. I left him a message, giving him the details about where to find Mac's truck and her phone number for any other questions. "Don't look so worried," I said to Mac. "This is a freebie."

Fab followed my finger-pointing directions. She put up with it as long as I didn't wait until the last few feet before the turn. "Did you give Spoon the almost-family discount on this job?"

"It's a freebie." I turned to look out the window, not wanting to see her expression. She loathed the word "free" when it came to jobs.

"That bastard is taking advantage of you." Fab beat on the steering wheel with her fist.

My eyebrows flew to my hairline. "I wouldn't recommend ever whispering *that* word in his general direction."

Fab fingered her neck. "He'd squeeze the life out of me."

"Not my business," Mac called from the back seat. "But free? You need to eat too."

"The agreement was that I'd do it for free as long as he didn't breathe a word about the fact that he thought I was perfect for the job. My ego suffered; in fact, I'm still sulking a little. I should have known that he wasn't going to offer me a job meant for Jason Bourne. Then I found out Mother had a hand in the decision..."

Fab tugged on a lock of my hair. "If I were a cat, I'd want to go to your house."

"Hell, yeah," Mac said.

"Look at Snow—her life just got a giant boost for the better. She's got food, her own comfy bed, Jazz sniffs her out a few times a day, and she doesn't have to pick up after herself. Now that's the life." Not having been paying attention to my hand signals, Fab hit the brakes and maneuvered through a wide turn.

I leaned back and closed my eyes, Fab's supportive words getting me over the last hurdle of pride.

"How many animals are there?" Mac asked. "What are you going to do if you can't find homes?"

"I was worried at first. Especially after I called several shelters. All were full to capacity; they seemed sympathetic but weren't very helpful. One told me, 'Good luck on placing the cats.' Apparently, there are more cats than dogs that need a home, and the demand is low. So I went through my phonebook, calling everyone listed, even if I'd only met them once, and asked them to spread the word. I lucked out and found homes for most of them. If I had to do it every day, I'd have many a sleepless night. Our friend at the bird farm took all the parrots and songbirds, two geriatric dogs, and three cats."

"That's why Spoon called you," Fab said. "I don't have any friends, and the others in my phone list would hang up on me."

"Hey," Mac yelled, "you got two friends—besides Madison, of course—Shirl and me."

Fab wouldn't admit it, but I knew she liked hearing that.

* * *

"I'm not sure why people call gravel a road," Fab griped, turning off on the "street" to Ruth's house.

Looking out the windshield, I surveyed the approach to the property. "Believe me, it looks better than it did. Though the rusted-out mailbox is still the only marker." I pointed up. "A tree trimmer has been out here, or Billy did it. He's handier than he looks. I gave him carte blanche; I figured if he spent too much, he could explain it to his boss."

"Who's Billy?" Mac asked. She had scooted up and hung her head between the seats.

"One of Spoon's men and perfect for the job. He doesn't have any sense of smell. The odor inside the house is overwhelming. I tacked on a huge bonus as incentive not to ditch me at the first opportunity. All billed to Spoon," I told them.

"That's why Madison does all the billing and collection." Fab exchanged a nod with Mac.

"What if he doesn't pay?" Mac asked. "Billy might not be comfortable pushing for it; he's an employee, and Spoon is scary."

"Then *I'll* pay him and tell Mother."

"I could threaten him, tell him he better not go all cheap on you." Fab half-laughed, pulling up across from the trailer.

"That's two bad ideas in a row." I tsked.

Billy sat, feet propped up, under an umbrella outside his motorhome. On our approach, one hand had moved to the back of his waistband. Once he recognized the SUV, however, he stood, stomping on a soda can, which he pitched into the trash.

My last trip out, the flies were out of control, buzzing the open cans. Now the old ones had been replaced by two plastic cans with well-fitting lids. A weed whacker had been taken to the grass, which was still a little scraggly, but a huge improvement.

"Hey William," I said, stepping out of the SUV.

Caught off guard, he hesitated, then glared. "Since you're not my mom, Billy will be fine."

"Let me make a note: 'no sense of

humor,'" Fab said, coming around the front of the car.

"I smiled," he defended himself, his lips quirking ever so slightly. "You must have missed it."

"Mac—Billy." I introduced them after Mac slammed the door, joining us. "What's the update?"

"All the animals have permanent homes, except for the dozen that were sickly but not dying. Yet. They would have if left untreated. I didn't think you wanted them nuked." One would have thought Mac asked the question, since he kept his eyes on her, checking her out from head to toe. Mac had obviously noticed; her cheeks turned pink.

Fab walked across the driveway, then around the back of the house.

"No, of course not! I didn't even like it when it was suggested that the already dead cats get tossed in the trash." I was pleased when Dickie and Raul had offered to cremate them; they'd buried them under a paver on the patio and written in the cement to mark the spot.

"You should know that I made a deal with a woman who lives out here. She's agreed to look after the sick ones, making sure they're fed and get their medication. She's a little down on her luck, so I gave her money for it, but I wouldn't ask for free anyway. I was hoping you'd help me find her a job once the cats are better. Husband up and died and left her with bills."

"Make sure she's overpaid, and I'll tell Spoon that she needs to be subsidized until the cats are healthy and new homes can be found for them." I glanced over at Mac, who was unusually quiet; she hadn't taken her eyes off Billy. He didn't seem to mind, his gaze constantly going back to her.

"You've been more than generous, and I suspect it would be the same if it was your money. The job went smoothly. I enjoyed orchestrating the cleanup—" Billy flexed his muscles. "—and tried to make sure the relocation of the animals wasn't a shock to them. Another upside: no one got arrested, and there were no code-violation tickets."

"I'm surprised they didn't show up," I said.

"They did, and lucky you, it was another friend of yours—Quatro from the Code Department. We gossiped some, and when I mentioned your name, he said he knew you and that, since the cleanup was almost complete, he'd close the complaint that had been filed against the property. He likes you a lot and took a cat for his neighbor, who just lost hers to old age."

Quatro was a friend of my aunt's who spoke at her funeral. It wasn't until her death that I found out she'd had a colorful parade of friends. All of them extended their friendship to me, which I never failed to appreciate. My aunt would have loved to know that her old friends were happy to do a favor or two for her niece.

"More good news: Miss Ruth didn't end up under court control."

I was happy to hear that, knowing a protracted court hearing would take its toll on her and eventually the daughter would be named caretaker anyway.

"That first night, I thought the biggest problem would be Miss Ruth, but when her daughter showed, she seemed to accept that she was in over her head and needed help." Billy sighed, looking relieved it had gone smoothly.

Fab came out of the front door, scowling. "This needs to be bulldozed. Even Miss Fix Old Stuff over there—" She pointed at me. "—can't do anything with this. There are a couple of places in the floor you should check out before you do anything. It appears to be more than a bad case of dry rot."

It surprised me that Fab knew anything about construction. "Why do you have to snoop through everything?" I asked.

"Why not?" She flicked Billy's shoulder and joked. "You find anything good under the floors, I get my finder's fee."

"Didn't you say you knew someone interested in buying the place?" I asked Billy. "The daughter would probably like to be rid of the place and the upkeep."

"Spoon's working out the terms."

"Sheriff come back?" Fab asked. "Kevin, I mean; he's a dick."

"Fabiana, language," I teased. She answered with an eye roll.

"Kevin showed up. Think he thought he had the property to himself; you should have seen the look of surprise on his face when I walked out the front door. I pointed out all the progress that had been made and commented that cleanup had gone faster than expected. Also happened to toss in that I was employed by Spoon, and he nodded and left."

"Get any final expenses to me, and I'll give the final accounting to Spoon."

"Are you going to continue to stay out here?" Fab asked Billy. "Word has probably already spread to squatters that there may be an open house."

"I'll check with the boss to see what he wants. I can drive by once a day, do a check. I can promise you that any trespassers will be happy to move along and not come back."

"I know you draw the short straw when it comes to being assigned to help the two of us with our problems. Thank you. You were the best man for the job; no one could have handled it better."

"You're forgetting the part about free food at Jake's," Fab offered.

Billy actually laughed and winked at Mac. Fab and I exchanged a secret smile.

Chapter 28

Fab and I stood outside the all-glass Boca Raton high-rise that held the foundation offices for Finn Kennedy.

"You look hot, by the way," I complimented Fab, meaning every word. The woman could make a paper bag look sexy.

"Didier picked this out." She smiled down at her black sleeveless dress, the lower half leather and molded to her hips. She'd accessorized with onyx earrings and a cuff bracelet.

"And did he say naughty things in French?"

Fab blushed a deep red.

I thought so!

"Did you update Brick?" Fab tugged my arm, heading away from the main entrance.

"Why do I have to do the dirty work?" I asked in exasperation. "I'm the sidekick, remember?"

"Oh good, what did he say?" She flashed a cheeky smile.

"We skipped the pleasantries when he answered the phone with, 'Speak.'"

"I hope you've got news. No need to call when you don't know jack," Brick grumbled.

I took a deep breath. "You hear back from your information guy? No? We did. Zilla Mirren is society darling Finn Kennedy, and we know where to find her."

Dead silence.

After a moment, Brick said, "I'll pay extra for the contact information of the person you use."

"Another snooper had to be called in, so don't bitch about the extra charge."

"Yeah, yeah. If this pans out, it will be worth it. Sitting here, I put together a plan for you. Blackmail her." He sounded proud of himself.

"I'm sure we couldn't have come up with that on our own." I didn't care how snotty I sounded.

"No, no, I got this figured out. You'll keep her felonious identity a secret in exchange for the money."

"Did you end it friendly?" Fab sounded hopeful.

Should I lie or not? The truth is more fun. "I heard the words 'piss-poor attitude,' and I'm almost certain he wasn't talking about himself."

Fab laughed. It took her a moment to pull herself together. "Today's it. If we don't collect now, we turn it over to Brick. Women can be more of a wildcard than men." Fab appeared worried.

I spun around, holding out the sides of my hot pink dress with a fitted bodice and full skirt. "How do I look?" I'd paired it with a gold collar necklace, diamond earrings, and a bracelet. Knowing that it's all about the jewelry and the purse, I'd dug out my knock-off designer bag, hoping it didn't scream "not the real thing" from across the room.

"The color hurts my eyes." Fab shaded her brow, looking up at the towering building. "I told you the jewelry would look hot, and it does."

"Your problem is that you need to introduce some color into your all-black wardrobe. And white is not a color."

"If we ever get around to having a real office, I want it to be in a glistening high-rise on Miami Beach." Fab looped her arm in mine. "We can't stand out here all day."

We walked around the greenbelt area before heading toward the lobby.

"Hate to burst your bubble, but I'm too cheap to pay my half of the rent," I said.

"You're always the practical one."

"The good news is it's not communicable." I ground to a halt in front of the directory just inside the door. "It's not too late to call in one of Spoon's guys, put him in a suit—if we can find one to fit over the brawn—and let him scare the dough out of her."

"Zilla is a crafty one, and I'd lay odds that she's not going to like finding out that her identities have been compromised. Be on the alert. Hopefully she writes a check and we leave, but the chances of the two of us getting that lucky are regretfully slim." She paused. "We won't be committing a jailable offense; it's not a crime to be a collector." She looked relieved.

We rode the elevator to the fortieth floor in silence. The doors opened into the reception area, where an attractive, auburn-haired woman sat at the front desk. She gave us a once-over and her gaze settled on Fab.

"We have an appointment with Finn Kennedy," Fab said in a haughty tone. "Fiona Milan, and my assistant." She waved dismissively in my direction.

"Please take a seat." She picked up the phone.

The muted tones of the walls, dark hardwood floors, and fancy furniture didn't exactly give off a welcoming, kick-up-your-feet vibe.

"Does your assistant have a name?" I whispered, settling into a suede chair.

"Now, Gertrude, you know I'd never forget your name." Her blue eyes twinkled with amusement.

Gertrude? I wondered if I had a last name.

"Ms. Milan." The receptionist cleared her throat, peering out over the countertop. "Ms. Kennedy's assistant will be right out."

A few minutes later, a thin, overly made-up blonde with thick black roots came through a side door, her black pencil skirt so tight it looked like it might hurt to move. She'd coupled it with a white button-down shirt and stilettos, and the diamond-encrusted watch on her wrist was a real eye-catcher.

"I'm sorry—Ms. Milan, is it?" she said, walking up to stand in front of Fab, not bothering to introduce herself. "We don't have you down for an appointment. Ms. Kennedy has a full schedule today. If you could tell me the nature of your business, I can help you."

Fab produced a business card. "I'm sure Ms. Kennedy can spare a few minutes. We're business associates of Zilla Mirren."

I squinted to read the card, but couldn't make it out.

The assistant glanced at the card, turned it over, then headed back to the same door she'd come out of, which she opened with a keycard.

Fab raised her voice to say, "We're here about a donation. If she still doesn't have time, tell her we will discuss the details with you."

I needed to hound Fab for lessons in perfecting that condescending tone.

Neither of us said a word as we waited. Finally, the phone at the front desk rang, and Fab's ears perked up.

"Excuse me," the receptionist said. She indicated the keycard-operated door. "You can go through those doors, and Ms. Kennedy's assistant will escort you to her office."

"If this works," Fab whispered as we crossed the lobby, "it will be the easiest job we ever had."

Ms. Kennedy's assistant was waiting at the open door and escorted us into the woman's office, which was decorated in an upscale tropical theme with high-end, solid wood furniture and soft blue accessories. The large windows behind the massive desk offered an impressive view of the park below. Everything about Finn Kennedy and her offices reeked of money.

"Make sure we're not disturbed," Finn instructed her assistant. As soon as the woman left, she turned on us, her face angry and full of contempt. "What do you two want?"

The hardened blonde had me thinking twice about sitting down; I noted that she didn't offer either of us a seat. However, I followed Fab's lead and sat in the chair next to her. The way Finn eyed us, she had already come to some sort of conclusion that I was sure she'd soon share.

Fab returned her sneer. "You have an outstanding debt with our client, Brick Famosa, and we're here to collect."

"I have no idea what you are talking about." Finn glanced at her gold watch. "My schedule is full today."

Not deterred, Fab leaned forward. "Famosa Bail Bonds put up your bail, which you guaranteed with worthless zirconia. You owe twenty large. We're authorized to accept a check, as long as—" She shook her finger at Finn. "—it doesn't bounce."

"Mr. Famosa accepted the ring as payment in full. Not my fault he's stupid."

"Get your checkbook out. If not, you can read about your dual identities in Boca Raton weekly." Fab reached out, flicking one of Finn's pens at her.

Finn's eyes narrowed. "Let's get something straight." She banged her hand down on the desk. "*No one* blackmails me."

"That's such a tawdry word." Fab flashed her crazy-girl smile. "Who said anything about blackmail? Think of us as debt collectors. No one will ever hear a word from us about your alter ego… unless you don't pay up. Today."

I held up my hand. "Before you give us the tough-girl speech about how you don't care what people think, we know you care—plenty! What would shock your friends more; the fact that you went to jail or that you owned and wore cheap jewelry? Once the first shock wore off, the next hot topic would be that you'd worn an ugly orange jail uniform and had cheap, scratchy cotton rubbing against your perfumed skin."

Finn's fingers wrapped around her pen with an iron grip; I expected it to snap in half momentarily. "Where's your proof?"

Fab removed her latest acquisition, a shiny new Ruger handgun, from her purse, shoving it underneath, then extracted several documents: "Zilla Mirren's" rap sheet and copies of Finn's face on driver's licenses under the two different names.

"Someone has clearly stolen my picture and used it on this fraudulent license." Finn's laugh didn't hide the trapped expression on her face.

"You already admitted to owing the money," I said, watching her carefully. Knowing that when a person felt trapped, they came out swinging, I copied Fab, shoving my gun under my purse. "But that's a good one." I clapped. "Your friends and business associates may come to eventually buy that story."

"How much?" Finn opened a side desk drawer. Instead of a checkbook, however, she produced a handgun, complete with silencer.

Impressive piece of hardware.

Fab was one step ahead of Finn; she already had her handgun pointed at her. "Put it down. Now."

"The problem with you blackmailers is that you always come back; it's never enough." She laid the gun down in front of her but continued to grip the handle.

"That's not the case here." Fab's full attention was on the gun. "Brick wants his money; he loathes getting screwed. Be happy that he found you attractive. If he hadn't, this could be ending in a way you wouldn't like."

Finn's eyes narrowed, the mixture of anger and desperation radiating off her.

"How is it that you run your own company?" I asked. "You can't shoot two people with your assistant sitting outside the door and expect to get away with it. By the way, did you know that when you're executed by electric chair, your body fries from the inside out? Not sure how long you stay conscious in the notorious Sparky; it has a tendency to misfire and has to be started up again."

"Put the gun away," Fab ordered. "You'll never get a shot off before I shoot you, and in the unlikely event that you *do* shoot one of us, the survivor will make sure your death is slow and painful, I promise." She flashed the mean-girl stare.

"You two are so full of it. I come from big money and bigger family connections."

"That wouldn't be enough to get you out of this. You ought to check the prison records; there are a few of your ilk doing life or waiting to fry. You have no manners," I said in my mediocre French accent and pointed my Five-SeveN in her face.

It surprised me when she complied, putting the gun back in the drawer and slamming it shut.

"Word of warning," Fab said. "Screw

Brick again and be prepared to look over both your shoulders, Finn/Zilla."

"Put your guns down," Finn demanded, clearly caught off guard and surprised that we'd come prepared.

"No! Crazy bitch. Start writing; I'm out of patience." Fab cocked her gun. "I believe I can make a case of self-defense."

"Don't think I'll forget the two of you." She dragged the corporate checkbook over in front of her. When she finished writing, she ripped the check off the book, handing it to Fab.

"Get over it. Don't be stupid. You're alive, not going to jail, and your shady reputation is intact." I stood, gun in hand.

Fab shoved her gun back in her purse, stood, and started for the door. "If you had a glass desk instead of a wood one, you would've known we were both packing." She smiled while imparting her tip.

I didn't trust Ms. Kennedy not to shoot us in the back, so I kept my gun leveled on her as I backed up, bumping into Fab. "I do have a question," I said, ignoring Finn's hateful glare. "Zilla—so unique." I wrinkled my nose. "Fan of monster flicks?"

"Get out," she yelled as we crossed the threshold.

"Do we run down the stairs?" I looked over my shoulder. "Or wait for the elevator?"

"Forty floors in stilettos? She's not going

to gun us down in the hallway."

I kept my handgun hidden, finger on the trigger. If need be, I'd find out if my draw and shoot lessons had paid off.

* * *

Fab and I split up in the parking lot, doing our best to disguise which car we got into, in case Finn had someone follow us to get the license number and showed up somewhere uninvited.

"What did you text Creole?" Fab asked once we were in the SUV.

"Job over. No one died. Love you."

"I need a drink or something." Fab shook her head. "Do you think Finn would have shot us both?"

"Probably," I said on a sigh. "How'd you manage to get the drop on her?"

"I realized in a split second that she had no reason to open the drawer. I'd rather choke out an 'I'm sorry,' than one of us take a bullet."

"A cocktail at the beach, on me?" I beamed at her. "You're not headed back to The Cove." I was stating the obvious since we'd passed the Turnpike and were now stuck in Miami traffic.

"Last-minute detour. We're going to blow up to the doors of Famosa Motors and lay on the horn. Bitsy can run her ass out and get the check, we drive away, and neither of us has to interact with the man himself."

"I nominate you to tell Brick why he's being charged the gun fee." I pointed to the left. "Speaking of… if you hurry, you can cut him off before he gets out of the driveway."

Fab laughed devilishly. "Hang on." With plenty of room to spare, she cut across the busy highway and entered the driveway faster than usual, blocking it sideways. Room enough for a bicycle to slide by, but not Brick's Range Rover.

Brick blasted his horn, shaking his fist.

"Now, that's not very friendly." I tsked.

He backed up and pulled into a space.

Fab pulled a wide turn, sidling the Hummer as close as she could get to his SUV without marring the paint job. She powered down the window.

"This better be good; I'm in a hurry," Brick barked, loudly enough that two of his salesmen stared in our direction.

Fab rotated her fist in her eye, handing him the check. "If I were you, I'd drive to her bank and cash it immediately."

Brick snorted.

"Okay, don't! But don't bitch at me when it's no good," Fab yelled.

Fab yelling at Brick surprised me; I'd never heard her do it before. If it surprised him, he didn't let it show. I leaned across the console. "If you're too lazy, sign it over to me."

"That's a great idea. Hand it over, and we'll call it even. We'll have it cashed in an hour, and it will be like it never existed."

"What—" Brick started.

Fab cut him off. "Don't forget the hazard pay, and before you get all high and mighty, Ms. Kennedy pulled a gun."

"Oh, here we go, snivel, snivel. You're always complaining about almost being shot. You look fine to me. I'm tired of being milked for extra pay; I'm not doing it anymore. You two aren't going to bleed me dry." He banged on the steering wheel one too many times and stopped to rub his hand.

"You don't like it, don't call us," Fab spit. "You're the one who let little Brick do the thinking when it came to 'Zilla.'"

"Fab," I whispered, my cheeks turning pink.

"Your multiple-personality friend scares me, and that takes a lot," Fab lectured Brick. "I suggest you be careful. If Finn/Zilla shows up on your doorstep, I don't like your chances of coming out unscathed. You listen to me: she shows up, don't turn your back on her." She threw the SUV into reverse and backed out, then jammed on the gas and squealed out of the parking lot.

"I have a bad feeling about Finn." I leaned my head back against the seat, closing my eyes. "I'm happy that she doesn't know our real names. The only one who might tell her is Bitsy. You and I know that if money is involved, Bitsy would sell us out in a second."

Brick's receptionist ran a side business selling and reselling information several times over.

"No worries about our bosomy friend. A long time ago, with Brick's blessing, I went through her desk and had a friend snoop through her computer files. Brick didn't know that last part. She had a file on us; The Cottages' address was the only one in it, and I made sure that was wiped. Brick only agreed because he didn't want any problems."

"I like your attention to detail. Good thing we take steps to keep our address private."

Chapter 29

Fab kicked my foot aside and flopped down on the daybed, laying Jazz on her lap. "Didier and I won't be here tonight; we're going out to dinner."

The daybed had been brought in on a temporary basis, but everyone found it a comfortable place to take a nap, and it didn't crowd the room. So I dressed it up with a slipcover that matched the rest of the furniture and restrained myself from the mountain of pillows I'd envisioned, though I did add a couple of throws on the off-chance it got cold.

"You're not going to get away with that," I said, putting my book down, lifting my displaced leg, and putting it with the other one, which rested against the wall. "I predict a fight with Didier. He'll put his foot down, and you'll both be here for dinner. He will not disappoint Mother."

"That's where you—"

"No," I interrupted. "Whatever weasel plan you've cooked up, you're on your own."

She pushed out her lower lip in a full-blown pout. "It's just that Didier and I have been busy and I want some alone time."

"Tell him and he'll make it happen. Does he ever say 'No,' except when your life is in danger? Let me know, and you can have the house to yourself; I'll go to Creole's." I patted her shoulder with my foot, which she flicked off, brushing at her sleeve. I bit back a laugh. "Brad's coming, and you need to be here to discuss the yellow house deal. We drag our feet too long, and it'll be sold. If that happens, you'll be the one explaining it to Mac."

"What about Phil? Why not have her get the information and we'll take credit?"

"Phil's on it. She called, and the only way to get information about a prospective buyer is from the realtor herself. Real Estate agents are required to keep the paperwork on their listings in their office, but a potential buyer's name wouldn't be included in the file. Our best bet is to find someone in her office who can get the information and sell it to us."

Fab raised an eyebrow, shaking her head. "Then what? Having the possible buyer's name doesn't mean we can get the client to sell to us."

"Yellow house is a rental being bought by an investor. It's not his dream digs. It's all about money, and maybe he'll take a couple of thousand to go away. Then, once the realtor's deal has fallen through, we make an offer on the house. Any bribe money would have to be factored into the offering price, of course."

"How does Brad fit in? His connections?" Fab asked.

"My brother knows everybody, and if by chance he hasn't met them yet, he can remedy that. He has real estate connections; I say we turn the problem over to him and see what he can do." I blew out a breath. "There's been some unsettling news: Another dead man showed up not far from The Cottages. Same MO. Phil didn't have details, but said she would get back to us."

"Find out if they have a likely suspect."

"Phil did say the cops have a ton of leads. I wonder how many of those tidbits are just people blowing smoke?" I shook my head. "Fingers crossed it will lead to an arrest before another body shows up."

* * *

The front door opened, and my family crowded in all at once. I glanced out the garden window to see where the tour bus was parked and, seeing only their cars, wondered how they'd managed to arrive at the same time. Mother led the parade, filling the island with shopping bags. Copying Fab, I stuck my nose in one of the bags and took a sniff, making a face.

Mother shook her finger. "I know where you learned that trick," she said, glaring at Fab, "and the two of you need to stop it."

Fab hugged Mother and had her laughing in seconds at whatever she whispered in her ear.

Scowling at Liam, I raised my eyebrows

in question. I was out of patience waiting for the pink bakery boxes to appear. I needed to know ahead of time how much room to save for dessert.

Liam wrapped his arms around me in a hug. "Not my fault," he whispered in my ear. "Mrs. Westin ordered dessert from that new Italian restaurant she insisted we try. 'Your palates need broadening,' she said."

"Are you mad at Mother?" I asked, surprised, knowing Mother would hate being addressed like that, especially by Liam.

"I told her that I'm going to call her Mrs. W until she makes up her mind what version of grandmother she likes. Just when you think she couldn't possibly come up with another variation, she does. Then I forget which to use, and she makes faces. Are all women this complicated?"

"Ask any man in this house; it gets worse." I laughed. "Consider this training for understanding our fair species by the time you are much, much older."

Brad joined us, hugging me. "You'll be lucky if you ever understand women. They don't think like men. I don't have a better explanation than that."

"This kind of talk means you're getting older, and I won't stand for it." I kissed Liam's cheek, then poked Brad in the side. "I need to talk to you."

Brad placed his hand on my lower back and pushed me past Spoon and Julie, who were taking orders from Mother, and out the doors to the patio. "Get a room," Brad admonished Fab and Didier, who were tucked into a corner of the patio.

"Cover your eyes, Liam," I said over my shoulder.

"Oh, please." Fab rolled her eyes. "We're kissing."

Didier anchored her to his side, kissing the top of her head.

"I don't want anyone to hear what I'm going to ask you," I told Brad. "Some people wouldn't understand." I grasped his hand and dragged him around the pool. "Let's adjourn to the no-eavesdropping zone."

We'd almost reached the far corner of the pool when a warm breath caressed the back of my neck. I stepped back, making contact with a hard chest, and sighed as arms wrapped around me. I twisted my neck to the side, giving better access to the teeth nipping my skin.

"I didn't like your text—the 'no one died' part," Creole rumbled in my ear.

"What about the 'love you' part?"

"Enough, you two." Brad laughed.

"Corner talk. What's up now?" Creole glanced between us, his frown deepening.

I turned in Creole's arms and gave him a quick kiss. "I just need a few minutes with my brother. Entertain Liam; his mother would flip if she knew what I was about to ask."

When we were alone, I told Brad about Mac and Shirl wanting to buy the yellow house and the realtor's less-than-friendly response. And that rifling her office and searching public records would most likely yield nothing. "Can you help us?"

"I've never used that realty office; the woman who runs it is abrasive and has zero personality. I've got a broker who wants me to use her exclusively, though; maybe she can strong-arm the realtor, or maybe she's got a connection in that office. Might cost you."

"Keep in mind that Mac and Shirl are on a limited budget. I suppose, if all else fails, I could send Fab to scare the hell out of her."

"Neither of you—" He jerked on my arm. "—are to do anything foolish. Let your big bro take care of this one." He flexed his muscles. "You'd owe me." He grinned.

"Name one time I said no to you." I held up a finger. "Just one."

He put his hand under my chin and leaned down until we were face to face. "I want the damn IOU, just in case. You two are to do nothing—and I mean nothing—that would put you in jeopardy of any kind." He hugged me. "Dinner time. I'm hungry."

"I'm suspicious that it came in bags I don't recognize. Liam says Mother's on one of her crusades to bring us a new food experience."

"You're the only resistant one. Open your food horizons."

"Sometimes you're a great brother, and then whammo, no sympathy."

"Here's my A-rated advice since you don't have a dog: use the napkin trick and sneak out later for a burger."

We both laughed. Growing up, Brad and I had perfected the art of disposing of unwanted vegetables in our napkins, making sure to get rid of them in the outside trash.

"Dinner's ready," Spoon boomed out. Mother poked him in the side.

As usual, Mother had taken into consideration everyone's food likes and dislikes, including my finicky eating habits. I'd been the reigning queen of picky eating for a long time before Fab came along and usurped me. All of the food looked good, though, and I recognized all the side dishes as ones I enjoyed eating.

Creole, who must have been first in line in the kitchen, held up a second plate and set it at my place. I wasn't sure how it had happened, but we had long ago assigned ourselves seats and never deviated.

Julie caught my eye from across the table. "How much notice do you need for me moving out of The Cottages? Depending on how long the renovations take, our new place should be ready in one to two months."

"I'll accommodate you in any way you need." Her declaration caught me by surprise, and I wasn't sure what to ask. "Are you staying in the area?" I did wonder if her brother had finally convinced her to move out of the "hell hole." Julie was one of the first tenants that I'd rented to, and I would be sad to see her and Liam go.

"They're moving into the building the guys are working on," Mother said.

Oh great, the last to know! I suppose it was my turn, but I hated it.

Looking at Liam, it was hard to tell what he thought of the move. I would miss having him around most of all. "You're welcome here anytime, no invitation needed. The basketball hoop can be moved over here to the driveway. No snack bowl, but the refrigerator is always full."

Reading my thoughts, Creole squeezed my hand under the table.

"That's cool, and I know where the key is." Liam nodded. "I need a favor. I'm doing a paper on careers for school. I chose Private Investigator and would like to interview you and Fab."

"No favor needed. We'd help you with anything. Fab is the professional; I'm the wannabe. She did her time and got her license." I winked down the table at my friend.

"Miss Wannabe has saved my backside a

time or two," Fab interjected. "Never take excellent backup for granted."

Julie patted his hand. "I thought you choose law enforcement and were going to interview Kevin."

Liam turned slightly and rolled his eyes. He'd never hurt her by squealing on Kevin, whose jerky moments bugged Liam more and more as he got older, something he'd mentioned to me more than a few times.

"I changed my mind," Liam mumbled.

"You've got lots of choices for a career paper," I said. "I know you have plenty of time to decide, but what's currently on the top of your career list?"

"I've thought about FBI or DEA," Liam answered.

"You're in luck. I've got a connection or two and can at least get you a phone interview with an FBI agent."

"That would be great. I'll have the best paper in class."

Mother clinked her glass with a spoon, calling for everyone's attention. "I've got news of my own." She beamed.

"Are you pregnant?" Fab asked sweetly.

If Fab had looked in my direction, I'd have burst out laughing for sure. Instead, I squeezed Creole's fingers so hard, he whispered, "Ouch."

My brother's face was hard as granite.

No one said a word, all eyes focused on Mother.

Mother giggled, which only made Brad's jaw twitch. He hadn't stopped to think logically that it couldn't happen, Fab's comment only serving to remind him of all the reasons he found Spoon unsuitable.

"Well…" I said, "it would end the grandbaby talk if you're preggo."

Brad's beer bottle hit the table so hard the silverware rattled. "What's the news?" he asked tightly.

"I'm moving to The Cove." Her brown eyes twinkled with happiness. "I have a contract on my house."

I liked the idea that Mother would be closer and I wouldn't have to worry where she was all the time, not to mention that I could find her faster. "The corner house is for sale."

"That's a great idea," Brad said, relaxing slightly. "I'm thinking about moving into Julie's old unit at The Cottages, so the whole family will be close by."

"Are you going to sell your house in Alligator Alley?" Liam asked, clearly not liking the idea. He and Brad were the only ones who thought it fun to tromp around out there amongst the tall grasses and bugs.

"Heck, no." Brad shook his head.

Liam gave him a thumbs up.

"I've already found something," Mother

announced.

My fork clattered against the plate. "So you decided you wanted to move, put your house up for sale, and signed a contract on something else? And not a word to your family?" I huffed. "Who thought all that sneaking around was a good idea?" I eyed Spoon, my voice rising. "Did you know? And condone the idea?" I tossed back the rest of my red wine.

Spoon held his hands up in defense. "You know how your mother is when she gets an idea."

There were a bunch of cowards at the table. No one said a word. They were probably making a mental bet as to who would break the uncomfortable silence.

Where's that wine bottle? Was I the only one who'd noticed that neither Mother nor Spoon answered the question?

"I'll go over the paperwork," Brad said tightly. "Make sure you're getting a good deal."

"No need," Mother brushed off his offer. "Spoon knows the developer."

"Where is this property?" Didier asked, venturing into the fray.

Brad was tapping his fingers so hard against the table that Julie finally covered his hand with hers. It appeared to be a tug-of-wills that she won. "What does he know about real estate?" He glared at Spoon, who glared right back. "I don't know of any new developments, so what's the address?"

The Cove had managed to stop further development of any high-rise condominiums, much to the relief of those who wanted to keep the small-town beach feel.

Mother smiled at Brad and then around the table. "I'm buying a loft."

"Where?" I narrowed my eyes. I only knew about one such development, and surely she wouldn't choose that area.

"It's a great deal," Mother cooed, snuggling up to Spoon. "I'm getting the top floor, a three-bedroom unit. I get to choose all of the finishes, and it has a water view."

"I know that building," Brad barked, his body rigid again. "You're talking about the docks and the sleaziest part of town."

"Who had this terrible idea?" Fab demanded. "It's a crime-infested neighborhood, which is why your boyfriend has barbed-wire fencing."

I agreed with Fab, but maybe Mother would hear the words better if they weren't coming from me.

Spoon scanned the table, glaring angrily. "I'd never let anything happen to Madeline. And I'd be right down the street."

Brad groaned. "This is a stupid idea. It better not be a done deal."

"The whole area is part of a revitalization

program, and the old building is being renovated from top to bottom," Mother said defensively. "Security is a priority. A card key will be required for the front entrance, elevators, and garage."

"Mother, I'm going to tell you the same thing you'd tell me: no way are you moving in there." Brad persisted. "Besides the deplorable condition it's in, I've heard there are structural problems. It needs to be torn down, not renovated."

The easygoing side of my brother had departed the patio. Smoke practically steamed out of his ears. "Anybody think this is a good idea?" Brad looked around the table. "No!" he shouted. "That should tell you something, Mother. It's a good thing that Madison has a house in a safe neighborhood, or we wouldn't have a place for family get-togethers; we certainly won't be coming to your new place." He pointed to Julie and Liam. "I'm not exposing either my girlfriend or the kid to crime." He paused. "One more thing…" He leaned across the table into Spoon's face. "*Anything* happens to my mother, and you're a dead man." He shoved his chair back, stood and said, "We brought dessert," and disappeared inside the house.

"Excuse me." I stood as well. "I'll talk to him."

As I followed Brad, I heard Liam say, "I love these dinners."

Chapter 30

The phone rang, and I opened one eye. Morning sun streamed in through the window. Creole's arm lay across my body, his leg hooked around mine, cocooning me in his body heat. His breathing was slow and regular. I felt protected, and Mother's shenanigans didn't seem so worrisome right now. Smiling, I reached out to brush back a lock of hair that had fallen over his face. "Don't answer it. It can't be good news."

He buried his face in the crook of my neck, and we lay there, drifting back to sleep. It seemed like seconds, but I knew it had been longer when his phone beeped from the bedside table. He woke up instantly and stared down at me, a smile curling on his lips as he reached up and grabbed my wrist.

One arm around me, he reached for his phone and quickly scanned the screen. "Another body's been found, and this time, an arrest was made. Might be a link to the serial killer case."

"Thank goodness for that. Is this the same body from a couple of days ago or a new one?"

"Few hours old." He snorted. "Got the

mugshot of the killer, want to see? It will cost you." He leered.

I stuck out my hand, and he handed off the phone. When I looked at the photo, I did a double take. "Is this a joke?"

"Nope," he whispered against my neck. "The chief doesn't have a sense of humor when it comes to murder."

As far as mugshots went, Macklin Lane's was decent; she didn't look all wild-eyed, hair standing on end, like the drunken Hollywood stars. And of course she'd smiled for the camera. I didn't need to know the facts; I already knew she wasn't guilty. Now how to prove it?

"Why wouldn't she call?" I asked, not understanding why I hadn't heard from her. "She needs bail." I rolled to the side of the bed. "And a lawyer."

Creole stopped my forward motion, his leg clamped around my bottom. "Not so fast. Mac has zero chance of getting bail if they suspect her of a half-dozen murders."

"Where are you going?" I asked as he retrieved his phone and got out of bed.

He tapped a finger against his lips. "It's not professional for me to call my superior when I'm in bed with a woman." He quirked his lips and dialed. "What's the update?" he asked the person who answered.

I liked Fab's and my system of listening in on each other's phone calls, but I didn't have the nerve to ask him to hit the speaker button. He made a few affirmative noises and didn't ask as many questions as I would have.

Creole laughed at the person on the phone. "You know Cruz operates on a 'what have you done for me lately' basis. Besides, the lawyer likes them. Not sure he has the same fondness for you. I've got an in, but if I used it, then you'd owe me." He hung up.

"As of now—" He slid back into bed. "—Mac is being held for the body found at her house, even though she was the one who reported it. The chief was fishing with the sheriff when he got the call; that's how he's up on what's happening down our way. No need to worry about Mac. Her first call was to Cruz, and he took it, even though the answering service had to wake him."

"That's my girl. I should have known Mac would know exactly what to do." I breathed a sigh, knowing Cruz would take care of her; criminal defense was his specialty, and he excelled at it.

"Having seen Cruz in action, I can say he's good at negotiating bail, although it'll all depend on the judge. Mac did make a second call, and that was to Brick," Creole related. "This murder had the same MO as the other killings, and Mac is the first suspect they've had. Expect the authorities to turn over every rock."

"First, we need to get Mac out of jail. We

know that she didn't kill anyone… unless the dead guy is her ex-husband," I said, snuggling into his arms.

"Not unless Mr. Mac's a bus driver. The dead man had a reputation as a hard worker, no family. Sure bugs the chief that Cruz accommodates you."

"I heard you tell him Cruz only cares about what's in it for him and that's the truth. The lawyer has a busload of relatives hitting town this week, and he needs Mac out of jail to babysit them. She plans all the sight-seeing, gets them dinner reservations, and generally keeps them happy; the only complaints we get are when we can't host a drunken brawl or an arrest." I thought about Mac. I had to see her to make sure she was okay, and I needed to deposit money in her jail account. "Can you get me a jail visit?"

"It would have been better if she'd been arrested in Miami. But I've got a connection or two down here. I suppose Kevin is out of the question since you're kicking his ass to the curb."

"If I could physically do that, he'd have been bumping down the street long ago." Imitating Kevin, I bounced my backside up and down against the mattress, making growling noises.

Creole tightened his hold, laughing in my ear. "No one makes me laugh like you do." He nibbled down the side of my neck. "Have you calmed down about your mother's antics?"

"Do you think her calling the docks home is a good idea?"

"I'm in agreement that she could find a better address. But I have my own theory. Having watched Spoon carefully, I don't think this real estate deal is signed on the dotted line. It was a scam your mother trotted out to gauge what the reaction would be. Expect her to come back with whatever it was she really wanted. Living with Spoon perhaps."

I squeezed my eyes shut and groaned.

"You were all too riled up to notice, but Spoon was seething at being criticized for all that. Your mother wasn't about to backtrack at that point and say, 'Ha-ha, just kidding.'"

"Mother… yeesh! If it's true, I wouldn't have wanted to be her once they cleared the door last night. If she's not careful, her antics are going to lose her a boyfriend. And if you're right, I need to apologize to Spoon."

"Fab's comments didn't help."

"I think she meant to lighten the mood. If it turns out that Mother was punking us, Fab will have a few choice words."

"You need to talk to your brother about his animosity. He can't control who your mother loves or what she does." He turned me over to face him. "I've got a meeting, but I want to hear about your latest Brick job."

"You mean Godzilla?" I went on to detail the visit. "Brick said he had no idea she'd pull a gun, and I believe him for a change."

"Shower with me." He clambered over me to get out of the bed and scooped me into his arms.

"Do you have to get up?" I murmured.

"Yes, and so do you." He set me on my feet, my body sliding down his, and kissed me until my toes curled.

"You're gonna be late."

Chapter 31

Creole carried me down the stairs on his back and dumped me in front of the kitchen island. Didier and Fab shook their heads.

"Bon Cheerio," I said a little too loudly. One would have thought I was drunk instead of it just being morning. "I'm making coffee. Anyone brave enough to drink a cup?"

Didier hooked his arm around Fab, holding up his coffee mug. "It's a little early for your version of a French accent." His blue eyes twinkled in amusement.

Creole beat his chest with his fist and swept me into a kiss. "No coffee for them, more for me."

"Do you two think you can go the whole day without brandishing a weapon?" Didier asked. He ruffled Fab's hair in response to her indignant look.

"Mac's been arrested," I said, imparting the few details that I had.

"Is that all you've got?" Fab snorted in Creole's direction.

"If I hadn't gotten the call, you wouldn't know that much," Creole defended himself.

I picked up the clear carafe and checked out the contents; it passed for coffee to me. Besides, even if it tasted like swill, Creole would never turn up his nose and gag it up like the French woman barraging him with questions. Taking pity on his friend, Didier kissed her into silence.

Filling a travel mug, I held it out to Creole, walking him to the door. We stepped out on the porch. "Stay safe. No getting shot at," I admonished and hugged him tightly. I watched until his truck drove by, headed toward the corner.

Opening the door to go back inside, I came within an inch of clocking Didier in the head. "Behave yourself."

"Humph," he uttered and kissed my cheek, then walked outside with Fab in tow.

I closed the door behind them and moved into the kitchen. Jazz had taught Snow that even when there was food in the bowl, a glare at any human in the house would get it refilled. They sat side by side, an unspoken "hurry up" on their faces.

After doing the cats' bidding, I fished my phone out of my pocket and texted Phil to check with her sources regarding Mac and get back to me.

Fab's phone started to ring as she walked back inside. I leaned over, and my brows shot up at the name that lit up the screen—Casio

Famosa. She slid it from my view. "Wonder what he wants? I can't remember the last time he contacted me. If ever."

Casio was Brick's older brother, a decorated detective for the Miami Police Department with zero tolerance for fools and felons. He had a no-nonsense demeanor that, the few times I'd met him, made me happy I wasn't a law breaker with him on my tail.

Then how did his name and number end up in your contacts list? I wanted to ask. The phone was still ringing. "Answer it already. Or hand it over, and I'll pretend to be you." My accent would never pass muster, and this wasn't a man to try and trick.

Fab rolled her eyes at me and accepted the call. A moment later, she covered the phone. "Brick's in the hospital." The call lasted another minute. Finally, she hung up and stashed the phone in the pocket of her skinny jeans. "Gunned down at the dealership, shot in the back. Lucky bastard, he's not dead and the bullet didn't do any real damage."

"Wouldn't be the first time he's been shot. I remember one a few years ago during the commission of a robbery."

"Casio says the person lay in wait, took the shot, and left. Didn't bother with his wallet and watch."

"Besides being cowardly, sounds personal. And not a professional, or he'd be toes-up in the morgue. I wonder if Zilla has an alibi."

"When I told Brick to be careful, it wasn't with the idea that Zilla would shoot him. Maybe she really was unstable enough to shoot us that day." Fab frowned.

"If you're going to shoot someone, don't you want to look them in the face?" I grimaced, another image I refused to allow to form.

"That mind of yours is a scary place."

"Hey, Pot, I guess that's why we're well-suited." I blew her an air kiss. "Are we going to visit Brick in the hospital?"

"He's got a huge family, and who wants to get involved in that drama?"

"I've met a couple of them, and they're scary." I shuddered.

"We'll send flowers."

"That's lame. I vote we break into his office, grab one of his cigars, and send him that—at least we know he likes them."

Fab belly-laughed. "That sounds fun."

"First things first: a latte with a double shot of whipped cream." I sighed at the luscious vision in my mind.

"So bad for you." She tsked.

"And a double espresso isn't?" I pressed my lips together. "Then we'll jet by the crime scene at Mac's, blend in with the other looky-loos, and maybe we'll garner some real information and not just speculation and gossip. Before that, we need to detour down to the docks and check out the new lofts." I told Fab Creole's theory that Mother had some trick up her sleeve.

Fab brushed her hands together. "If true, it's a little messy, but problem solved."

"And if Mother's serious, then I'll play my ace—you!" I grinned. "You'll swoop in, guns blazing, and scare the developer so bad that the next time Mother comes within a block, they'll tell her, 'Sold out.'"

Fab shook her head and pulled her invisible six-shooters, blowing the kitchen to pieces, complete with sound effects. She blew on the muzzles, reholstered them, and turned on her heel. "You coming?" she asked, opening the front door.

* * *

"Stop already," Fab said in exasperation. "The cup's empty; you drank it all."

I swirled the straw around the bottom, making two last sucking noises, then ran my finger around the inside rim of the lid, not wanting to waste the last of the whipped cream.

We were taking the scenic route down to the docks. I hung my head out the window and waved at Spoon's Auto Body as we raced by. There was never any sign of activity; all work took place behind the locked gates. It had been whispered in the past that his business wasn't on the up-and-up, and he always countered with "show me proof." I believed him. I knew he worked hard to be an upstanding citizen but still reveled in his badass rep.

"I thought this area was under renovation?" I twisted in my seat, checking out the block.

The building Mother was interested in was under construction, although no one had shown up for work in what appeared to be quite a while. The contractor also had a sign on the neighboring property but nothing on it about a start date. I could see the potential of the area, but it wouldn't appeal to me to live in a commercial zone with mostly fishing-related businesses. Still, once the first loft building sold out, more would likely pop up. But that would take some time.

"If your mother's unit is really under contract, she'll need a place to live for a long time before this dump is ready." Fab pinched her nose as though there was a foul odor in the air. "Bet you don't hear another word about your mother moving here—Spoon will see to that. I don't know what she's up to, but we'll probably find out soon enough."

"I'll pass on the bet; your terms are usually too steep."

"Okay, no wager, but promise me Didier and I can choose the restaurant for our next night out. And no complaining."

"Gee, that sounds fun." I didn't want to tell her Creole was tired of the dress-up dinners.

"If you don't choose something tropical and fun—as opposed to black tie and stilettos—we're not going. Creole and I would rather eat greasy burgers on the beach."

Fab clutched her chest. "You're a terrible friend."

I sniffed, squeezing my eyes shut a few times; hard as I tried, not a single tear rolled out.

* * *

"This is a cute little house," Fab said as she drove past Mac's single-story beach cottage. It was typical of the neighborhood, built back in the 1950s as a vacation home. Generally, they had two bedrooms and not a lot of square footage. Very few of the old houses remained, as most had been torn down and rebuilt up on stilts at least one story off the ground.

"Is our 'stay out of jail' pact still in place?" I asked. Fab looked at me like I'd grown an extra head, which I took to mean the answer was yes. "Then I suggest that we respect the crime scene tape draped across the driveway and not cross over or under it."

"We'll park at the corner and go for our morning walk in this direction," Fab said.

"There's no one milling about. The excitement must be over, and the neighbors have gone back inside." That was unusual. Based on our past experience with sheriff's calls, there was nothing like a dead body to bring out the lawn chairs. "Since there's only one squad car and a forensic van clogging the street, I'd say the investigation is winding down." My phone beeped with a new message. "Mac's been transferred to county. I've got a jail visit set for tomorrow."

"Do you think the deputy that mans the desk at the jail ever wonders how you manage to get an appointment when most people have to wait days?"

"People slog through their daily, and when I've been there, he hasn't paid much attention. He's not going to recognize me; besides, I haven't been there in a long time. If he does, he'll think all my friends are criminals. I wouldn't be the first Floridian to know only felons."

"Tell Mac I said something nice. I'm not going; hate that place." Fab backed into a parking space and hopped out.

I shook my head. "I'll do my best to make up something and sound sincere."

"Keep up." Fab motioned for me to follow.

"I'm not playing 'follow the leader' unless I'm in the lead."

Fab paused for me to catch up. "If we go this way, we can get a few answers, and maybe by then, the deputy will be gone." She pointed to a six-foot-high bush in the opposite direction. "I recognize those tighty-whities."

I groaned. "When I told Crum he had to

wear something over his underwear, I should have extended the edict to off the property." It was hard to fathom how he could have a never-ending stream of women; he had a limited personality and zero social skills. "He can't even get into the 'no shorts, no shoes' places."

Fab snorted in disgust. She'd never admit that she too had a certain fondness for the man, but it definitely didn't extend to being seen with him in public. "Hands up," she shouted. "Slowly, I'd hate to have to shoot you."

Crum stepped out onto the road, clad solely in his underwear, an undershirt slung over his shoulder, and waved. "Terrible about Mac. You never know what might drive a person to kill, but I'm certain she's innocent. Rumor has it she didn't know the sap. If you need a property manager, I'm your man." He puffed out his mostly bare chest, showing off a few stray hairs. "You know I have experience."

If I actually entertained the thought of Crum taking over at The Cottages, it would bring on a migraine. It could be loosely said that he had experience, but I remembered his previous job responsibilities had been limited to running squatters off the property.

"I'm not replacing her. She's getting out of jail." I didn't know exactly when or if it would happen, but it sounded better than *no way in hell.*

"I'd be manager before you," Fab informed the disappointed man.

That would never happen either, I thought, a little hysterically.

"Now. What do you know?" Fab demanded.

"The body was found on the back patio in one of those big deck boxes. The deputies took bags of stuff out of the house, not much from the garage. Kevin's lurking around. Be careful of him; he's in one of his snotty moods. Threatened to have me arrested if he saw my ass in the vicinity of the house."

Fab poked me in the side, nodding down the street. Out of nowhere, Kevin stomped towards us. "Stay away from the crime scene. I'd hate to have arrest you." He grinned.

I pasted a smile on my face; at least, I hoped it looked like one. "Do you have any evidence that Mac killed your John Doe?"

"A dead body." He continued to grin. "If you don't have any actual business here, I suggest you leave." He turned on Crum. "I already warned you."

"He's with us," I said. "I guess I need to point out that it's not illegal to stand on the curb and talk. And that we're half a block from the crime scene."

That wiped the grin off his face. "This isn't a game," he said. "I better not see you again." He turned and stalked away.

"If you really don't want to see me again, it would help if you moved away from The

Cottages," I yelled at his back.

"Gotta go," Crum said. "Got a date, and I have to get washed up."

"You hear anything, better give me a call," I said.

Crum saluted, pulled his bike out of the bushes, and started singing as he rode off in the opposite direction.

"If you'd offered him a ride," Fab said, "I'd have left you here with him before he could get to the door."

I put my head on her shoulder and laughed.

Chapter 32

Fab flew up the Turnpike and took the cutoff to the hospital where Brick was recovering. Neither of us was eager to make this social call, so we'd run every errand on the list first and even threw in some shopping. Now visiting hours were over, so we were late. Fab cut around a slowpoke, leaving more maneuvering room than usual. Praise had the opposite effect on her, so I kept my mouth shut.

"Thanks for stopping by Jake's so I could cop a couple of Mother's best cigars."

"I thought we were taking a girlie magazine." Fab skidded into a parking space in front.

"That idea made me squeamish." I flicked through Fab's phone. "Room number is 1201."

"Don't make eye contact with the receptionist," Fab instructed. "Act like you know where you're going. If that fails, we'll say we're headed to the coffee shop. That's open all night in a hospital, isn't it?"

"It's not generally staffed all night, but they usually have vending machines."

Fab and I were relieved to find that,

instead of a receptionist, there was a placard saying, "Dial 0 for information."

"If Brick's asleep, don't poke him awake," I said as we stepped into the elevator. "We'll scribble a note and leave."

The elevator doors opened, and we saw Brick's brother, Casio Famosa, standing in the upstairs hallway. "Just the two I want to talk to. Saves me time tracking you down." He motioned for us to follow him into the waiting room, which wasn't currently occupied.

Fab and I sat down, but not before signaling "What's up?" to each other. We knew Casio had a reputation for not playing by the rules, and I suspected Fab was as uncomfortable as I was with this encounter.

I broke the silence. "Mr. Casio Detective, sir." I flashed a smile that I hoped looked sincere. "How can we help you?"

"You're a smart-ass," he declared.

I didn't bother to tell him that his statement wasn't a news flash.

"While you two engage in this little love fest." Fab stood. "I'll go say hello to Brick and drop off the cigars. You're not his favorite anyway," she said to me, holding out her hand.

I fished the cigars from my skirt pocket, smoothing out the one with the smooshed end and handing them over. *Oh well, it will smoke the same, won't it?*

"I know Fab is part of the Famosa family,

but I thought that you were no longer doing his dirty work and all." Casio dragged a chair over in front of me.

The Famosa family – eww! I suppressed the shudder that went through my body. "I made a clean getaway. Then, after a chat, we came to terms. We all agreed that he's a dick, and now I'm back in the fold."

"Runs in the family." Casio looked at me like I was a choice piece of beef. "If I weren't married…"

I grimaced. "My boyfriend would kill you and then leave me."

"Hmm… There is that. Creole's a good guy and a damn fine detective. If you tell him I said that, I'll laugh it off and have you arrested."

Another couple entered the waiting room, acknowledging us with a nod. Casio stood and motioned for me to follow.

Fab joined us in the hallway. "Brick was only awake long enough to tell me where to stash the contraband." She sidled up to me and put a hand on my arm. "Done? Good," she said, without waiting for an answer, and started for the exit.

"I'll walk you out," Casio said and moved his body in between the two of us. "Either of you got any idea who shot my brother?"

Fab and I exchanged looks, and Fab shrugged. "Yeah, maybe," she said. She told him about the latest case we'd done for Brick.

"We can't finger Zilla definitively, but she's worth checking out," I said. "We warned Brick. We both had a bad feeling about her and made sure she couldn't track us down. You arrange face-time with her, be careful. If the hair on the back of your neck stands on end, heed the warning."

"No neck hair." Casio ran a hand over his bald head. "For me, it's a jolt up my spine, and it's saved my life a couple of times." He held the elevator doors open for us and pushed the button to the lobby.

"Give me your phone." He held his beefy hand out. "I'll put in my info and text you my email; you can send any info you have on Zilla to me tomorrow."

"I have your number." I pulled my phone from my pocket, finding him in the contact list and calling. "All you need to do is save."

He frowned at me when his phone rang. "If this pans out, I'll owe you one."

"Just don't kill her," I whispered.

"You need to stop listening to gossip."

Chapter 33

The next day, I was left to my own devices. Fab refused to go on a jail visit; she even drew the line at sitting in the parking lot. Another factor in her decision was that Didier showed up at the last minute with a twinkle in his eye, which sealed her plans for the day; naturally, she chose the gorgeous Frenchman. I couldn't complain; I'd rearrange *my* day for a romp on the beach with Creole.

Heading to The Cottages, I made a mental list to check for any problems. Thankfully, all the units were booked, so I didn't have to sit in the office all day. On the drive over, Creole called and informed me that the jail was on lockdown and all visits were cancelled for the week. One of the women had snuck in cigarettes and got caught smoking, and then a brawl had started over who told on whom. Creole assured me that he'd called in jail-perk favors for Mac.

As I rounded the corner, a lime-colored matchbox car with a realtor sign on the door caught my eye. The fact that it was parked in front of the yellow house irked me. I slid into the open parking space in front of the office and went directly across the street.

Janice Pincher, who I recognized from her ads, was locking the door of the house. Her clients, a husband and wife in their sixties, stood off to one side.

I waved wildly over my head. "Has a dead body been dumped on this property yet? Another one was found—number seven, or was it eight? Not on this block again, thank heavens, but a few blocks over." I acknowledged her clients with a cheery smile.

"Uh…" Janice stumbled, a deer-in-the-headlights look crossing her face.

I cut her off. "You have the hardest time with tenants." I said with faux sympathy. "Didn't the last bunch also end up in jail? I hope they don't come back and vandalize the place like the last ones did." I made a face.

It amazed me that I wasn't struck dead by the murderous glare Janice flung my way.

The older couple appeared horrified and immediately put distance between themselves and Janice, the wife practically sprinting to their car, a dark sedan that had one tire up over the curb.

Janice watched her retreating clients, then closed the distance between us and snarled, "The next time you have something to ask me, do *not* do it in front of my clients."

"I thought you had this sale in the bag. No offers?" I said sweetly. She clamped her lips shut, continuing to stare. "I've got an all-cash, no contingency offer for you. You'd never have to show this place again; just cash your commission check."

"If nothing else comes in, I'll give you a call," she said in a "don't hold your breath" tone and stalked over to her clients.

I waved to the three of them and hustled back across the street and into the office so I could peer out the window. I knelt on the couch and poked my nose through the blind. The man looked a bit irate. Janice had pasted on a phony smile, and I'd bet was offering assurances that this wasn't a crime-ridden neighborhood, pointing the finger of blame at me and saying that I didn't know what I was talking about.

The conversation lasted another minute before the couple pulled away from the curb, heading in the opposite direction from their realtor.

I whipped my phone out, lay down on the couch, and called Brad. He answered and deep-breathed into the phone. "This isn't high school," I said in annoyance.

"You're no fun."

"Need I remind you that every time we had too much fun, we got into trouble? Realtor Janice was just showing the house across the street. I'm hoping I quashed whatever interest her clients had by dropping little bombshells like dead bodies and possible serial killers."

"Thought maybe the deal was dead now that Mac's in jail?"

"You and I could partner and buy it. If Mac gets sprung anytime soon and she and Shirl are still interested, we'll flip it to them. If not, we'll keep it. One of us should own it; it's a great place to sit on the porch and watch the happenings at The Cottages."

"Turns out Janice was saving the listing for an investor friend of mine. That information cost a couple hundred. The deal isn't happening, and Janice knows it. The owners want their asking price, and the numbers won't work for an investor unless they lower the price."

"I just offered an all-cash deal, and she turned up her overly long nose and pranced off. Now what?"

"Leave it to me. I'll make the deal happen, and it won't be at full price," Brad assured me. "But you owe me, and I'm collecting. Found Mother a house and a condo. I'm going to take her to lunch and then to see both properties. You need to back me up."

"Hate to be a buzzkill, but Mother may be up to something." I told him Creole's theory. "Be subtle, order her Jack Daniel's and then spring the surprise on her."

"Neither property is a dump. Personally, I think the condo is a better idea, considering her age."

"Bro, I'd leave the age mention out of the

sales pitch." I shook my head.

Brad lumbered on, not listening. "The condo has amenities that a loft won't have, and she won't need a guard to get out of her car at night. There's been a rash of vehicle break-ins down there; if she ever parked on the street, her car would disappear. Just recently, two cars were left on blocks, the tires gone."

"Unless the thieves can swap out tires like a NASCAR pit crew, I'd think that would be a good way to get caught and end up in the pokey."

"There was one arrest, but that's not a deterrent. Where are you? You can go to lunch with Mother and me." He laughed. "You working the office? That will drive you crazy; you might have to hire someone. What about Crum?"

I groaned. "If you're going to torment me, I'm hanging up."

* * *

Locking up the office, I headed to the pool area. Halfway there, screams coming from Crum's bathroom window had me skidding to a halt. I whipped out my gun, creeping closer, and listened. My face flushed bright red when I realized the screams weren't distress but those of a woman vocally expressing her rapture, going up and down the musical scale.

An older couple came in through the side gate holding hands. I recognized them as registered guests; their unit was just across the driveway.

The woman squealed, "Look," pointing at my gun. "It's so exciting around here."

I reholstered it in the small of my back. "I'm sorry." I wasn't. Not sure what to say, I finished lamely, "I thought someone was in distress."

"Oh hon, those two are loud. At first I thought… well, I'm not sure…" The woman giggled.

The husband rolled his eyes and stared at the ground, the toe of his shoe scraping back and forth against the concrete.

"This won't be happening again," I apologized. At least not before they checked out.

"Oh," the woman said, looking disappointed. "How… hmm… can we watch?"

Her husband tugged on her arm, and she jerked it back.

More of Cruz's relatives. I had a hunch he rented them from somewhere, but I lacked the nerve to ask. He'd be annoyed if one of them reported back that I'd stood in the way of their fun. "If you wouldn't mind standing back?"

They backed up a half-step.

I took a long-legged step over the planter, careful not to squash the flowers, climbed up on an old rusty meter, and poked my head in the bathroom window. "Keep it down in here," I yelled. "Close the bathroom window. Whatever you did with the screen, it better be back in place by the next time I visit or you'll be evicted." I climbed down, reached up, and with a hard shove, banged the window closed.

The woman scowled at me. "I thought you'd use your gun."

"If I shot my tenants for noisy sex, I wouldn't have any."

"I suppose." She clearly wasn't convinced. "Isn't it exciting about that nice Mac Lane getting charged with murder?"

Would this woman enjoy lounging about in a six-by-eight cell, her only view through steel-barred doors, without an iota of privacy? "Mac didn't murder anyone, which I'm sure your… um… relative, Cruz, would tell you, since he's representing her. I'm sure she'll be out soon." I needed to tell Mac how much I appreciated her when I saw her next.

"We never thought she did." She sighed, looking sheepish.

Her husband gripped her bicep, maintaining his hold this time, and dragged her away. She turned and waved.

Crum hobbled out his door, buttoning a dress shirt that hung down to the tops of his bare thighs, his feet crammed into mismatched loafers, one leather, the other canvas. "Sorry about that. I'll get the window fixed."

The fact that he didn't look sorry put me in a fighting mood, but it was Starletta peering around his shoulder that sent me over the edge. "What the hell are you doing here? You're officially banned, which means don't set one of your grubby feet on this property ever again."

"And to think I was going to offer to fill in for Mac while she languishes in jail." Starletta flashed a tight smile.

"Come back again, and I'll call the sheriff and have you arrested."

Starletta looked down her nose, mimicking her boyfriend. "They'll laugh at you."

"You're standing on private property, and I have the final say about who comes and goes." I fished out my phone, sticking it in her face. "Shall I call? Test out who's right—you or me?"

"You bitch." She stepped out from behind Crum in a hot pink bra and a black G-string. That was too much nakedness; she resembled a skeleton with a hank of hair. *My poor eyes.* "Do you mind if I get dressed?" She stalked inside without waiting for an answer.

It didn't escape me that Crum had thus far remained silent. "You have until the count of three," I yelled after her, "so make it snappy."

"It won't happen again," Crum mumbled. "I'll go to her house."

"Can't you find a nice, older woman?" I flinched, realizing I sounded like my brother when he was trying to sell Mother on a new boyfriend.

"Yeah... but... they don't want to... you know." He tried, but couldn't maintain eye contact.

"The last couple of your women friends have been mental-hospital crazy." I hadn't had a headache in a long time, but I did now. "They may be good in bed, or whatever it is you require, but there's a price to pay. I can give you a list of men who had to learn the hard way."

Starletta flounced out the door in bright-yellow, patent leather, four-inch heels with her flowery dress gaping open in the front, not having bothered with a single button. She stood on tiptoes, wrapped her arms around Crum's neck, and laid on a wet, smoochy kiss, complete with sound effects.

"Get going. Before I get sick on you."

She gave me the finger and slithered down the driveway.

Chapter 34

It had been over a week, and calling Cruz Campion, Mac's attorney, was a dead end. His assistant, Susie, put me on hold and never came back. I took it to mean mind my own business, though in the past, she usually just blurted that out. It wasn't like I tried to weasel details about the case out of her; I'd stopped doing that when I realized it only raised her irritation level and made getting ahold of Cruz more difficult.

My phone rang, and Creole's face smiled back at me. Putting my coffee cup down, I picked up the phone, sliding onto a stool at the island. "Mac's got a bond hearing this morning," Creole said.

"Brick just got released from the hospital." I was worried about the bail issue since he was still recuperating.

"Cruz's got it covered or he wouldn't have requested the hearing. I've never seen him go to court without a bondsman sitting in the front row. Fingers crossed he gets a friendly judge. It will just be a matter of how much the bail is set for. She'll get it since most of the evidence corroborates her story."

"I'll have to do something really nice for you for calling me with the information so I wouldn't worry."

He unleashed a rumbling laugh that never failed to send tingles up my spine. "This weekend—you and me, we'll hide out, no phones, and do nothing."

I sighed. "Looking forward to that."

"Mac's house is no longer considered a crime scene, but I don't recommend that she go back there until they catch the real killer. If you have an open cottage, you might want to put a hold on it for her."

"If I don't have any openings, I can make one. That would brighten my day." I laughed. "Stomping over there and kicking a few tenants to the curb."

"If it weren't for you, a couple of them would have to live on the beach; no one else would rent to them, or at least, not for long." He chuckled. "I'll see you later."

I heard a male voice in the background shouting his name and knew it was back to business. I smiled, setting the phone on the counter.

* * *

It was mid-afternoon and everything was quiet around The Cottages, not a face in sight, which I appreciated. The troublemakers were either not home or staying inside and out of trouble.

Mac had called when she got released. It had taken most of the day because she had to be fitted for an electronic monitor. Cruz informed the court she'd be staying at The Cottages, and her intention was to stay with Shirl. I let her know that she had another option: number ten was available and reserved for her.

I hustled to the grocery store and put together all the foods she liked, including her favorite beer, and had them arranged in an electric-blue enamelware bucket I knew she could find a use for once she'd eaten everything. I also grabbed a bouquet of flowers, shoving them in a vase and putting them on the coffee table.

* * *

Shirl called to let me know that they were back and to thank me for helping her friend. They'd stopped for dinner on the way; Mac had complained about the food served in jail and said she was starving. When she got to Shirl's place, she took a long hot shower, scrubbing off the cooties; she told Shirl it would take more than one shower. Afterwards, she promptly fell on the bed and went to sleep.

I told Shirl to tell Mac that her job was waiting for her and if she even thought about quitting, I'd sic Fab on her. I needed her and appreciated that she kept the property from being overrun with undesirables.

Chapter 35

Several days went by with no unpleasant surprises. One day, after Didier left for a meeting, Fab and I hit up the Taco Wagon. We ordered more food than we could possibly eat, bringing it home and spreading it out across the island. I retrieved pitchers of flavored water and iced tea out of the refrigerator, filling our glasses with ice.

We were half-finished with lunch when Fab groaned, putting her taco down, and crossed to peek out the kitchen window. "Kevin's coming up the driveway. He blocked in both our cars, so our only option is to sneak out the back and down the beach. That's worked for more than one felon with an outstanding warrant."

"We're neither felons nor wanted," I felt compelled to remind her.

There was no mistaking the pounding on the door. A cop knock had a distinct sound all its own.

I tugged at Fab's wrist as she started to stand. "He'll go away eventually."

"Wouldn't count on it." Fab took another taco from the tray. "You kill anyone lately?"

Kevin pounded louder and longer.

"Could be another felony, but I haven't even jaywalked lately. Are we compelled by law to open the door just because he's making a racket?"

"I'm certain he has to announce, 'I'm kicking your door in,' and that 'warrant' has to be in the sentence somewhere." Fab downed her iced tea, tossing Jazz a piece of shredded beef.

Both of us jumped off our stools when the banging moved to the garden window, rattling the potted plants on the shelf. "Open the door," Kevin bellowed.

I princess-waved and turned back to my lunch.

"You know he's going to be family one day," Fab reminded me.

"If you're trying to ruin my lunch, talk like that will do it."

"He's going to break the window." Fab stood up. "I'm letting him in."

"Not without a warrant."

Fab cracked open the door, sticking her nose out. "What do you want?"

Oh man, I love that girl. I should tell her more often, but then she'd be more insufferable than ever.

Fab stuck her hand through the opening and said something I couldn't hear. Probably that she wanted to see the warrant. To my surprise, she stood back, opening the door and ushering him in with a brush of her hand.

"Mac here?" Kevin barked, looking around.

I bent over and looked around the bottom of the island. "Nope. Not here."

"When he mentioned that it was about Mac, I thought we should hear him out." Fab shrugged and telegraphed, *Sorry.*

"She's at The Cottages, which I'm sure you already know," I said.

"Mind if I look around?" Kevin started in the direction of the patio.

"As a matter of fact, I do." I stuck my leg out, trying to scoot forward to affix my toes to the cupboard and block his way. "You might get better cooperation from me if you didn't call me a liar and accuse me of felonies whenever we run into one another."

Fab stepped between me and Kevin, forcing him to deal with her. "Mac isn't here. Is there a problem?"

"She's missing," Kevin grunted.

"She'd never violate the terms of her bail." I frowned. *She'd go back to jail and not get out.* "She has an ankle monitor that will give you her location."

"She's not at The Cottages and not here, unless you're lying, and if I find out you are, I'll be back to arrest you on an accessory charge. Any idea where else she might have gone?"

His lack of response about the monitor didn't go unnoticed. I knew he'd never share information, and I didn't expect him to, but it had been worth a try. Judging by his reaction, he'd checked the monitor already and hit a dead end. Why?

Fab slid the keys across the countertop and into her pocket. "This has been fun, but we have to meet a client. If we see Mac, you'll be our first call."

The only problem with Fab's words was that they lacked sincerity.

I stored the leftovers in record time, looking at my watch. "I know, call her lawyer. Maybe she's with him. Do I look okay?" I twirled in front of Fab. "I forgot about the appointment."

"Can't you be cooperative just once?" Kevin seethed. "I'll be back."

"I know you won't believe me, but we've been truthful," I said. "If you come back on business, make sure it's all legal-like, as Creole will be here and he's a stickler for the rules."

Fab crowded in behind Kevin, giving him no choice but to move toward the front door. She was so close on his heels that if he stopped suddenly, her nose would be planted in the middle of his back. I was right behind her.

Once everyone was outside, I double-locked the door and checked the knob twice, then ran to the SUV, jumping in. "What appointment?" I asked as Fab gunned the engine, glaring out the rearview mirror as she waited for Kevin to move.

"Something's up with Mac. The cops should know exactly where she is unless she's no longer wearing her ankle monitor. For that to happen, she'd have to have removed it, which we know isn't easy to do. Maybe with a knife. You and I know she wouldn't do that." She opened the driver's side door and laid on the horn. "Kevin's enjoying this."

"Start at The Cottages," I said as soon as Kevin's car slowly backed out, unblocking the driveway.

Fab went down the street in the opposite direction of the way she usually did. My guess was she wanted to lose Kevin so he wouldn't know where we were headed.

"Mac would never run," I said as she turned onto the highway. "She didn't kill anyone. When she found the body, she reacted like an innocent person, calling in and reporting it." I tossed my phone on the console. "I texted Creole; Mac's phone is turned off."

My phone rang, and it was Cruz's office. *This can't be good.*

"This is Susie. Mr. Campion would like to know if you know where his client, Macklin Lane, can be found."

"We're looking for her now. Any reason she'd run off?"

"Mr. Campion says, 'Find her.'" She hung up.

I stared at the screen. "What did I ever do to that woman?"

Fab laughed and listed off: "Snuck behind her back to speak to her boss, ambushed him in court… You know she's territorial—no one talks to him without going through her—and you've eluded her several times."

"It's been a while; she could get over it." I sniffed.

Fab careened into The Cottages' parking lot. "Kevin will be here any minute. He was sitting down the street, hiding in someone's driveway. I want to know how he got ahead of me."

"If he asks about the meeting, we're waiting for our client in the office. We can't help it if the person is a no-show."

Fab hit the steering wheel. "I knew I didn't have to worry and that you would think of something."

Fab was right; Kevin pulled into his parking space a moment after we pulled up. He got out and stood, arms crossed, at the bumper of his cruiser, glaring at us. After a minute, he ambled into his cottage.

"That was anti-climactic," I whispered.

"He's a bastard when it comes to us, but he's a good cop." We both got out, slamming the car doors. "Never mind him for now. How are we going to find Mac?

I tossed my head towards the back of the

property. "We'll start with him."

Joseph was leaning back in his chaise, baseball cap pulled down over his forehead. Svetlana occupied the chair next to him, surveying the property. If she could speak, I bet she'd be the best source of gossip on the block. And reliable. Joseph appeared to be asleep, but I knew better. There was too much activity going on around him; he'd want to be in the know so he could brag at the bar, sell his tale for a beer.

"Where's Mac?" I asked, jerking his hat off and dumping it in his lap. His eyes were already open, darting first one direction, then another.

"She cut off her ankle monitor, left it on the floor, and split. She ain't gunna like life on the run." He held out his palm. "That was your freebie. I'm out of cash, or I would have finessed you some."

Fab jerked him upright by the back of his collar and peered down into his face. "You worm."

Kevin's door flew open. "You need assistance, Joseph?" he yelled.

Fab dumped Joseph back in his chair.

"No, I'm fine," he shouted back.

Out of the corner of my eye, I noticed that Kevin continued to stand in his doorway. I knelt next to Joseph, whispering, "You actually see Mac leave?"

Fab waved to Kevin and moved behind

me, blocking the deputy's view.

"This better be good and truthful," I told Joseph. "There are worse things than letting Fab come back and kick the hell out of you. Such as calling Spoon," I threatened, having grown immune to the feeble-old-man routine.

Joseph's grizzled skin paled at the mention of Spoon. It never failed to scare the hell out of anyone who knew the man's reputation, and most knew better than to test out what he would or wouldn't do.

"I do need a few bucks," he whined. "It could be a loan."

I flashed him my mean-girl stare, crossing my arms in a fierce stance, and did my best not to laugh at myself.

"Yeesh, I'm a sick old man." He glanced up, checking to see if I was in a pushover mood. After a long pause, he spit out, "Oh, okay. Two deputies showed up here about an hour ago. Mac's door wasn't locked, and as you know, there's not a lot of places to hide inside, so they were in and out."

"Unlocked? Then what?" Fab growled at him.

"They went door to door. The tourists that were home hadn't seen anything, but afterwards lingered on their front stoops. Crum, who I know was inside, didn't open the door; haven't seen him since yesterday afternoon. Miss January was drunk on the porch. She had a hissy fit at being woken from her stupor, mumbled incoherently, and stumbled inside."

"What about Shirl, she at work?" I asked. He nodded. "You see anyone lurking around her place?" Upon her arrival, Mac had opted to stay with her friend.

"Since Mac got out of jail, she's kept to herself." Joseph's eyes continued to dart around. "First time you get out, it takes a while to shake the jittery feeling of not knowing what to expect next."

"You call me if you hear anything, and don't screw me." I fished my ringing phone out of my pocket. "Creole," I mouthed to Fab and pointed at Joseph, rubbing my thumb and forefinger together.

"Go." Fab waved me off. "I've got cash for a change; I'll take care of our extorter here." She cracked her knuckles.

Didn't her mother ever tell her that doing that would give her man-hands? Mother had threatened me with that, and I stopped.

"Find Mac yet?" Creole asked. He knew I'd never abandon a friend in need.

I caught him up on the events of the day, updating him on my conversations with Kevin and Joseph. "Can I go into her cottage and look around? I wouldn't give it a thought, but Kevin is here and standing watch."

"Legally, no. Sneak around the block and enter from the side the apartment building is on.

Climb through the hedge, and Kevin won't be able to see you. Did that a few times when I lived there." He chuckled. "Or call Shirl, get permission, and still sneak around so you don't have to answer any questions from Kevin."

"I'm happy you didn't suggest climbing in the bathroom window."

"I still can't believe how many of your old tenants used that as a getaway option."

"I'll call you later."

"Hold on a second. If you need help with anything, and I mean anything, you call. Promise me."

"Promise." I blew a kiss through the phone. "After we check Shirl's cottage, we're headed home; nowhere else to look. We're out of options. All we can do is wait for Mac to show back up or call. Unfortunately, when she does, she'll be going directly to jail."

Fab finished with Joseph and came to stand by my side as I was ending the call. "Creole know anything?"

I shook my head. "He said to be careful sneaking into Shirl's cottage."

"That's good advice." She smirked. "What? You're thinking too hard."

"Mac's truck is parked in her space. Why? Any reason to think she's guilty?" I asked, not waiting for an answer. "Or scared and doing something stupid? She could get a long way, just by swapping out the license plates from some old beater car. That means she had to have help. I never heard her mention any friend other than Shirl, and she would've talked Mac out of such a bad idea. She has mentioned a drunk or two she's befriended lately, but they're horribly unreliable. Doesn't feel right."

"I called Shirl. She's working a longer-than-usual shift due to a couple of sick nurses. She knew nothing about any escape plans and is just as worried as we are." Fab looped her arm in mine. "Let's go for a walk."

Fab led me down the street in the opposite direction of the way I wanted to go. "Stop struggling." She jerked on my arm. "We're going to cut around the corner and trespass through old man Rodney's property and end up one house over across the street. If he's out sunning with a washcloth over his goods, we'll whistle and yell hello."

"Washcloth?" I scrunched up my nose. "How do you know this?"

"I know every property on this block that has a cut-through path." Fab sniffed, in a "duh" snit. "He's into nude sunbathing but doesn't want to get his… you know… burned."

"Isn't he a hundred?"

"He's sixty-six and just retired. I had a talk with him, told him the leathery look was ruining his skin and sunbathing might shorten his life if he got skin cancer."

"If you used that same sunny personality

on everyone, people would like you instead of being wary when they see you coming."

"Being liked by everyone is overrated. Let's hustle around the next corner so no one knows which way we went."

As we cut down the side path along Mr. R's property, I slowed and craned my neck to look around the yard. "You promised entertainment, and there is none." I pouted.

"Next time." Fab sprinted across the street. I followed and steered her away from the bushes, showing her the slim break where the hedges came together. She peeked around Mac's cottage—coast clear. She tried the knob, and I was surprised to see that the door was still unlocked.

"It appears that Mac was living out of a suitcase." Fab lifted the lid and ran her hand through the contents. "Wouldn't she want to take a change of clothes? Running from the law is stressful enough as it is."

"Look at this." I pointed to the flowers I had bought, now lying on the floor surrounded by broken glass.

"Don't touch anything. The sheriff's department might not be done here." Fab took two pairs of gloves from her back pocket and tossed me a pair. She held up a set of keys, having scooped them off a side table. "These are Mac's; who else has a troll doll key ring?"

From behind the recliner, I dragged out

an overly large purple canvas tote bag. I turned it upside down, knowing it had a false bottom, as I had the exact same bag in leather. "No way in hell she would go anywhere without this," I said and held up the Beretta, displaying it on the end of my finger.

"It appears she walked out the door, leaving everything behind, including her gun, identification, and money." Fab walked around the room, opening drawers, tossing the place in her well-organized way. "Let's go find out if Crum's home and what he knows." She peeked out the door. "Kevin's car is gone. Must have been the one I heard go by earlier." She pointed to my gloved hands. "Save those. You might need to use them again."

I tugged on her shirt, forcing her to come to a halt. "You don't think Mac could be so distraught that she'd kill herself?" The idea had ebbed its way into my thoughts earlier, but I'd dismissed it immediately. Now I wondered… "I don't want to believe that she was that upset and I didn't notice."

"Stop it." Fab shook her finger at me. "She'd leave a note. A list of instructions for a grand send-off. She'd want Dickie to do her proud: a funeral that was the talk of the town."

I knocked on Crum's door. Not waiting for an answer, I beat on it, administering a couple of kicks, taking out my frustration and worry. Not hearing anyone milling about inside,

I knocked again.

Fab cupped her hands against the window and strained on tiptoes to catch a glimpse through the cracked blinds, moving from window to window around the side of the building. Seconds later, lockpick in hand, she reappeared from the back of the building. "He's either passed out on the floor or dead," she whispered.

She popped the lock, drew her gun, and burst through the door.

I drew my own gun and stayed on her heels.

Crum lay on his side in the middle of the floor. I rushed over and dropped down next to him while Fab checked the bedroom, bathroom, and two closets. "He's been stabbed," I gasped, placing two fingers on the side of his neck. "He's got a pulse, but not much of one. Call 911." I ripped my shirt over my head and wadded it up, applying pressure to the blood-soaked area.

Fab raced to the door, half-yelling into her phone.

"Don't you dare die on me." I enveloped Crum's hand in my free hand and squeezed it gently. "Do you hear me?"

His eyelids fluttered. "Mac," he murmured, his voice barely a whisper.

"Mac did this to you?" I asked in shock, finding it hard to reconcile with the woman I had come to know. No way she would stab someone, a friend no less, and leave them to die.

"Help Mac. St—" He broke off. After a long pause, he whispered, "—got her," and closed his eyes. "Crazy bitch," he gasped out.

I knew I had to stop asking questions; he needed his energy to live.

Shirl burst through the door, black bag in hand, and dropped it and herself on the floor next to Crum.

As I scooted back to give her room, I noticed a sparkly blue phone case peeking out from under a chair. I knew it belonged to Mac and caught Fab's eye, pointing it out. She reached down and stuffed it in her pocket.

"Let me know if you need help," I told Shirl. "Please don't let him die."

Fab burst out the door at the approach of blaring sirens. The 911 call would also bring deputies, but hopefully, the paramedics would arrive first. Crum's skin tone had faded to a translucent white; his breathing took on a rattling noise.

"Don't worry." Shirl patted my hand. "I'll be riding to the hospital with him. He's lost a lot of blood, but we'll fix him up. You go outside and get a breath of fresh air."

"We'll meet you at the hospital," I said over my shoulder, stepping out of the way of the paramedics.

Fab grabbed my arm and led me across the driveway to the hose, turning it on and washing the blood off my hands and arms. "Breathe. Nice and slow." She rubbed my back.

"Crum said, 'Help Mac.'" I said, my voice trailing off. "Why wouldn't she stay and help him?"

Fab grabbed my shoulders, giving me a shake. "Repeat exactly what he said."

"I can't remember exactly." I tried to repeat it word for word. "There's something wrong with people," I whined and laid my head on her shoulder, nodding in the direction of the four guests lined up in beach chairs at the opposite end of the driveway.

One of them motioned for Joseph and Svetlana to join them. The sexy blond was far more popular with the guests than Joseph. They always made it clear that any invitation included Svet and that he shouldn't leave her home by herself.

Fab took my hand and dragged me over to the Hummer. "You need to change your clothes. All the blood makes you looked unhinged, and it doesn't help that your hair is a wild mess today." She fluffed the ends, frowning and making a face.

It had been my idea to keep a change of clothes in the back of the SUV for those "you never know" moments, like the current one. I peeled off my skirt behind the open driver's door and swapped it for sweat shorts. Having left my t-shirt with Crum, I ditched my bloody bra and finagled my top over my head carefully, in case I had blood in my hair, not wanting to get it on my clean shirt. I rolled my stained clothes into a ball and stuffed them in the back corner of the SUV.

Fab had stood watch while I changed, noting the comings and goings. "Hurry," she whispered. "We need to get out of here before the deputy over there tells us we can't go anywhere."

"We can't. We're witnesses. They'll arrest us."

Fab switched her focus to the building next door. "Which one of those units is Starletta's? 'St,' Crum said—obviously Starletta. But why would she stab Crum? Mac, I'd understand; Starletta hates her."

"You really think it's her?"

"It's a good place to start, and she fits the crazy part."

"We need to text the guys."

"After." Fab shook her head, giving the idea no thought. "We don't know anything yet. Might turn out to be nothing."

"They might buy that excuse. Probably not. If they pitch a fit, I'm blaming you. I'll say I was traumatized and only did what you told me." I returned her scowl with one of my own.

I followed Fab, who scooted through the opening in the hedge, made sure the coast was clear, and signaled to me. A young guy was skateboarding down the driveway of the apartment building next door. I recognized him from The Grill restaurant, where he worked.

Fab flagged him down. "Which one does Starletta live in? She's not answering her phone."

He pointed. "Upstairs, back one on this side." He flew out into the street and off down the middle of it.

"I think we should knock first." I tugged on the back of her shirt as we walked up the stairs. "If we kick the door down or shoot the lock off, she could have us arrested. And would. I'm not on her favorite-person list either."

"You let me handle this," Fab said in her superior tone, which made me smile. She slipped her pick out once again, along with her latex gloves, and nudged me to put mine on. She picked the lock quickly and quietly pushed the door open. Empty.

It was a small, one-room efficiency, and it wouldn't be hard to spot someone if they were there. Starletta could have hidden in the bathroom, perhaps, but the door was open. She kept it neat and clean, the bed covered in colorful sheets. There was a strip kitchen, the counters clear, and one oversized chair in front of a television with rabbit ears.

The desk and chair in the corner drew our attention, and we stared in open-mouthed shock. Hanging on the wall was a bulletin board covered with newspaper stories about all the recent murders, along with pictures of the deceased that had been cut out with a jagged instrument, probably the serrated knife that affixed several other articles in place. Lined up along the bottom were candid color photographs of the year-round tenants of The Cottages, plus Mac, Fab, and myself. Bullseyes on every face and a knife in the throat of Mac's picture.

"This picture makes me look fat, don't you think?" Fab leaned in to inspect it closely. "It's not my best side."

"I'm fresh out of 'you're hot and sexy' compliments." My eyeroll behind her back was lost on her.

"As much as I hate to admit this, for once we need to call in law enforcement. I don't know what I expected, but not this." Fab pointed at a picture on the board. "This is the dude from The Cottages trash." She flicked up the photo to show the post mortem close-up underneath, then tapped another snapshot. "This one was found at Jake's."

It took everything in me not to turn and run out the door. "We found the serial killer?" I didn't want to believe that the pictures of the men were all of the unsolved murders. Maybe Starletta was just a weirdo following the cases. But the glossy pictures did not come from any newspaper, and where could she have gotten them? "It's unusual for a serial killer to be a woman; this will make headlines."

Fab pulled out her phone and photographed every item on the wall and desk, then walked around, snapping pictures of every inch of the room. "Got a burner phone in the office?" she asked.

I nodded. Mac always kept a couple of throwaway phones on hand, charged and ready.

"We'll leave the door ajar, giving the deputies cause to enter. When we get to the office, I'll call 911 and report hearing screams." She motioned for me to follow.

Fab led me on a silent trek down the back stairs and along a footpath that ran along the rear of the building. Stepping around trashcans, we reached the end and squeezed through an opening in the fence into the driveway of the house next door, then cut across the street and down a weed-strewn path. Coming out on the next street over, we looped around and through a grove of eight-foot-high banana plants and back to the office.

I breathed a sigh of relief that no one had spotted us trespassing, triggering another emergency call. So far, no sirens in the distance.

I stole Fab's space on the couch and stretched out. She found a pre-charged phone on the shelf and made the anonymous 911 call. She hung up and handed me a bottle of cold water. Just then, someone banged on the office door. I put a finger to my lips, but Fab shook her head and opened the door. An officer I hadn't seen before stood there. I breathed a sigh of relief that it wasn't Kevin.

"Madison Westin?" he asked Fab. "Deputy Walker."

Fab pointed to me.

"I need to ask you a few questions."

I appreciated his calm demeanor and that the first thing he said wasn't, 'Did you stab Crum?' "Can we do it in here?" I asked. "I'm feeling a little faint. Would you like a cold water or soda?" I was overplaying the drama, but I felt safer inside.

I had just finished relating the details about finding Crum when a siren raced by the window, barely clearing the property before it shut off. More guests. Fab and I exchanged raised eyebrows. That was a fast response to her call; law enforcement wasn't wasting any time.

Deputy Walker excused himself, saying, "I'll be right back."

Fab hustled to the window, lifting the blinds. "There are two squad cars parked in front of the building next door."

"Where do we start? Mac left and took nothing. Based on the knife stuck in Mac's picture, she might not even be alive. On the other hand, other than the pics of the dead people—already-dead people, I mean—everyone else on that board is still alive and well."

"You're Dickie-pale." Fab felt my forehead, then pushed my legs over and sat down.

"That was mean." Dickie's skin tone could easily be described as pasty, a lack of color that I still found creepy. "We have to find Mac, and I mean alive and not dead." I grabbed one of the throw pillows and hugged it to my chest.

"If Mac were dead, the deputy probably would've mentioned it. But then, only if the body has already turned up. For now, we're going on the assumption that Mac's still breathing."

"Starletta's display might not mean anything other than that she has a fascination with unsolved murders. No way she could hoist a body into a dumpster by herself. Maybe we're on a goose chase."

"We need to warn the guys to be on the lookout. Your house is the only one of your properties that hasn't been used as a dumping ground." Fab was back on her feet, pacing the room.

"What do we do if Starletta shows back up? Pretend we didn't snoop around her place? If she sees the police cars out front, she's apt to make a run for it. What does she have to lose? Unless she's innocent." I wanted to close my eyes and block out the day.

"Sitting here doing nothing isn't going to help find her anytime soon. Starletta may be our only link to Mac. We have to find her before the cops take her in for questioning, and they will put an APB out on her once they get a look at her wall." Fab ignored my scathing look. "You're forcing me to come up with a plan."

I squeezed my eyes tighter, wanting to stick my fingers in my ears.

"First stop: Mac's house. We'll check out that murder scene ourselves. What about her ex?"

"That's a dead end. The marital house got sold, and they split the proceeds; he's moved to a new place with his barely legal girlfriend." I rolled on my side. "Bet you your idea comes with police tape, and you know how law enforcement hates it when you ignore the keep-out warning." I handed over her phone, which had fallen out on the couch cushion. "Forward the display of Starletta's photography skills to the guys and include a 'we're fine' message. The pic that woman took of me… I had no idea she was anywhere close by. That creeps me out."

I'd only just hit send when my phone rang from where I'd left it on the desk. I flinched at the ring tone—Creole's. He'd found out that we hadn't texted, telling him of our new destination. I held out my hand, and Fab slapped it into my palm.

Not giving me a second to say hello, Creole boomed, "Damn it! You better be okay, or I'm wringing your neck."

Fab rubbed her ears, laughed, and mouthed, "Say hi to Creole."

"I'm fine," I whispered and related the details of our breaking and entering next door. I told him that I was lying on the couch, awaiting the return of the deputy, not wanting to risk arrest. I hoped that would earn me points with my irate boyfriend. "If you look at the pics Fab sent you in order, it'll be like a tour. Girlfriend is very organized about her picture-taking."

Fab waved and slipped out the door.

"You should have called *before* you entered whack-job's apartment."

"It was all so shocking, we didn't think about it." That part was true.

"You're coming straight home after you finish answering questions."

I knew an order when I heard one. "I want to stop by the hospital and check on Crum." I heard Creole's sigh.

"Call and inquire about him first. He might be in surgery or just out and not his obnoxious self and ready for visitors."

"I'll call Shirl and remind her to keep me posted on his condition and let me know when I can go and say hello."

"Do I need to come get you?" Creole grouched.

"What's your professional opinion? You deal with lowlifes all day long."

Creole didn't answer right away, which

had me worried. "I think you found the serial killer. As for Mac, my guess is Crum's last words, coupled with the knife in her picture, mean she's in trouble. Which means that you two need to let law enforcement do their job. Go home; I'll call a couple of my contacts."

A small detour wouldn't hurt.

"I can hear you thinking of ways to get hurt or worse. Promise me you're going straight home." Creole had clearly come to the end of his patience.

"That's the plan," I reassured him.

Fab opened the door and slipped back inside as I hung up. "Talked to Joseph. He was unhelpful." She shook her head in disgust. "Called Shirl. Crum's out of surgery, in stable but serious condition. She'll call as soon as he wakes up."

"Did you ask about Mac?"

"Of course." Fab sighed out her frustration. "Here and her house are the only places she'd hide out, which Shirl assured me that Mac would not do. The only way she'd kill someone is if it was self-defense. Shirl was quite certain there's no relationship between Mac and Starletta. Mac can't stand the woman, and the feeling is mutual."

Fab stopped to answer a knock on the door.

Deputy Walker came back in, made himself comfortable in one of the chairs, and started his questioning, mostly about finding Crum. Then he switched to Starletta Wells and did I know her and what did I know. He wanted a run-down on the area in general and who lived where. He said he'd just transferred in and wanted to catch up.

Short straw. I filled him in on everything I knew about the neighbors, most of whom minded their own business and stayed out of trouble. I also handed him a card for Jake's and told him to stop by the bar for the law enforcement discount—which meant free, but I didn't want to suck up too much.

Finally, he turned to Fab. "You have anything to contribute?"

I answered for her. "She's not friendly. Unless you're an old man."

Fab flashed a slightly deranged smile and shook her head.

The deputy checked her out from head to toe, then turned back and handed me his card. "You think of anything, call me."

Chapter 36

Fab swerved to miss a car that shot through the stop sign. "We're going to drive by Mac's, check it out for ourselves, and possibly catch a clue that someone might have missed. And if that doesn't work, we're out of options. I know you promised that we'd go straight home, but the guys will never know about a little detour."

When was she going to learn that they find out everything?

Several turns later, Fab slowly circled Mac's street. There was no sign of activity anywhere on the block. The yellow police tape strung across the driveway was noticeable a block away.

"Look." I twirled my finger, twisting in my seat as we drove by the house. "Right there in front. I'm sure that's Starletta's lowrider Impala. No one else around here drives that particular eyesore."

Fab doubled around the block and pulled into a vacant space at the curb. She glanced at me and said, "We'll walk."

"Hold on a second." I grabbed her sleeve.

"Why would Starletta be here? This doesn't make any sense. It's one of the first places the cops will check when looking for Mac."

"We'll check out Mac's, then the neighborhood. Maybe we'll luck out and find someone sitting on their porch. And hopefully get the kind of person that knows every time their neighbor sneezes. Mac probably knows all of them, so that could work in our favor." As we neared Mac's place, Fab sidled up next to me. "Pay attention. Last thing we want is to get caught off guard. Starletta is dangerous. You watch the street, and I'll check the place out. If I'm not back in two, shoot your way in and try not to hit me."

If Starletta's in there, we call 911. Fab crept down the side of the house and around the back, out of sight.

I barely had a chance to give the block a once-over, checking for a porch-sitter, before Fab appeared at the far corner of the house, finger over her lips, and motioned me forward.

"Mac and Starletta are both in the living room. Mac's hands are bound, and she has a black eye and marks on her cheeks. Starletta is pacing frantically back and forth, wringing her hands, a gun stuffed down the front of her jeans. The window's cracked open, but I couldn't make out her mumbling, only that she's becoming more agitated. It sounded like she was arguing with herself. I can't imagine what ramblings are going on inside her head—the woman reeks of desperation. Starletta is on the edge; on some level, she knows she's compromised her killing spree. Anything could set her off. We've got to get Mac out of there."

Both of us jumped at the sound of the front door slamming and ducked out of sight. Starletta raced across the grass to the trunk of her car, retrieved two red gas cans, and disappeared back inside. She kicked at the door, but it didn't close completely, and her incoherent screaming could be heard moving around the house.

"I'm going around the back." Fab twisted the back of my shirt. "Keep watch on the front." She moved quietly around the side of the house.

I snuck up the front steps, thinking I could be more useful checking out the front, thereby eliminating any more delays. Gun in my hand, I crept across the porch, and squinted through the six-inch opening. Starletta crisscrossed the hallway, splashing gas on the baseboards and walls. I could swear I hadn't made any noise, but she jumped around, frozen and wide-eyed, her mouth going slack at the sight of my gun trained on her. Extending the can out in front of her, she pulled her gun from her waistband.

"Go ahead, shoot me," she screamed, "and we all burn together."

My gun was trained on her chest, but the

gas can was in the way. If I shot that, it would cause an explosion; if I shot her elsewhere, the pain might cause her to squeeze the trigger reflexively. We were in a standoff. She let loose with a high-pitched, hysterical laugh, her eyes darting toward the door.

I held out one hand. "Let's discuss this like rational women. Join forces. We can help one another. No one has to die today," I said, trying to sound casual. I knew Starletta was dangerous, but hopefully she wasn't completely unhinged. If I could stall her, keep her talking, Fab could get in through the back and get the drop on her. It was a half-assed plan, but it would have to do.

"You're such a Pollyanna, makes me want to erp," she said and punctuated it with a gagging sound. "Now get in here before I burn your fat friend to a crisp."

It surprised me that she didn't ask for my gun. I shifted it behind my thigh.

"Don't be getting rid of that," she said, waving her gun in the direction of my leg. "Once I determine whether you've brought anything of interest to this tête-à-tête of ours, we'll play shootout, old-west style. You know, count the paces, turn, and one blows the other to hell." She was dressed for her little scenario, wearing a knee-length, ruffled full skirt, a matching bandana on her head, and cowboy boots.

If I didn't know Fab was right outside, I'd take

my chances with her shootout scenario right now.

I looked around, spotting Mac in the corner. She was tethered to a chair, disheveled and on the verge of shock, one side of her face and eye puffed and swelling. Her eyes brimmed with tears that spilled down her cheeks. Noises could be heard from behind her gag, which was nothing more than a bunched-up rag that Mac worked her jaw to dislodge without much success.

"Set your damn gun on the floor. I'm not ready to play yet." Starletta produced a lighter from inside her boot and flicked it open.

If I had any doubts that she was delusional and crazy, they were gone now. I ignored her request, weighing my options. Putting my gun down wasn't one of them, and I decided to chat in hopes of distracting her. "You're not going to like burning to death. You might want to give that some thought before igniting a flame that you can't control. Besides, it seems to me your track record so far has been to only kill men; why switch now? You know you're going to be infamous. I'm not the only one who would like to hear why you killed all those men. You'll exceed your fifteen minutes of fame with all the headlines and news coverage." I willed myself to maintain eye contact. If I could figure out Starletta's next move, maybe I could keep anyone else from dying.

"You've got this all wrong. She's the

killer." Starletta pointed to Mac. "I know because I spied on her."

Mac wiggled ferociously in her chair, making gurgling sounds, her head swinging side to side.

"If that's the truth, then why become her executioner? Why not let the court do its job?" I shot Mac a reassuring look, then turned back to Starletta. "Come on, tell the truth, it was you that murdered those men. Why?"

Starletta's eyes widened. She started nodding to herself, as though contemplating her next words. "You know how it is. When a relationship is over, who wants to see the man again, be forced to speak to the bastard knowing you wish they were in their grave? You know they're going to end up there anyway; why not a little earlier than planned?" Her eyes weren't quite focused, a dreamy smile on her face, and her hands shook.

"A civilized 'I never want to see you again' and then avoiding the man would have worked better than all the bloodshed," I said. "The added bonus is then you're not looking over your shoulder, waiting for the police to show up and arrest you."

Starletta didn't seem to notice that I had spoken. She made a crowing sound. "Homer was my first one, and he's never been discovered. I figured why the hell not? I loved him, and how did he repay me? He beat me and did other vile things. I broke into his house that day and hid until he got off work, then shot him as he came through the door, before I lost my nerve. It's true what they say: you always have a soft spot for your first. After that, it became a game and just plain fun."

I tried not to shudder at the way she related the story with a complete lack of feeling.

"Poor Homer's probably been eaten by animals by this time. Left him face down in the woods off the Turnpike in Central Florida. Great dumping ground out there. Did you know you can unload your clip in the forest and no one comes a-lookin'? Good thing." She gave another high-pitched laugh.

"I'm in awe of your talents," I managed to say without stumbling on my words. I backed up a step. "The man that you left in The Cottage dumpster, how did you manage to get him into it?" I hoped to keep her talking about her exploits; she seemed to revel in her murderous rampage, enjoying the retelling as if they were fond memories.

"I paid Skippy Newman to haul out the trash. Got to find me a new hauler, though. He caught a conscience and is no longer with us." She wiped a non-existent tear and giggled.

Poor Skippy.

Where the hell is Fab? Out of the corner of my eye, I caught movement from the doorway leading to the hallway.

"Why Mac?" I asked.

Starletta leaned in Mac's direction. "Bitch," she hissed in her face. Mac flinched. "It was bad enough that she wouldn't rent to me, but then Crum and I got into an argument and he took her side. That's when I decided to set her up, make those stupid cops think they had their killer, and disappear up north. Reading my news articles, I realized I have to get creative and not kill them all the same way. Then they'll be chasing a dozen people instead of little ol' me."

Sooner or later, they'd catch up to her. I hadn't met anyone stupid in law enforcement, and that included Kevin, who I didn't like.

"Soon as I get done here, I'm going to stop by The Cottages and do a little house—or should I say cottage?—cleaning." Starletta laughed hysterically and turned, tossing the gas can at Mac, hitting her in the side of the head, gasoline sloshing down her clothes. Mac hung her head, shaking it back and forth. Starletta retrieved the second can from nearby, swinging her arm back...

The hallway door hit the wall and splintered. Fab stormed into the room.

I took advantage of Starletta's distraction and aimed my gun at her, but before I could shoot, she dropped the can.

"Put your guns down, or I'll set us all on fire." She flicked open her lighter.

I had already determined that, with all

the gasoline puddled on the floor, one flick and the house would quickly roar into flames. The wooden structure would burn to the ground with the four of us trying to get out.

I was damned if we were going to die.

"Okay, we'll put our guns down. Won't we, Fab?" She nodded without looking at me. "We can come to a win-win agreement." I held my weapon out, capturing Starletta's attention.

There was a deafening explosion and a shriek. Starletta stared open-mouthed, an expression of surprise and confusion on her bony face, as Fab rushed over and kicked her to the ground. She had her divested of her gun and lighter before she had a chance to move. Blood gushing from a hole in her shoulder, Starletta grasped her shirt and shrieked again, trying to sit up. She fell back and her head hit the floor. She'd be lucky if she ever had use of the arm again.

"You're going to jail," Starletta squealed, "when I tell the cops you're trying to frame me to help out your friend." She gasped and struggled, until finally she fainted and her body went slack.

Fab pointed her gun in Starletta's face and gave her a stiff kick. A faint "umpf" could be heard. At least she wasn't dead.

"What happened to your shoot-to-kill edict?"

"Too much paperwork."

Mac stared, wide-eyed, as I ran over to snatch the gag from her mouth. "What took you two so long?" she choked.

"You didn't leave one damn clue," Fab yelled. She snapped a knife out of her back pocket and made short work of the tape around Mac's ankles and wrists.

"I'm calling 911," I said.

Mac pointed to the window, where sirens could be heard in the distance. "Too late, someone beat you to it." She stood and enveloped Fab in a bear hug.

"Get off me before I shoot you too," Fab barked. "You really owe me. I got a video recording of the crazy woman's ramblings." She held up her cell phone. "The picture part isn't so great," she grouched.

Mac burst into racking sobs.

I patted her on the back. "I know Fab's mean. You can hug me."

"It's not that." Mac hiccupped, tears pouring down her face. "I thought I was going to die. Worse yet, I kept hoping smoke inhalation would knock me out before I burned to death." She made gulping sounds. "Starletta murdered those men and…" She shrieked, "Crum."

"It takes more than that skinny bitch to kill Crum." Fab found a roll of paper towels and handed her one. "He'll be back on his feet and prancing around in his underwear in no time."

The sirens were now on the next block

over. "We need to take this party outside and set our guns on the porch." I put my arm around Mac. "When the deputies arrive, it's best to have our hands in the air."

"What about…" Mac pointed at Starletta.

I leaned down, pressing two fingers to her neck, just to be sure. "She's not dead. I suppose EMS will transport her to the hospital. She needs to go directly to the prison ward."

"Before Starletta comes around…" Fab rooted through the drawers, pulling out a scarf, and descended on the woman. She nudged her over on her stomach and tied her hands behind her back.

"Bitch better not die," Mac said with venom. "The families of those dead men should have the opportunity to face her and unload on her ass."

"You have bloody scratches on your face and some bruising. Don't touch them." I batted her hand away and tugged her out the front door. "They might provide DNA evidence. With any luck, we can talk the paramedics into looking at you first."

Fab followed us out onto the porch and suggested Mac sit on the step. I stood behind her.

Two police cars squealed up in front, and Kevin got out of the first car. It wasn't a friendly face, but at least it was a familiar one.

Chapter 37

The next few hours were a flurry of activity. Once Mac and Starletta had been taken away to Tarpon Cove Hospital in separate ambulances, Kevin stalked in Fab's and my direction. We'd been separated for questioning, and I was quite sure Fab had ignored an order to stay put where we'd been sitting, several feet apart, when she showed up next to me. I was just happy that we got to stay outside; I never wanted to see the inside of that house again.

I slumped over on the grass.

Fab dropped to her knees at my side. "You faker."

I opened one eye and smiled.

Fab called to Kevin, "No need for a paramedic; she's coming around." She hit me on the back.

"Ouch. Dammit."

"Get up. You're not leaving me to answer all the questions alone." She tugged on my arm.

"Ohhh," I moaned. "Can you help me sit up so I can catch my breath?"

"You're so good at this phony stuff. I'm demanding my IOU back from your mother; the instructions I got didn't cover this nonsense. I was gypped."

I watched as the tips of shiny black shoes approached me. I moaned again and leaned into Fab's chest. "Send that video to Cruz and Creole and get the lawyer on the phone, or we'll be sitting here or at the station forever."

Fab stood and mumbled something about the bathroom. Kevin nodded, and she went in the direction of the house.

"You okay?" Kevin asked.

He actually sounded sincere. I squinted up at him. "I don't envy you your job."

"Some days require more coffee than others." He gestured toward the vacant chairs on the front porch and started walking that way, expecting me to follow. "Starletta's been yacking her head off, saying Mac's the serial killer. The best part is she claimed you and your cohort helped with the logistics and body disposal."

Would it be believable if I "fainted" again? Instead, I stood and followed.

"This will surprise you," he went on, "but I didn't believe a word from her lying lips and almost laughed at the mental picture of the two of you dumping bodies. 'Trouble' over there," he said, pointing over his shoulder at Fab, "wouldn't get her designer jeans dirty. And although Mac is… quirky… I know she's straight up. Besides, killers don't generally report finding bodies on their property when they're the ones who put them there. They tend to dig a hole and kick the deceased in, or they come up with something too gruesome to be believed."

"Well… I agree with you. Is this the start of a friendship?" I asked.

"Let's not get carried away." He chuckled. "Are we waiting for your lawyer?"

I shook my head. Then I began at the beginning—the beginning of the end, at least—and told him about finding Crum and the paramedics taking him to Tarpon Cove Hospital. I skipped the part about checking out Starletta's apartment, and instead told him that we'd decided on the way home to stop by Mac's as a last resort, hoping to find a clue to her whereabouts, and that we'd walked in on Starletta preparing to torch Mac's house with Mac in it.

"I'm surprised you didn't offer to rent a cottage to the charming Starletta."

The twinkle in Kevin's eye told me he thought he was amusing. "Oh, she tried, but Mac has 'crazy' radar and told her we didn't have any vacancies. Which was true. It was the part about 'and we never will' that probably set Starletta off and started the feud between the two."

One of the deputies tried to interrupt Fab's phone call, and she could be heard informing the man that she was talking to her lawyer. Then she handed him the phone. A couple of minutes later, the phone exchanged hands again and she appeared at Kevin's side, handing it over. "Cruz told me to give this to you. It's evidence. He also told me to tell you that we are available at your convenience. A little notice would be nice." She sniffed.

Kevin arched his brow. "What's on here?" He looked down at the phone.

Fab told him about how she had gotten a partial confession on tape, saying the audio was clear and grumbling that the video wasn't what she'd hoped for. "Cruz wanted me to tell you that he represents Mac and the two of us." She wagged her finger and turned on me. "And he told me to tell *you* not to refer the defendant to him—he's not interested."

"Can I have your phone?" Kevin asked me, thrusting out his hand.

"Is it possible to call Creole first?" I asked.

"I took care of that." Fab winked at me.

"You two stay here," Kevin ordered. "No sneaking off. I know where you live." He left with a big grin on his face, leaving us to stare at his back.

"He's awfully nice today." Fab sniffed in suspicion. "I forwarded the videos and texted Didier and Creole. I told Creole you were fine after collapsing. *You* can tell him it was a hoax and your idea."

"Be smug now, but I predict that hell hath

no fury like Creole worried about his girlfriend—" I poked myself in the chest, "—especially for no reason."

"How long are we going to have to sit here?" Fab was always out of patience when law enforcement was involved; she preferred to say as little as possible and leave.

"As long as it takes. Instead of making barn animal noises, go to your calm place, sit cross-legged, and breathe."

Fab crossed her arms and scowled. "I've never been in a barn."

I looked away and laughed.

Chapter 38

When our interview with the deputies was over, Fab and I all but ran to the SUV. We left them trying to do crowd control, all the neighbors suddenly out for a walk and wanting to trample the crime scene.

When Fab pulled into my driveway, it didn't escape our notice that both our boyfriends' vehicles were parked across the street.

Before Fab could do a disappearing act into the house, I grabbed the back of her shirt. "You try and get away, and I'll bust a cap in your butt. Knowing you, it will make you look sexier to have a bullet hole back there."

Fab leveled her intimidating stare at me. "With what? Have you forgotten we got our guns taken away? Again."

"You listen to me—if I'm going to get the safety lecture, then you're going to sit through every excruciating word. No skipping upstairs for fun and games."

"You think I don't get my share of lectures?" She let loose an unladylike snort. "Well, I do. Once Didier figured out I tuned him out like that odious elevator music, the sneaky devil started making sure I paid attention to every word."

"Probably has something to do with that S-word."

"The word is sex," she said in disgust, then opened the front door and pushed me inside.

I ground to a halt. Creole lay on the daybed. "Nice to see you two ladies in *one piece*." He crooked his finger at me. The narrowing of his eyes made him look impressively menacing.

Fab shoved me out of her way and flew into Didier's arms. "I've had a hard day."

Creole surged to his feet, grinned at Didier, and strode over, scooping me up into his arms. "Later."

I struggled and kicked, but his arms were like bands of steel. "Put me down."

"Behave yourself." He tossed me over his shoulder and headed for the door.

I winked and waved to Fab and Didier.

* * *

Creole had been given five days off, and we planned to hide out in his house, indulging in our favorite things: swimming, walking on the beach, and generally lazing around.

"No phone for a week, since you can't seem to stay out harm's way," Creole admonished.

"Ohh." I stuck out my lower lip in a full-blown pout. "You're so mean." I tried to sound attitudinal, but almost burst out laughing. He knew that my phone had been taken into evidence, and I had no desire to replace it for at least a week.

He squinted at me. "You don't care. And don't you dare deny it."

"Bliss to me is five days alone with you, no visitors, and no phones." I shook my finger at him. "But when Fab calls, are you going to answer?"

"She doesn't have a phone either." He smirked.

I rolled my eyes. "You don't know our friend very well. She'll be calling."

"Didier seems to have more control over her than we'd guessed. Or so he boasts." He stretched to reach a bottle that he'd placed on the bedside table earlier. He unscrewed the top and squeezed some of the thick lotion into his hands, then began rubbing it into my foot.

"You two, uh… don't… discuss personal girlfriend stuff, do you?"

"I'm not a teenage boy; I don't need to boast. To you, maybe." He puffed out his chest. "We compare notes on how to keep you safe but not a word about us sitting here naked, your foot in my lap." He kissed one of my toes.

He took his time, not neglecting the arches of my feet, my ankles and toes getting equal attention, then moved up my legs to my knees. It was as if he was committing every nuance to memory.

"Love you."

"I knew you were mine from the first kiss," he said smugly. "Just had to be patient. I knew that boyfriend you had would lose his shine, and when he did, you weren't getting away."

"You know what sealed the deal? Besides the toe-curling kisses?"

"My good looks." He waggled his brows and flexed his muscles.

"You were always there for me, giving me support, not asking me to change. And you fit into my family."

Creole groaned. "For a while there, Madeline only wanted a second son and campaigned heavily against our dating."

I moaned and stuck my other foot in his lap. "Don't get bored before this one gets the same treatment."

The slowness of the massage was hypnotic. I stretched blissfully on the bed, content with having the hands of the man I loved on my body.

He tightened the pressure on my foot.

"Oww," I groaned.

"Just making sure I have your full attention. I don't want you taking any job where you go off by yourself. Fab is getting the same lecture about those secret clients of hers. You two are better as a team, regardless of what that bastard Brick says; you each bring a different set of strengths to your partnership."

His encouraging words spread a new warmth through me. "Fab will probably give Didier a hard time, but I know she doesn't want to run solo anymore. I've hung on her designer jeans long enough that she's comfortable with me as backup." I sighed. "I need to call Brad and tell him I need another gun. I like getting them as gifts."

He dropped my foot and reached under the bed. "I've got that covered," he said and handed me a box with string for a bow. "When I bought the first one, I also got this, knowing the other one would end up in the police evidence room before long."

"Aww, nice." I pulled the handgun from the box. "Heckler and Koch P30. This is better than candy any old day."

"Never had a girlfriend who could name her guns. And shoot them. Kinda hot." He brushed my lips.

Chapter 39

Creole's phone alerted continuously while we were gone. Mother slammed him with messages, refusing to be ignored even after he told her we'd gone fishing and would see her in a week. After that, he didn't respond to the next barrage of messages, and she stopped, which made me suspicious. I wondered if Didier's phone was now blowing up with messages. He had a way with her, speaking sternly to her in French. It didn't matter that she didn't understand a word; she would calm down. Spoon had growled a couple of times that Didier could get her to behave when no one else had the power.

Finally, Mother had had enough of Fab and me being under house arrest and decided to throw a party on Spoon's boat. She sent a message all in caps that ended with "DRESS UP."

"I think I'm going to be sick that night." I clutched my stomach and let out an ear-piercing moan.

The sides of Creole's lips quirked. "She might believe it coming from me, but you'd never get away with it."

"I know! You get sick, and we'll tell her you gave it to me. How could you?" I frowned.

"If we call in sick, she won't be satisfied unless she sees a doctor's note. Who gets dressed up on a boat?" he grumped. "Let's show up in shorts and say we forgot."

"I dare you. You'll think that your ears will never stop burning."

On the day of the party, we left the beach house and, with no traffic, made it home in record time. Fab had the door open before I got halfway up the driveway. She barreled out and threw her arms around me. "We'll talk later," she whispered. "It will be fun tonight. I raided your closet, and Didier came up with several selections; they're hanging on the closet door."

I hugged Creole's side. "We're flu-ish and not going. You can tell Mother, support our story."

"To use one of Joseph's favorite words, 'baloney.'" Her hand shot out and she pinched my arm.

"Arrest her," I yelled at Creole. "That's assault."

"Come on." Fab egged me on, jumping into a boxer's stance. "If I go to jail, you're going with me."

Didier's arm shot around her waist, lifting her off her toes. Hugging her tight, he carried her, single-armed, back into the house.

"Fabiana," he huffed as he went.

"I'd feel sorry for him if he wasn't so happy," Creole said.

The two of us trailed in behind. As Creole laid his suit bag over the railing, I flicked my eyes towards the stairs.

"Sit," Fab commanded. "We got a bottle of wine to toast our friendship."

"Since you asked so nicely..." I wrinkled my nose.

Didier and Creole laughed.

"It's been quiet around here since Madeline showed up early one morning and caught us half-dressed. After that, it was all phone messages." Didier released the cork on the wine bottle and filled the glasses. "Friendship," he toasted.

We all raised our glasses and drank.

"Did you bring something appropriate to wear?" Fab asked Creole, running her eyes up and down him.

Didier whispered something, but Fab ignored him.

"No need to worry," I said. "I picked out a pair of shorts and a tropical shirt for him, and I have a beachy cotton dress in the same colors."

It amused me when her mouth flopped open like a fish's. Not for long, though; she soon snapped it shut. "I'm sure you'll look fine," she bit off, clearly not believing her own words.

I stood, holding out my hand to Creole.

"We'll go in separate cars."

"We're going together," Didier said, aggravated.

* * *

"What are you doing?" I propped myself up on the pillow, watching Creole tap the screen of his phone.

"We're supposed to be downstairs in ten minutes, dressed and ready to go. Considering our current state—" He ripped back the sheet, flashing me. "—we're not going to make it. I don't want your friend kicking the bedroom door with one of those pointy shoes of hers."

"It's brave of you to text her. Fab thinks it's okay if she's late, but not when anyone else is."

"Didier," he corrected. "Telling them to go ahead; we're going to be fashionably late."

"Then text Mother, oh brave one, throw that thing on the floor, and come back over here." I held out my arms.

* * *

Fab wolf-whistled as Creole and I came down the stairs. "Look at you." She checked Creole out from head to toe.

I raised my eyebrows, having thought the two of them had left.

Fab read my mind. "No way we were leaving without you two."

Creole's black suit hugged his large frame, a white dress shirt, unbuttoned at the neck, adding to his sexy appearance. His black hair was slicked back, still damp from his shower.

I looked into his eyes and smiled, pressing my lips against his.

"That's not what I picked out," Fab said indignantly, pointing at my dress.

"You like?" I twirled in my black dress: a short tulle skirt with a beaded top.

Didier shot us two thumbs up. The "it" couple were also dressed in black, he in one of his custom suits and Fab in a ridiculously short black dress with capped sleeves and a pair of red-soled designer stilettos.

The drive across Tarpon was too quick. Fab asked from behind the wheel, "What is your mother up to with the dressy invitation?"

I couldn't lean into Creole any further without shoving him out the door and both of us ending up in the street. "I just hope that all this step-daddy talk isn't about to become a reality. Brad will have a heart attack."

"You're so dramatic." Fab tossed her long brown hair, which hung in waves down her back.

"Hey, Pot," I yelled from the back seat. Fab ignored me. "You can bet Mother's up to something," I whispered in Creole's ear.

Chapter 40

Fab zipped into the parking lot and slid into an open space. "Your mother has been busy."

The gate to the dock was framed in lights, which continued along both sides of the walkway that led down to where the boats were moored. So much for the one overhead light bulb that usually provided all the light, barely even casting a shadow. We walked in silence, following the voices that floated across the water.

The first person I spotted was Mac, standing at the top of the stairs. My jaw almost dropped at the sight of her in a royal blue knee-length A-line tent dress and a pair of low-heeled pumps. We had exchanged messages, so I knew she'd been released from the hospital within a couple of hours with a clean bill of health, but I hadn't seen her since the showdown with Starletta.

Mac exchanged hellos with everyone as we climbed on board. My next shock came when Billy sidled up next to her, dropping his arm around her shoulders and pulling her in to kiss her cheek.

When did this happen?

"You look very pretty tonight," I told her. "Just like one of the ladies at the yacht club."

Mac hooted, and her eyes danced with happiness. "I know you already know Billy." She smiled at him. "We're, uh… what are we?"

"Together," he said tersely, but smiled back at her.

"He came to The Cottages with flowers when he heard about me being held at gunpoint by a madwoman." Mac beamed at him, then sobered. "It still makes me mad that Starletta got the jump on me, and I couldn't take her out."

"I'm just happy you're alive. Selfishly thinking about myself, of course; how would I replace you? Since you're going to be around," I told Billy, "we'll give you a title—Problem Solver—and I'll bill Spoon."

"Call anytime. You've got my number." Billy turned Mac to face him. "Any trouble, I want to hear ASAP, not after the fact."

"Yes, honey." She grinned up at him.

Mother came over and grabbed my arm, pulling me into the main cabin. She'd managed to run a table lengthwise to accommodate family and friends and still leave room for other seating. We were the last to arrive, and everyone yelled hellos. The night was full of surprises: Phil waved while her date, Chief Harder, kept his arm around her. *I wondered how and when they'd hooked up.*

"Sorry we're late." I kissed Mother's cheek.

Spoon handed me a glass of wine and kissed me on the cheek, then gave Creole a bottle of beer.

Creole nudged me, casting a glance at his boss.

"I'll be getting the details on that hook up later," I whispered.

Brad appeared at my side with Liam and Julie, who looked great in a tropical-style halter dress. "What's Mother up to?"

"Why does she have to have an ulterior motive?" Julie asked.

"Because she usually does," Liam chimed in, which made us all laugh.

Mother quieted everyone down, welcomed us with a toast, then waved us all to our seats.

On the way to the table, I crossed paths with Phil. "I want details," I whispered. "Not skimpy ones either." She giggled in response, and I turned to Harder, raising my voice to say, "Nice to see you, Chief. I hope Mother has a sense of humor and seats you across from Fab."

Harder growled. Honestly, he sounded like a wild animal. He nodded at Creole. "Meeting tomorrow, usual time."

Mother had hired Cook's son to serve, and he looked cute in his uniform; I winked at him as he brought out the salads. I picked around the assortment of greens, looking for my favorites, and let the rest go untouched. Next came the main course, and dinner went by quickly, with a lot of laughter, everyone trading stories.

After the table was cleared and stowed away, it made room for more-comfortable seating. Creole pulled me into an oversized chair, and I snuggled up to him.

Mother didn't keep us waiting long; she grabbed our attention by standing and holding up her glass. "I bought a condo," she announced. "It's right as you come into town, and it overlooks the water. I have my son to thank for it." She toasted Brad. "He helped me to find the perfect location and convinced me that it was better than a house."

It would be a good move, I thought. Given more time, Brad and Spoon would find more things that they had in common, and then Brad would be supportive of whatever Mother decided to do about her relationship. A girl can hope.

Mother then satisfied everyone's curiosity about the guest list by telling us that she'd invited the chief for an update on the case. Creole groaned into the back of my neck.

Even though she didn't know Chief Harder well, my guess was that she'd poured on the southern charm and had him agreeing to dinner before he knew what hit him.

Harder cleared his throat. "I'll tell you the same thing I told Madeline. I can update you on everything that has already been made public. Starletta is in jail; she won't be charged at this time for *all* the murders we think she committed, but we've got a good case on the two we did charge her with. I predict the death penalty in her future. She entered a not-guilty plea, and her attorney mentioned he was making a self-defense case."

"That might work with one victim," Creole said. "She going to claim they *all* attacked her?"

"She'd be better off to try a nutjob defense, because she is one," I interjected.

"We also charged her with the attempted murders of Macklin Lane and Professor Crum. I offered to buy him a pair of pants or shorts for his court appearance, and he laughed at me. So I threatened him with a seventy-two-hour psychiatric hold. Then he went off on me with his five-syllable words, and I just laughed, knowing a judge would do the same and admonish me for wasting the court's time."

"Shirl and I have news," Mac said excitedly. "Brad rocks; he helped us get the paperwork together in order to buy the yellow house. We're closing in a month. You can sit on our porch anytime," she told me. "We'll hang out and watch when the deputies come to roust

The Cottages."

Everyone laughed. The chief squinted at me, and I shrugged in return. "What? Stuff happens."

Liam had moved and was now sitting on an end table between me and Creole and Fab and Didier.

"Announcements are over; we can go home," I said in a low voice.

"Not so fast," Liam said. "My mom's got something to say."

Julie overheard. She smiled at Brad and clinked her spoon on her wine glass. "As you know, the renovations on the apartment building have hit a permit snag, so Liam and I won't be moving for a while. Kevin says he's moving, but he hasn't found a place yet. You'll have to be patient; he hates the idea of packing and moving again."

Packing what? His last place burned to the ground and the cottages come furnished.

"I don't understand why you and Brad don't just shack up," I said.

"Oh Madison, really," Mother reprimanded me.

"You want to know what else I think on the subject of co-habitation?" I managed not to laugh.

"No, I don't," Mother barked.

Spoon smirked and shook his head; I was waiting for him to wag his finger at me.

Creole tightened his hold and whispered, "Please don't start a brawl."

Brad stared Mother down but didn't say a word. Normally, when it came to a stare-down with Mother, my brother or I flinched first, but not this time.

"I guess we all have news," Brad said, hooking his arm around Julie. "You're going to be seeing more of me. The man I hired to run the fishing trips is working out; he's happy and so am I. Didier and I are going to be looking for more hovels to renovate and sell or rent."

Brad and Didier clinked glasses over Fab's head.

Everyone started talking amongst themselves then, so I assumed announcement time was over.

Creole set me off his lap and stood. "Let's dance." He led me to a miniscule space in front of the galley.

"This is a good way to get your toes broken," I muttered.

"Do you trust me?"

"Of course I do."

"I've got a plan to sneak us out of here. No one will notice until we're long gone. I'm going to hold you close; you follow my lead, and I'll dance you out that door to the side deck." He nodded toward it. "Then we'll sneak to the other side of the boat and go down the stairs."

"Fab's got the car keys, or most likely

Didier. We could hotwire it, but that would be mean, leaving them stranded." My words came out somewhat muffled because I was speaking into his chest. I looked up. "I know—we'll boost Spoon's SUV; I saw it out there. Send him a text, though, so he won't order a hench-dude after us."

"I'd love to see the big man's face when he realized his ride was gone. For the first time in my life, I would blame a girl—you." He laughed. "At least you didn't suggest we steal the chief's car."

Creole slowly twirled me around a couple of times and then right out the door. I concentrated on not stumbling or, worse, falling down. I knew the latter wouldn't happen, though; he had too tight a hold on me.

"I'm so happy you thought of this."

Creole spun me out onto the deck that wrapped around the cabin. The sea air whispered against our faces, and I was so caught up in wondering if we were going to get away with dancing out of sight that I didn't notice we'd reached the railing until I found myself up against it and melting against him. He reached out and turned my head, kissing me deeply. His lips tasted of his favorite beer as he quickly slanted them across mine. In the next second, the railing behind me disappeared and I lost my footing. He grabbed my arm, tightening the hold he had on me, and ordered, "Don't let go." Hard as I tried, my fingers slipped through his, and he couldn't stop my fall backwards into the water. He went down with me, and we hit with a splash, disappearing under the inky blue water.

We resurfaced not far from one another, coughing and treading water. I spotted him easily in the light that danced over the side of the boat and swam into his arms.

"Madison," he said in a stern whisper against my mouth. "You better be okay."

I buried my face in his chest.

"You okay down there?" Brad yelled, tossing down a life ring. "The water's kind of dirty for a late-night swim." His laughter floated down to us.

"We're fine." Creole's voice was laced with sarcasm. "There went my shoes." He shifted from side to side, shucking them underwater. "They weren't comfortable anyway. I'd like to take my pants off as well."

"You will not." I tried to sound stern, but giggled. "What happened?"

"There was an opening in the railing that I didn't see. I'm going to have a talk with Spoon about safety violations."

I wrapped my legs around his torso. "You're so romantic, taking me on a moonlight swim."

"How am I ever going to top this?"

He kissed me again, and I found myself molded against him. I should have protested just a little—at least suggested we get out of the murky water—but he was kissing me hard and slow and oh, so deeply, and all rational thought fled my head.

ABOUT THE AUTHOR

Deborah Brown is an Amazon bestselling author of the Paradise series. She lives in South Florida, with her ungrateful animals, where Mother Nature takes out her bad attitude in the form of hurricanes.

Sign up for my newsletter and get the latest on new book releases. Contests and special promotion information. And special offers that are only available to subscribers.

Visit her website at
http://deborahbrownbooks.com

You can contact her at Wildcurls@hotmail.com

Find me on Facebook:
https://www.facebook.com/deborahbrownbooks

https://www.facebook.com/DeborahBrownAuthor

On Twitter:
https://twitter.com/debbrownbooks

On Pinterest:
https://www.pinterest.com/debbrownbooks/

Deborah's books are available on Amazon
http://www.amazon.com/Deborah-Brown/e/B0059MAIKQ

Made in the USA
Middletown, DE
23 September 2019